The Sign Of Fear

The adventures of Mrs. Watson
with a supporting cast
including Sherlock Holmes,
Dr. Watson and Moriarty.

Molly Carr

Paperback ISBN 978-1-907685-00-2
ePub ISBN 978-1-907685-04-0
Mobipocket/Kindle ISBN 978-1-907685-02-6
Published in the UK by MX Publishing
335 Princess Park Manor, Royal Drive, London, N11 3GX
www.mxpublishing.co.uk

Cover design by www.staunch.com

Chapter One

"Och, not another blessed pearl!"

I'd heard the postman just as I was putting the finishing touches to my toilette before going down to breakfast, and the sound of eager footsteps as they mounted the stairs. When my employer's youngest daughter Flora appeared at the bedroom door with a happy little smile on her face and a letter in her hand instead of a small parcel it was all I could do not to express my surprise.

However the letter, when I tore it open after hurriedly sending Flora back downstairs, proved to be as anonymous as the pearls which had been coming for me on this very day every year since 1882 addressed to Upper Camberwell care of Mrs. Cecil Forrester. I had, of course, kept very quiet about them as I didn't want anyone accusing me of stealing the things, although the temptation to show off or sell such lustrous jewels was almost overwhelming. If I had tried to dispose of even one pearl the fat, I was sure, would have been in the fire –for who would expect a governess to own such a thing? But the letter was different. It called me a wronged woman who should have justice. I went at once in search of Flora's mother to ask what I should do.

She suggested I go immediately to see a person called Sherlock Holmes. Well if he was, as she said, an upper-class consulting detective who'd unravelled 'a little domestic complication' for her, I thought I'd better be careful how I presented myself, at the same time as I was full of curiosity about what my employer's little domestic complication might have been. Was she going to be sent down for shoplifting? Or did she want a detective to track down Mr. Forrester,

3

last heard of in Reigate posing as a police officer and resisting all attempts (except Holmes') to bring him home?

There wasn't much in my wardrobe but I went through it as quickly as I could, discarding a peacock blue dress with a low neckline as too daring and an orange and yellow suit as too garish for this particular errand. I also rejected the idea of wearing my red dress with the close-fitting bodice. It outlines the figure too well, and I didn't want to distract anybody from my main problem. Not yet, anyway. I finally decided on a beige walking-out dress and matching hat. That fool of a husband of mine called it a turban. But it was more like a toque, and had a tiny white feather on one side. Going through my gloves, I found a pair that hadn't been darned too much and which fitted me, I thought, rather well. At least, that's what Sherlock's friend said. He especially mentioned that I was well-gloved when he finally decided to publish an account of what happened to us all. However, that was in the future. Before leaving the bedroom I sat at the dressing table practising pulling my mouth into as pretty a shape as I could, and saying a few words to try out a new London accent. Not cockney, of course, just sufficiently refined to hide my slight Edinburgh burr. I also posed in front of the pier-glass until I'd got the right kind of demure look, all downcast eyes and sweet womanly modesty. It was quite an effort, believe me. But I certainly didn't want this man to know what I was really like. According to Mrs. F., Holmes is very astute.

After taking one of the Road Car Company's horse-drawn Omnibuses from Camberwell (the first to have a staircase suitable for women who preferred to ride on the top deck) I duly arrived at number 221B Baker Street; where a plump motherly woman let me in and, as soon as she knew my business, asked for my card and took it upstairs on a brass salver to what I later saw was a large, airy sitting-room. I followed demurely behind her up the seventeen steps, and was just in time to hear her say, "A young lady for you, sir."

When I went in I could not help noticing how untidy the room was, or the large armchairs placed one on each side of an empty grate as if waiting for the blazing fires of a British winter. Stuck in the centre of the wooden mantelpiece was a huge jack-knife skewering some unopened letters: and on the hearth a coal scuttle which didn't seem to contain any coal. Instead it was half full of quite good cigars, although a Persian slipper near it also appeared to contain tobacco – but of an inferior kind. What quite spoilt the cosiness of the room was an old deal table in the far corner. It was heavily stained, and littered with retorts, broken test tubes and racks of evil-looking chemicals. However, I was glad to see a half-full bottle of whisky and a gasogene on a small table next to one of the armchairs. It gave the room a comfortably masculine look, enhancing what were obviously bachelor quarters.

So fascinated was I by all this that I didn't notice at first that Sherlock Holmes, who had been minutely described to me by

Mrs. Forrester, had another person with him: quite a handsome man, with a very fine moustache and plenty of hair on what I thought of as a particularly well-shaped head. I saw that he kept his handkerchief up his sleeve. An old soldier, obviously. I bowed and he smiled and Mr. Holmes asked me to sit down. *His* hair-line, and a nose like a hawk, made sure he wasn't at all handsome, but he did have a way of putting a woman at her ease. I told him that, ever since my father Captain Morstan of the 34th Bombay Infantry disappeared, I had been very anxious to find him. He was my only living relative and whenever I was hard-up, which was often, the only human being I could rely on to send me any money. Dad had asked me to come down from my school in Scotland to meet him at the Langham Hotel, a popular place to stay for men returning from the Colonies. But I was told when I arrived there that, although my father had indeed checked in his luggage, he had later gone out for the evening and never returned.

I showed Sherlock the letter which asked me to come to the Lyceum that evening at seven o'clock with, "if you are distrustful," two friends. Since I immediately said that I didn't have any friends it was natural for the men in front of me to volunteer. Considering the part I'd chosen to assume, I rather wished it had been some other theatre, even though actresses are nearly all the same whichever one they work in, because a rumour persisted that an underground passage existed between the Lyceum and a nearby brothel. It had, so they said,

6

been put in when the old Lyceum was rebuilt in 1834. I went back to Baker Street at six muffled in a dark cloak, a precaution I hoped would save me from being recognised by any of the regular prostitutes walking the pavement –and deliberately getting in the way of the hansoms dropping off parties coming to see the play. Holmes said something about the actor Henry Irving, who owned the new Lyceum, and we took our places by the third pillar as instructed in the letter. It wasn't long before a man accosted us. He was dressed as a coachman and seemed a very sharp-eyed cove indeed. I had to swear the two men with me had nothing to do with the police before he signalled a young and ragged little street arab to bring over a four-wheeler and we three got in. In less than a minute the coachman had vaulted onto the box and we were off. The old soldier sat next to me and started a long and boring account of his adventures in Afghanistan. It was all I could do to keep my eyes open, even though I tingled with excitement at the thought of what might lie ahead.

When it came to writing up everything for an American Magazine called *Lippincott's,* my name was taken in vain and it was said that I remembered a tale of a musket looking into this man's tent and how he fired a tiger cub at it. Maybe that agent of his suggested putting in a little humour. If so, it was too daft to laugh at as the saying is. Later, when we travelled with one of the Sholto brothers to Pondicherry Lodge, I heard him tell the man (a confirmed hypochondriac) to be careful not to take more than two drops of castor oil at a time, but that any amount of strychnine would be beneficial if he wanted to relax.

"He'd relax all right," I thought to myself with a grin. I ought to have realised there and then that the old boy wasn't a proper medico, even if the ever-prescient Holmes had introduced him as "My friend, Doctor Watson, who assists me in these cases."

When we got to the house, which turned out to belong to the other Sholto twin, I had to stay with the housekeeper while the three men went off on their *Boys' Own* adventure together. I wasn't very pleased at being detailed to comfort the frightened old trout, who had more than a sour look on her wrinkled phiz. But I had to stick to my role of delicately nurtured, womanly young female, even though I'd reached the ripe old age of twenty-seven. Talking of that, it was high time I had a husband and I could see Doctor Watson was already smitten. He might get a bit of a shock on the wedding night but I knew a trick or two to deal with that.

Well the mystery was solved, the treasure all the fuss was about got lost in the Thames and I became, in double-quick time, the wife of 'John H. Watson, Late of the Indian Army.' Really, the blockhead made so many mistakes. He was with the *British Army* in India and not, like my father, commissioned directly into an Indian regiment and expecting to spend all his military service in that part of our vast Empire.

8

To my chagrin, however, it wasn't long after we were married before John was off on another investigation with Holmes. Instead of coming home from his Practice as usual one evening he took it into his head to visit Baker Street. The next I heard both he and Holmes had become involved with an actress named Irene Adler who lived in a part of London called Serpentine Mews. She, the actress, was, mark my words, no better than she should be and had been carrying on with someone who called himself, can you believe it, the King of Bohemia! I don't know what my husband imagined I'd be doing while he was away. No doubt he'd assume (if he thought about it at all) that I'd be sitting at home twiddling my thumbs and telling the slavey not to serve up the dinner yet. But whatever might be going through his mind I certainly didn't keep up the pretence of being the mild Victorian wife, with her endless bits of needlework, when he was out of the house. I was already finding that too much of a strain when he did condescend to be at home.

One evening when this was the case, and I *was* doing some dratted embroidery, we heard the door bell ring. The next moment a woman rushed into the room and flung her arms round my neck. When the world came to be told about this incident in *The Strand Magazine* Watson said that it was always the way: anyone in trouble "came to my wife like birds to a lighthouse."

9

Et ma tante! When I discovered it was Kate Whitney who was clinging to me and sobbing her heart out I could have stuck a knife in her. She had been the ring-leader of a set of girls who tormented me for years when, as a motherless child, I was sent home from India to the school in Edinburgh, the same one I had come from to join my father in London so many years earlier. What Kate didn't know about ways to hurt someone as vulnerable and defenceless as I was then wouldn't have covered a three-penny joey. Now she had found out her husband was in an opium den and she prevailed upon John, with false smiles and crocodile tears, to fetch him out of it, for "How could she, a young and timid woman, make her way to such a place?"

Well, she was young. But timid? I didn't see why Watson should help her, but he insisted on going. And who do you think he met there, on some shady business of his own, but you-know-who. The upshot of it all was that Whitney was sent home alone and unconscious in a cab. Kate Whitney went to join him, and no doubt give him a rollicking, and I received a note to say my loving spouse had 'thrown in his lot' with Sherlock Holmes. They were off to solve the mystery of some other foolish frequenter of the opium den, which I later discovered was in Upper Swandam Lane.

Since my life was rapidly becoming intolerably boring, so much so that I even missed being a governess in Mrs.

Forrester's house, and still more my occasional nocturnal adventures, I decided to do something about it. Sherlock Holmes had said I was a model client who had the correct intuition, and that if I hadn't got married might have been most useful in detective work. I had preserved the map of the Agra treasure that I found among the rest of Dad's papers when I removed his luggage from the Langham, an act which Holmes considered showed real genius. The next time John H. Watson went off, I would also be off – this time on an adventure of my own.

"You have been looking a little pale lately. I think that the change would do you good," I had said in a rather prissy manner over the breakfast table soon after a telegram arrived from Sherlock, who was away to the Boscombe Valley to investigate a murder and needed company. I was determined a change would also do me good and as soon as the house was empty I dressed myself in my best clothes, put on my newest hat, jumped on a bus and went strolling down the Haymarket. I didn't intend to be picked up, and was very annoyed when an old man fell into step beside me. He was thin and extremely tall, although a stoop made him seem shorter. But the queerest thing about him was the way he kept twisting his face from side to side, oscillating it on a scraggy neck like an angry vulture. I turned away and stared into a shop window. Instead of taking the hint, he came and stood beside me so that our reflections were together in the glass. Looking straight ahead of him he said in a sibilant whisper, "You know, my dear, one villain can always recognise another villain, be it man or woman."

I was about to say something curt about my certainly not being a villain, but the knowing look in his extremely deep set grey eyes, a greyness completely in accord with the rest of him, showed me it would be a waste of time. After we had both turned away from the window and walked a few more yards he said, still in the same soft voice, "Shall we step in here and elaborate?"

'Here' was a Draper's Emporium. I toyed with the idea of buying something that would embarrass him, but soon decided he wouldn't be fazed by anything I could do. Instead I followed him into the shop and sat, lady-like, on a chair hastily brought by the manager while he asked to look at some gentleman's gloves. I didn't worry about anyone I knew seeing us together and letting two and two make five. He was nearly old enough to be my grandfather, and as ugly as sin. After a moment or two he said in a voice even lower than before, and while the assistant's back was turned, "My name is James Moriarty and there are many ways in which you could be most useful to me."

I nearly jumped out of my skin. I'd never heard of the man, but while speaking to Kate Whitney I had inexplicably called my husband James instead of John. I mentioned this to my new acquaintance, and he smiled in such a sinister way I was quite frightened. But, "A portent, my dear. A happy portent," was all he said, and we left the shop together.

He asked me to come to Green Park the next day, when he would be waiting "with my back to the entrance and wearing a large hat with an enormous brim, on the first seat to the left of the main gate." If he thought such a thing was a good disguise he was sadly mistaken. It made him the most conspicuous man in the Metropolis. When I turned up he said, "This is the first time I have dealt directly with a person I hope will become one of my agents, but you are very close to the fountainhead and therefore in an excellent position to influence Holmes. I want you to get him off my back."

"I don't know how you think I could do any such thing," I said, "since I hardly ever see the blighter. My husband often asks him to the house but he's usually too busy with his horrible chemicals to come."

"Well, in that case use your influence with your husband. See that he hampers Holmes with lots of inane questions. That tiresome busybody is coming uncomfortably close to some of my most profitable operations. I can't put up with it. Indeed, I *won't* put up with it."

"I think he hampers him already with inane questions, as you call them."

"No doubt, but I would like him to do it even more. At the moment his questions only serve to make that ass of a detective think he's cleverer than I am. Have you read the latest copy of *The Strand Magazine*? 'Your native shrewdness, my dear Watson, that innate cunning which is the delight of your friends, would surely prevent you from enclosing cipher and message in the same envelope.' And 'Good, Watson, good! But not, if I may say so, quite well enough.' If it had been me I'd have up and shot him with an old service revolver. I'm told Watson keeps one handy." Moriarty chuckled, so chillingly that an uncomfortable frisson went down my spine. "Anyway, Porlock's certainly done for. I defy anyone to find his body, above or below ground."

"Porlock?"

"One of my men, who I discovered was in the pay of Holmes."

I thought it best to change the subject. "Are you really so very clever then?" I asked, hoping to flatter him.

"Didn't I write a treatise on the Binomial Theorem which earned me a Chair of Mathematics before I was twenty-one? It's true I had to leave the University shortly afterwards because of a spot of bother and am now coaching boobies who want to get into the army. But my book *The Dynamics of an Asteroid* is so difficult nobody can be found capable of reviewing it intelligently enough to do it justice."

I saw over his shoulder that Mr. Moriarty had begun savagely biting his nails. "If you consent to work for me the rewards will be astronomical," he said. "But if you breathe as much as a word to anyone…" He turned round, fixed me with a terrifyingly malevolent look and drew his hand slowly across his withered throat. If I decided to become one of his agents I was to leave a letter at the Wigmore Street Post Office. "Just one sheet of paper, with the letter Y on it, addressed to S.M. and marked 'To be called for.' Go back next day and ask if anything has been left for Miss Muriel Blatherskate. This will tell you what to do next."

I didn't care much for the pseudonym, but perhaps it could be changed. I had been told to sit still for five minutes until he left the Park and then to go home. I watched him carefully as he sloped across the grass in that ridiculous hat and then made my own way out of the place, once more boarding a passing bus. Back in the house, I took a piece of paper out of my escritoire (which I always keep locked) and marked it with a great big Y in red crayon. Then I folded the paper in half, slipped it into an envelope, stuck down the flap and wrote as Professor Moriarty had directed. I was trembling with excitement, and knew I'd get no sleep that night.

The following day I left my letter where I had been told to do so. But the next twenty-four hours saw me unable to settle to anything. When at last the time came to re-visit Wigmore Street I was a nervous wreck. I noticed that the pavement outside the door was being dug up. I had to tread carefully to avoid getting red clay on my best costume. John, if he had been at home and planning to visit the Post Office, probably to send a wire to his bookmaker, would never have noticed it of course. But I didn't want to soil my outfit if I could help it. When I walked up to the counter and asked if there was anything for Miss Muriel Blatherskate the clerk handed me a cheap envelope with a great thumb print in the top left-hand corner. "Very careless," I said to myself. Whoever handled it had obviously never heard of the developing science of fingerprinting. The writing, too, was illiterate, although I admit it's quite difficult to spell Blatherskate. I carefully tucked the envelope and its contents into my pocket and left.

The journey back to the house was tedious in the extreme. The horses were jaded so the bus crawled along at an exasperating rate. The little ragamuffins who earn a penny or two sweeping the roads kept getting between the horses' hooves, slowing us down still more. It would be just my luck if one of the boys had an accident and we were delayed while he was taken away. But perhaps I imagined the journey was taking longer than usual, I was that anxious to read my instructions.

When I reached home I ran into the bedroom and tore the letter open. 'Stand outside the largest divan in the Strand between four o'clock and half-past,' I read. 'Not a minute before or a minute after.' Was it a hoax? It certainly didn't sound very exciting, although divans were not the places for a lady to be seen at, much less in. But out I went again and the exact time saw me staring through a nearby plate glass window, trying to avoid the appraising glances of several gentlemen going into the adjacent building to play chess and smoke a cigar or two. Just as I thought nothing at all was going to happen a fussy little man in white spats, with a handlebar moustache and bright green eyes, appeared at my elbow. "*A vôtre service, Madame,*" he said with a low bow. "Auguste Poirot, Bank Robber. Retired."

He took a whistle out of his waistcoat pocket and blew it once. A hansom cab travelling in the opposite direction immediately wheeled round and came towards us. M. Poirot stopped it with a flourish, and we both got in. My little companion tapped on the roof of the cab with his silver handled cane, and when the driver opened the trapdoor and asked in a beery voice "Where to, Gov'nor?" told him to drive to the Savoy Hotel. I was beginning to be rather bored. The place was comparatively new having been opened in the summer of '89, and the offices of the D'Oyly Carte Company (which produced the so-called Savoy Operas) were there. I preferred something a lot more rumbustious than Gilbert and Sullivan, although I had let John persuade me to go with him to a performance of *The Gondoliers* at the Opera House. I began idly to hum one of the best known drawing-room songs of the century called *You Should See Me Dance the Polka,* at the same time tapping my feet in time to the music.

"That's not Sullivan," said Auguste, showing some surprising knowledge for a foreigner.

"No," I said. "It's George Grossmith. He and his brother have written a very popular book. But George is also famous for his Gilbert and Sullivan roles."

"Oh, I see you talk of M. Pooter and his amiable wife Caroline. Such an Englishman. Always the correctness. But no *sang-froid.* I assure you the book, it has been very well received on the Continent."

We had reached the hotel by this time and I saw with surprise that a private room had been booked for us. Once there, the little man took out a plan and showed it to me. He told me something about what was going to happen, and how I would be involved. I nearly danced round the room I was so excited, and my eyes shone. "You are *une tres jolie femme,*" said M. Poirot appreciatively. "But now I must be off to catch the boat train to Dieppe. That son of mine is the bane of my life. I cannot be away too long as I never know what he will be up to next. In spite of all my efforts, to say nothing you understand of my example, he tells me he wants to be a policeman, or even" –here the little man grew red in the face and began to splutter –"or even a detective!"

"I must go too," I said. Mr. Clever-Dick Holmes might have solved the Boscombe Valley murder already, and John be at home. "But I've really enjoyed meeting a Frenchman."

"*Belge*," he said crossly, and vanished.

A couple of weeks later I was doing a little shopping in the Burlington Arcade when I noticed a thick-set man with flaming red hair gazing into one of the shop windows, just as I had done to avoid Moriarty. As I passed I perceived that he had his wallet in his hand and, as I thought then, accidently dropped a piece of folded paper which he had just taken out of it. I picked up the paper and was about to hand it to him when I caught a glimpse of the letters M.B. Trembling with excitement, I read the message: 'Put an aspidistra in your front window whenever your husband is away with Holmes.'

Looking round, I saw that the red-headed man had disappeared. I went at once to buy an aspidistra and arranged for it to be delivered that very afternoon. Since John had come home by then, I put the plant on the hall table. But the next time he was off helping his detective friend and I told him I was going to my mother's I was determined I would put it in the window as directed and sit tight to await further events. Both he and Holmes had forgotten that, after we were told during the investigation into *The Sign of Four* that my father had died of a heart attack in Major Sholto's house, I didn't have any relatives. I discovered I was able to vary visits to my 'mother' and my 'aunt' with impunity. Sometimes I simply said I was going 'away on a visit'. It was all the same to John, he was that keen on helping to catch criminals. As soon as the door closed behind him I grabbed the aspidistra, did with it what I had been told to do and kept my fingers crossed.

That afternoon there was a ring at the door bell and the slavey announced a gentleman to see me. Well, she wasn't wrong. An extremely genteel person came into the room carrying a large parcel. He was also young, handsome and with a rather regal bearing. After we had bowed to each other he said, "This evening we are going to the Haymarket Theatre. The Prince and Princess of Wales will be there so you're to wear these clothes and this tiara." He passed over the bulky parcel and took another, smaller, one out of his pocket. I couldn't resist examining the contents of this second parcel straightaway, and was completely bowled over by the beauty of the sparklers. My good-looking visitor made immediately for the sitting-room door prior to passing out into the street –evidently a young man in a hurry –and as he opened it said over his shoulder, "Don't forget to wear a veil."

What a disappointment. With a tiara on my head *and* a veil I'd look like Queen Guinivere in one of Moxon's Illustrated Editions of Lord Tennyson's *Morte d'Arthur*. But the dress and fur cape were beautiful. Whoever put the outfit together had even remembered to include matching shoes, bag and long white gloves. When my escort, in dress-clothes which included knee-breeches and several decorations pinned to his manly chest, called for me that evening I tripped out of the house like a two year old filly at Epsom. It was such a pleasure to travel in a gentleman's carriage instead of a growler. He handed me in with a flourish, tapped on the roof of the vehicle in the same way M. Poirot had done on the way to the Savoy Hotel and said in a loud voice, "The Haymarket, Kirwan. As fast as you can."

Of course there was a terrific crush at the theatre, and we had to be in our seats before the Royals arrived. I discovered delightedly that we were to be in a box with someone called the Duchess of Loamshire. As we made our way towards it, a gangling, slightly foreign-looking youth bumped into us. "Be careful," I said to my companion. "There are always a lot of pickpockets in these places."

"That's no pickpocket," he said, laughing. "Didn't you see the notebook in his hand and the pens in his top pocket? That's Belloc. His father's a Frenchman, you know, although his mother is English and runs a printing press. He's working on some nonsense rhymes for children, has been doing so since he was a kid himself. He likes to visit theatres, says plays stimulate his brain. But the book probably won't be published for years."

By then we had reached the Loamshire box and, after looking me up and down for some time through her lorgnette, the Duchess smiled graciously and said, "Good evening, Mr. Clay. Perhaps you would be kind enough to…"

"This is my sister, Lady Helen Stoner." Honestly, his bow wouldn't have disgraced Sir Henry Irving himself.

"Not one of the Stoners of Stoke Moran?"

"The very same."

Before another word could be exchanged we heard the sound of the National Anthem being played, badly but enthusiastically, by the theatre orchestra. Everyone stood up with their eyes on Prince Edward and his astonishingly beautiful wife, the Danish Princess Alexandra. The royal party took their seats, the lights dimmed and the play began. The Prince looked bored. He preferred Mrs. Langtry in her part as Rosalind (complete with tights) rather than what was being served up this evening.

Halfway through the first act a voice hissed in my ear, "Out!" We were sitting behind the Duchess and her party and half ran, half slithered from her box and along the corridors. Clay's coachman had already brought the carriage round and I don't think I've ever entered a vehicle as fast as I did that night. Even so, it wasn't fast enough for him. I almost fell into Clay's arms as Kirwan whipped up the horses and we went rattling at a furious pace down Jermyn Street towards Piccadilly Circus.

"I'm pretty sure she hasn't noticed anything yet," gasped Clay, referring to the Duchess. "Even if she has, she won't make a fuss until after the Royals have left."

"Noticed what?" I asked crossly. I was afraid my dress had been torn, and I'd nearly lost one of my shoes.

"The loss of her necklace, of course. I reached over in the dark, put my hand carefully between her chest and her double chin, then one snip of these tiny pliers and I'd palmed it. These hands," he spread out his long thin fingers for my inspection, "are my pride and joy. I'm the most dexterous man in Britain, just as Clean Willie is, or was, the most agile climber –before Edward Pierce's coachman did for him."

"Show it to me," I said eagerly, lifting my nuisance of a veil. I'd caught a glimpse through the gauze of a magnificent rope of diamonds. But seeing them now, and so close, would be much better.

"I can't show the necklace to you," he said. "I haven't got it."

"Did you drop it?" I almost screamed, recalling that hectic race through the theatre.

"No."

"Then where the hell is it?"

"Watch your language. Remember you're a respectable doctor's wife."

"You still haven't told me where the blasted thing is."

"In your reticule," he said wickedly.

"*What!*"

"The Duchess knows me. She's never met you before. If we'd been caught, I'd be the one most likely to be searched. Give it here so I can pass it up through the chain. If it doesn't get to the Boss at once my life won't be worth a moment's purchase. I'm told he's still smarting over the Countess of Morcar's blue carbuncle, which his arch-enemy Sherlock Holmes recovered for her. By the way, I told the Duchess of Loamshire you were wearing a veil because you are pock-marked."

"In Britain, in the nineteenth century?"

"I said you'd caught small-pox in India."

"It's my husband who was in India," I said testily.

"Ye-es?" said Clay in a funny voice. He signalled his coachman to stop. "I've got to be out of these togs and in Saxe-Coburg Square in an hour. Kirwan will drive you home. Tomorrow make up a parcel and take *your* togs to…"

"Yes, yes," I said impatiently, "Wigmore Street Post Office. S.M. To be called for."

"Certainly not," he retorted, shocked. "S.M.'s much too

important for that. Just mark the parcel with a couple of stick figures. The woman who comes for it will know what to ask for."

"I shall begin to be too well-known in Wigmore Street," I said uneasily, somewhat piqued to hear Moriarty had other women besides me in his organisation. I'd been rather hoping to keep my things, although when I'd get a chance to wear them again goodness only knew. As for the tiara, even John might eventually notice it and begin to ask awkward questions.

"You can always wear a veil," Clay said mockingly, blowing me a kiss and springing out of the coach. He bowed to me from the pavement as we drove off –and that was the last I ever saw of him.

Chapter Two

After that little episode with Clay, things quietened down for a while. I regretfully packed up my party clothes and took them back to the post office, and John and I settled down to our usual monotonous existence for a few weeks. He said he was busy with his medical chores and, in between, sat in his study chewing the end of a pencil. There was much talk of Editors, deadlines, incipient boredom because he hadn't seen Holmes for a while and a slight disagreement over the slavey. I wanted to get rid of her. As a doctor's wife whose husband also seemed to be carving out quite a lucrative literary career for himself, I felt very much in need of a larger establishment. A bigger house, with a cook, parlour-maid, out-door boy and a manservant to call a cab if one was wanted (although I secretly hoped we could have a carriage of our own eventually) was what I aimed for. But my husband felt sorry for the girl and said if she was as bad as I said she was then she'd never get another job and might even descend into prostitution. He did, however, say he would look out for something more suitable for us to live in.

Perhaps you can imagine my frustration when he bought a house large enough to have a consulting room on the ground floor. It was a very good address, however, and the aspidistra had pride of place in the hall. But if Holmes abandoned him he'd be at home all the time. The plant might never move to its place by the window. I had been told if we ever changed house I was to be sure to inform S.M. and had almost given up hope when John suddenly said he had to visit Holmes in a hurry, "To solve the mystery of an engineer who has lost his thumb." Well, that was a new one. But I didn't ask questions. Just whipped my precious plant off the table as fast as I could onto the window sill, and sat down to await results.

Sure enough a note soon came through the door, delivered apparently by a coster. Did I have a pistol? If not, I was to look in the empty water butt outside the scullery. Did I have a pair of built up shoes? That was a facer. But never mind. The note informed me there was a pair hidden in the long grass at the bottom of the back garden. If I was interested to know what the pistol and the shoes were for I was to go after dark to a house in Upper Swandam Lane (that had a familiar ring) where a lascar would tell me what to do, and give me a long cloak and a heavy veil. "Not again," I groaned. But as soon as the sun went down I was off.

When I plucked up enough courage to knock at the door of the decidedly seedy place in Upper Swandam Lane, which itself could hardly be called salubrious, a lascar came to the bottom of the stairs leading to the first floor and told me I was to prove myself by shooting somebody at a particular address. I didn't need to know the name, or what the man had done to deserve it, but the Boss would be highly gratified if I could empty both barrels into him. I asked the lascar if he had ever met the Boss or knew who he was. A look of the most abject terror appeared on his swarthy face. "No, ma'am, I haven't met him and I *don't want* to meet him. I don't know who he is, and I *don't want* to know."

I was a bit nervous at being given such an errand, and highly conscious of the gun in my stocking-top, but it didn't take me long to find the address. What did frighten me to death when I was admitted to the house by a servant was the sight of two pairs of boots behind a curtain. One pair I knew belonged to my husband, and I guessed the other pair belonged to Holmes. "So much for the engineer and his absent thumb," I said to myself and ran as fast as my legs could carry me away from the place. Little did I know that John and Sherlock were doing the same, thankfully in the opposite direction. I was too shaken to go to bed and when Watson came in I heard him, late as it was, call for hot water for a bath. When he sauntered into our sitting-room in his nightshirt and dressing-gown he was surprised, but I thought pleased, to see me. I could tell by the expression on his face that he had something shattering to impart.

"I was in a muck sweat," he said. "Holmes and I had to run for it. He's lighter than I am and vaulted over the wall easily. But a servant caught me by the ankle and I had to kick out, before we both ran for at least a mile without stopping over Hampstead Heath."

"Why?" I kept my voice steady. I certainly didn't want to let on that I'd seen his boots. But I was intrigued to know how he had come to be in the same place as I was, and exactly what Hampstead Heath had to do with it.

"The shots awakened the household and we didn't want to be found inside the building."

"What shots? And why," I repeated, "did you have to run away from wherever you were?" A nice touch that: "from wherever you were." I'd nearly given myself away.

John, scratching his head and answering my second question first, said vaguely, "I don't rightly know. Some scheme of Holmes'. He wanted to steal papers from a blackmailer. But, before we could do anything, a great tall woman wearing a thick veil came in and riddled the man with bullets while we were hiding behind a curtain."

I was puzzled as well as frightened. There was the explanation for the built-up shoes and the veil I'd been told to wear, but why had I been asked to go to the house in the first place? Was it simply to test my nerve, as the lascar said, and a coincidence that someone got there before me? Or did Moriarty want me to be caught red-handed with a pistol but had sent somebody else, someone with more experience, to actually do the job? Watson would be discredited through me, and Holmes would be discredited through him. The Professor was obviously even more devious than I thought –and more than a little revengeful. The blackmailer had probably been holding out on him, not giving him his cut. I recalled Moriarty's warning to me if I ever betrayed him, and shuddered right down to my shoes.

In order to hide my agitation I started fussing round John, bringing him hot cocoa and his favourite book –one of the 'yellow-backed' sort usually found on railway stations and left in hotel rooms. "Don't stay up too long," I said, planting a quick kiss on the top of his head. "It's already very late."

Once in our bedroom, I began to think seriously of the map M. Poirot had shown me in that private room of the Savoy Hotel. At the time I thought it was an impossible operation, but now I knew Moriarty was capable of anything. Would he test me again, or would we get on with that job? A month or so later, and after receiving a note from a crossing-sweeper, I used one of my usual excuses and told Watson I'd be away on a visit. The aspidistra was beginning to wilt, and I was tired of waiting for Holmes to turn up. John didn't enquire where my visit was going to be, or who with. Indeed he seemed not to have heard me, he was that preoccupied. Over the breakfast table he suddenly burst out with the news that Holmes had asked him to go abroad for a week, and that "anywhere would do."

"It's so unlike his normally precise nature," John said, buttering his third slice of toast and covering it with jam. "But he seemed unduly agitated, even talked about climbing over our back garden wall." He bit into the toast and said through a mouthful of crumbs, "Holmes did, however, ask after you –and I told him you were away from home."

"It's just as well that I will be then," I said tartly. "It saves you telling any lies!"

M. Poirot had told me that on a date to be arranged I was to go to a certain hall in the East End of London normally used by Methodists, where I would meet other people engaged in the same errand and be given more instructions. The call finally came on a bright day in early spring. I was to be in the East End at two o'clock on the very day John would be leaving Paddington Station for foreign parts and a holiday with Holmes.

I guessed the Methodist Hall had been hired to lend an air of respectability to the proceedings, and reached my destination in good time. There were a few men and considerably more women standing around and, when we were asked to take our seats, I was amazed to see someone I already knew from the newspapers. Famous in public life for philanthropy and the utmost probity, his name was a by-word in every middle-class home and every poverty-stricken hovel in the country. His face, as he mounted the platform, shone with benevolence. He had

31

donned a half-mask of black silk but there was no mistaking the uplifted, and uplifting, look in his fine eyes. I wondered at the mask. Surely everyone had, like me, twigged immediately who he was? We were there, he said, to organise blowing up the Houses of Parliament, Westminster Hall and the Tower of London. That would take an awful lot of dynamite and we were to pick up a stick each, tuck it in our bustles and march down Whitehall. What rubbish, I thought. There was a place on my map indicating where in the lobby of the House of Commons I was to place my explosive, but surely the police would want to know why so many women were streaming through London on a sunny April day just right for taking nothing more strenuous than a stroll in the park?

And what good would it do Moriarty? His specialities seemed to be forgeries, robberies and individual murders, carried out with the utmost secrecy; always for substantial gains, and sometimes for a very satisfying revenge. He excelled in planning, and revelled in his network of helpers and spies knowing that nobody could possibly guess who was behind the mayhem he caused: not even his senior henchmen if one discounted S.M. Blowing up buildings seemed an altogether too public a pastime. It was crude and not at all aesthetically pleasing, requiring only the most elementary mathematics.

"We've told the police it's a rally of the Women's Franchise

League," said the voice from the platform, "with a few male sympathisers. Now consult the maps you were given, find your groups and be off."

As I was preparing to leave the hall a tall young woman wearing rather a narrow bustle came up to me and hissed, "Don't bother to find your group, just look casual and follow me out of the hall while everybody's milling around."

"Did you collect your stick?" I asked breathlessly as soon as we were outside.

"Certainly not." She was walking resolutely away from the hall at a furious pace and had longer legs than me so that it was an effort to keep up with her. "We're all likely to be blown up ourselves marching down Whitehall. I hope you left your stick behind?"

"Well no, as a matter of fact…"

"We'll have to chuck it in the river," said my new acquaintance, moving faster than ever. The bang frightened the mudlarks, all those appropriately named destitute children scavenging on the banks of the Thames, out of their wits. They scattered like chaff in a high wind, while we fled before the river police could find out what was going on.

"Have you any idea why someone wants to blow up so many buildings?" I asked, wondering why we hadn't been sent to Buckingham Palace.

"No, unless it's to get the contracts for re-building; or to disrupt everything so much they can take over the country and run it for themselves."

That sounded much more like Moriarty. Only he would arrange for the Royal Family to be murdered and put up two of his most able henchmen as President and Prime Minister, while he continued to pull all the strings in secret. I'd wanted excitement, but this sounded altogether *too* gothic. I intimated as much to my companion who said, "It wouldn't have come off anyway. Burton and Cunningham tried it in 1885 and all they got was penal servitude for life."

"Yes," I said."But there were only two of them."

"Why, you goose, don't you know they had a large organisation behind them?"

"Maybe so," I said to myself, "but not like Moriarty's." Of course, it could have been Moriarty's gang once again foiled by Holmes. No wonder the Professor hated his guts. Aloud, I asked her what she was planning to do instead of helping to blow up buildings. "Find the Ripper," she answered coolly.

"The Ripper? Everyone says he's dead."

"There's such a thing as imitation. Prostitutes are still being cut to pieces. The police are so fed up with their lack of success in finding out who's doing it this time that they've given up. Which only leaves me."

I refrained from asking why she thought she was qualified for such a task and merely enquired what she intended to do at this minute. "Take you home and dress you up in something shabby. If we go into Whitechapel looking like this we'll be stripped naked, and not for any pleasurable reason I can assure you." Looking at me keenly she added, "You are game, I suppose?"

'Home' turned out to be a large villa standing in its own grounds near Hyde Park, with a well-lit dining-room in which some cold meats had been laid out on a small side-table. "Eat up," said this strange woman, grabbing something for herself. "Then we can go upstairs to change before sallying forth into the evening air." She sounded like a knight in armour. Saint George in search of the dragon.

"You do realise," I said briskly, "that I've no idea who you are?"

"Nor I you."

"Muriel Blatherskate." It was best to be cautious.

She looked at me sceptically and, holding out her hand, said in a cool voice, "Emily Fanshaw." Neither of us believed the other. But we would be Muriel and Emily for as long as this adventure lasted. I asked her how she had known about the march to the Houses of Parliament and who had given her a map.

"Map, what map?"

"The one which shows you where to plant your stick of dynamite."

"I don't know what you're talking about. I just happened to be passing, and went in to see what all the excitement was about."

Throwing an old cloak over me and calling for a stable boy, she ordered him to bring round the carriage and horses. "Get inside," she said to me as soon as it arrived and jumped onto the box, plying her whip with tremendous energy and swearing like a Billingsgate fishwife. It wasn't long at this rate before we reached a livery stable. "Here's where we leave the nags and walk," she shouted. It was only then that I realised she was in male attire. "It gives me freedom to walk about the streets, and will be some kind of protection for you. If people think I'm your brother there'll be less chance of your being molested." The shabby clothes weren't sufficient protection then. I began to wish I hadn't thrown that pistol back into the water-butt.

Walking as fast as ever, Emily led the way through a maze of dilapidated dwellings and past buildings which seemed to be kept standing by faith alone. They leaned precariously against one another, and from what we could see of the dirty rooms inside were crowded to suffocation. But there were an even larger number of pathetic scarecrows in the streets, with hordes of children scrabbling about in filthy gutters and relieving themselves when and where they pleased. In spite of our own ragged dress, I felt we gave ourselves away by being a picture of health.

"Some of these places are so dangerous that even policemen carrying guns are too scared to meddle here," said Emily, putting her hand into the pocket of her trousers and fingering the pistol I had seen her pick up before we left the house. "But most of the men you see lounging about here are cowards. The great thing is to look confident, and not to show the sign of fear."

This was easier said than done. I began to wish for my comfortable home and busy servants. Even John, with his old service revolver and Eley cartridges, would have been a comfort if he'd suddenly materialised. These 'slums' (the word had only recently come into common use) filled me with terror. If this was Whitechapel they could keep it as far as I was concerned.

"What's the matter?" asked Emily suddenly. "Lost your nerve?"

"No," I said, trying to stop my teeth from chattering. "But it would be helpful to know what we are to do next."

"This is in the nature of a reconnaissance. I'm looking for Leather Apron. If I can find his dolly mop…"

I didn't bother to reply since it was all Greek to me. She went into one of the houses, leaving me trembling on the pavement, and when she came out said, "What a bit of luck. I know where she is and if she's any kind of a judy she'll know where he is. But will she tell *us*."

I felt my interest in this adventure definitely on the wane. We were going deeper and deeper into a den of thieves and cut-throats and I wondered when, if ever, we would get out of it again. When we came to such a vile alley that I wished I had my scented handkerchief with me, or better still a bottle of smelling salts, Emily stopped in front of a recumbent bundle of rags and prodded it with her foot. "Leather Apron," she shouted. "Where is he?" The bundle of rags moved and a feeble female voice told us to go away, adding words even I didn't know –although Emily seemed familiar enough with them.

With a coarse laugh she took a small coin out of her pocket. "If I bribe her with any more," she whispered, "somebody here will murder her for the money." But the bundle would have none of that. She emerged from her rags for a moment, bit on the coin, secreted it somewhere about her person and, going back into her comatose state, said nothing.

"All right, if you don't mind the risk," growled Emily and gave her a guinea. The result could hardly be called electrifying. We had to bend down to catch a very few words, and once they were spoken this horrifying relic of a degraded humanity retreated into whatever world her soul was being allowed to occupy.

"She can't last much longer, poor creature," said Emily. "But at least we know where her pimp is."

We had come out of the warren and were walking down Whitechapel High Street when we came across a butcher's shop. I use these words rather than others because I feel that no-one who reads this could possibly have any idea what it was really like. Blood streamed everywhere, and animals were being slaughtered willy-nilly in the lurid glare of a dozen gas lamps. These not only served to show what was going on but gave a demonic appearance to the whole scene, one which mimicked hell in all its horror. There was no regard for the dying animals' terrible sufferings. And not only was the noise deafening, but the stench was as bad, or worse, than the one we'd just left. I turned aside to be violently sick, but nobody would notice *that* among all the other filth.

In the middle of this mayhem stood a man wielding a gigantic cleaver. To say he was ugly would be an understatement on my part, but to say he was weedy would be a downright lie. Tall and heavily built, he was one of the largest men I'd ever seen in my life. His leather apron, tied round his waist with a dirty piece of string, couldn't hide his huge calves and, because he wore only a singlet, his arm muscles were also very much in evidence. They rippled with menace, and he was obviously taking a sadistic delight in his work. The apron was covered in blood, shambles and other material I didn't want to think about. Even Emily was disconcerted. "I'm here," she screamed above the tortured racket of living animals having their legs broken, "to make a citizen's arrest for the murder of …" But the rest of her words were lost in the infernal din.

To say that the giant was momentarily halted in his tracks is also an understatement. He stopped with the cleaver in mid-air and his mouth open in the most enormous gape, showing black and broken stumps of rotting teeth. It would have been funny if it hadn't been so frightening. The next second he had sprung out of the abattoir with an inhuman yell of rage, and would have cut us down if four bobbies hadn't suddenly appeared from nowhere and come rushing towards us.

Even four men had trouble in restraining this ogre, and were whistling frantically for reinforcements. But he was handcuffed at last, bundled into a Black Maria and taken away howling imprecations at us, the coppers and the world in general. "I would advise you, madam, to leave catching killers to the police," said one of the constables gravely, "and get back as quickly as you are able to your own sphere." He had seen through her disguise all right, in spite of all her planning. As we went away, Emily took off her cloth cap, flung it disgustedly into a gutter and we ran at full pelt back to where she had left her carriage and stabled her horses. I'm sorry to say that on the way home she took it out on her animals more than ever. Did she, too, have a sadistic streak? One would naturally assume there wasn't quite so much scope for it in Bayswater as there was in Whitechapel. I felt that, although at first appearing to be shocked, she had secretly enjoyed some of the things going on in the abattoir.

Shortly after we reached our destination and I was thankfully climbing back into my own clothes, there was a ring at the door-bell. Since it was so late and the servants were in bed, Emily opened the door herself and I heard a familiar voice say, "My, but you're still a fine filly, Mrs. St. Clair." I had never heard such language from him, even though I knew he was fond of racing. But surely that couldn't really be John? I ran downstairs in time to see him putting his hat and stick on the hall table, and was amazed when he didn't show the slightest sign of surprise at seeing me.

"Do you two know each other?" I demanded, glaring at Emily. Miss Fanshaw my foot!

"Doctor Watson and Mr. Sherlock Holmes rescued my husband from a noisome den in Upper Swandam Lane," she said in the demurest voice imaginable, turning to me with a well-bred expression on her duplicitous face. But all I could think of was that Upper Swandam Lane was beginning to haunt me.

41

"That's right," said John heartily. "By the way, how is Hugh?"

"Surely you mean Neville?" I saw her smile sweetly at Watson, indicating most graciously that his mistake was quite understandable. He wasn't to feel bad about it. "My husband's at a bit of a loose end since your friend warned him off begging, but we jog along nicely. At the moment I'm afraid he's away from home on business."

"Yes. How silly of me. Neville, of course," John stammered. "A great pity we can't meet again and have a good laugh over that very convincing make-up of his, and the red wig Holmes twitched off his head after applying a wet sponge to his face. You could have knocked me down with a feather when my friend bent down and took that sponge out of his Gladstone bag. I had absolutely no idea where it had come from, or what he would want with it."

"Yes," said Emily in a cold voice. "I was told Mr. Holmes took advantage of my husband while he was asleep. He even used the water from a jug in the room where Neville was confined to dampen the said sponge so that it could do its work. We had to sell the house in Kent."

Watson, obviously very discomfited, gazed vaguely round the room, twiddled absentmindedly with a small ornament on a nearby whatnot, politely declined Emily's offer of refreshment, picked up his hat and stick, ceremoniously offered me his arm and finally said, "I've very much enjoyed meeting you again and chatting about old times. But now I must take Mary home."

Chapter Three

I didn't say much on the way back to the house, except to ask John how he knew where to find me. "I was coming from Paddington Station on my way home from that so-called holiday with Holmes when I recognised the livery, and then spotted you sitting inside the carriage. There seemed to be someone quite wild in the driving-seat. Had me worried for a minute."

"Mrs. St. Clair keeps a queer coachman," I said hurriedly, clinging to John's arm like the proverbial ivy.

Once indoors, while I was hanging up my hat and cloak and he was changing his boots in favour of his scorched slippers, I asked after Mr. Holmes –only to be told he'd gone over some Swiss Falls!

"It turned out we were evading Moriarty. I was decoyed away by some tale of illness at our hotel, those two beggars met, there was a fight and, still locked in each other's arms, they fell from a narrow ledge into the raging torrent. I'm afraid, my dear, that Holmes is dead as mutton."

"I've never heard you speak so lightly of him before."

"To tell the truth, I was getting a little tired. Not of our adventures, I shall always remember them with relish, but his continual sniping. It's wearing to be put down so much."

"Yet you let it be included in all your reports."

"Holmes insisted on it as a condition of publication. I suppose he needed a boost to his ego, although you'd never think so if you heard the way he spoke sometimes. Of course, I'll be just as fulsome as I ever was in what may be the last account of our time together." My husband put his feet on the fender, as was his habit, even though the coals were not lit. "I've decided to call it *The Final Problem.* Ring for some brandy will you? I've got something else to tell you."

Once the brandy was brought and the servant out of the way he said, with a sidelong glance at me, "Have you ever heard of anyone changing their name by deed-poll?"

"No, I can't say I have."

"Well, I did. I was born Ormond Sacker."

"And you changed it?"

"Wouldn't you?" John picked up one of the fire-irons and started poking at the dead coals.

"Yes, I certainly would," I said. "But why change it to Watson?"

"That seemed as good a name as any, plain and much less exotic than Sacker, to say nothing of Ormond. As a matter of fact, it turned out that 'John Watson' would prove highly appropriate. But that's a tale that can wait for another time."

John stopped poking ineffectually at the cold grate and shifted uneasily in his chair. It appeared that he had even more confidences to make. "While we're at it," he mumbled, "I might

45

as well tell you that I'm not a doctor either."

"*What?*"

"I started off as a ward orderly at Netley. It's a military hospital near Southampton."

"That explains why you played down your expertise and let Holmes do most of the talking when it came to discussing anything medical." I could hardly believe my ears.

"Well, I was allowed to say something after Huxtable fainted at the beginning of our investigation into the events at the Priory School, and Holmes said a description of the way I dealt with an engineer's severed thumb should be included in one of the so-called *Adventures*. I was occasionally called upon to assist a client with the vapours or to say something about rigor mortis, as I did when it came to writing about Blessington. In my very first outing with Sherlock, long before I started writing for *The Strand,* I told the readers of *Beeton's Christmas Annual* how I successfully identified an aortic aneurism. But it was when Holmes pointed out the absence of powder blackening on a body to prove a man hadn't been shot at close range that I nearly came unstuck. A genuine ex-army surgeon would have spotted that at once. Mind you, although I was anxious not to undeceive my fellow lodger, as a conscientious author I couldn't assume my readers would know as much as I did about the subject. It was better to give Holmes his head on this occasion, even if it did make me appear somewhat stupid."

"What about the so-called Civil Practice you mentioned?" I screamed.

"A ward orderly gets to know a lot about dressings and such like. He also picks up things from the doctors if he's intelligent and keeps his eyes and ears open. I learned enough to get by reasonably well in general practice, where it's mainly cuts and bruises and the occasional sprained ankle. There were also plenty of broken arms and legs to be set where the soldiers at Netley were concerned, I assure you." John paused and took a large sip of the brandy. "Mind you, I was always glad to have Anstruther or Jackson take over, or even Verner, while I was once more off assisting Holmes in yet another of his investigations."

I began to think my head would burst and rushed upstairs into our bedroom. After a few minutes frantic searching I came back into the sitting-room angrily waving a book at him. "It says here you met Holmes in one of the laboratories of St. Bartholomew's Hospital and that a former dresser –a dresser mind you, someone who would train under you if you *were* a house surgeon – introduced you to Holmes."

"All eyewash," said Watson. "I met Sherlock at the racecourse, where he was busy poking his nose into some crooked bookies' business."

"So what are we going to live on if you're not a doctor and can't write up any more adventures with him?"

"I could go back in time, for example before we were married or before he was silly enough to get himself killed. I've done it before. Or I could sell another of your pearls."

"Pearls?"

"You've obviously forgotten they weren't sunk with the Agra treasure, and that I suggested you give them to me for safe keeping. It was while we were holding hands in the garden, like two children."

"One mug and one crook you mean," I retorted bitterly, remembering his account in what he had called *The Sign of Four*.

He looked very hurt and said, "I've always used the proceeds of any sale for your benefit as well as mine. How do you think I managed to buy this house, with its fashionable practice?"

"If it's that fashionable it's a wonder you haven't been found out. It would be better if you'd worked in the slums, where nobody knows anything.''

"And where nobody has any money. I'm surprised you think I'm that altruistic. Surely you realise my present 'patients' only want their toenails cut, or someone to listen sympathetically to the symptoms of their largely imaginary illnesses? If you knew the number of nostrums I've sold to bored society women you'd be absolutely amazed."

I relented a little at the sight of his sad face and said, as kindly as I could in such terrible circumstances, "Very well, then. Write a new story and screw as much out of the Editor of *The Strand* as you possibly can for it." John didn't seem to notice my language or the change in me. I was suddenly seized with the idea that he might have known all about me from the beginning. What had Moriarty said? One villain can always recognise another one, however heavy the disguise.

After a week in his study he emerged with a dog-eared manuscript and laid it on the dining-room table. I picked up the crowded pages and read them very carefully while he watched me from the window, looking out now and then as if he half expected a patient. But I had persuaded him almost immediately after his confession to sell his Practice, and a fully qualified young man with impeccable references was now temporarily occupying our front drawing-room while he looked for somewhere else to see his patients. The last thing we needed was trouble with the police. Turning my attention once more to the tattered-looking tale, I read: 'It was the evening of our wedding day and my wife and I were commiserating with one another that my old friend Sherlock Holmes could not be with us on such a momentous occasion.

"Oh well," I said good-humouredly, looking down at my new

boots that were later to receive such critical attention from Holmes, "even we must give way to Presidents and Foreign Royalty, to say nothing of the Emperor of China."

"Certainly," said my wife. "But did you happen to notice the old gentleman in Mr. Holmes' place at the church?"

I confessed that I hadn't, adding gallantly that at such a time and in such a place I had eyes only for her.

"He looked *like an amiable and simple-minded Nonconformist clergyman.*"

I replied laughingly that in using the word "simple-minded" I hoped she meant unsophisticated, and not that the stranger was wanting in the upper storey. It was while we were engaged in this friendly badinage that we both heard a ring at the door-bell.

I sat up in my chair and my wife laid her needlework down in her lap and made a little face of disappointment. "A patient," said she. "You'll have to go out."

"Hardly a patient," I replied, "since no-one knows yet that I've come back into civil practice." *I had bought a connection in the Paddington district. Old Mr. Farquhar, from whom I purchased it, had at one time an excellent general practice, but his age, and an affliction of the nature of St. Vitus's dance from which he suffered, had very much thinned it.*

My wife picked up her needlework again. "Could it be Mr. Sherlock Holmes?"

While I was pondering on this *we heard the door open, a few hurried words, and then quick steps upon the linoleum. Our own door flew open.* It was indeed the friend with whom I had co-operated so joyfully in *A Study in Scarlet* and *The Sign of Four.* "Mrs. Watson," he said *with that easy courtesy for which he was remarkable,* I must ask you to lend me your husband in the next five minutes as I am at present engaged in a case that threatens to undermine the whole fabric of our society. Besides, *I am glad to have a friend with whom I can discuss my results."*

"Then of course you must go," said my wife, rising and handing me the case I had packed that morning. My experience of camp life in Afghanistan had at least had the effect of making me a prompt and ready traveller. My wants were few and simple so that in less than the time stated I was in a cab with my valise.

"Bravo, Doctor," said Holmes, *with the easy air of geniality which he could so readily assume.* "Here we are at Baker Street at last." He jumped down, signed to me to pay the cabby (which of course I was only too delighted to do) ran up the front steps and put his key in the lock. As we climbed the stairs together to what had once been our shared sitting-room I was afraid there might be a repetition of his lecture to me on the subject of seeing but not observing with regard to the number of steps. But to my relief he merely glanced at me quizzically, flung open the door and invited me ceremoniously to enter.

The room was much as I had left it that morning, apart from the absence of my own few bits and pieces which I had arranged to be transferred to my new abode before the wedding ceremony. The bench in the corner was still strewn with test tubes, retort stands and sticking plaster, while the gasogene bubbled happily away on its side table. I sank gratefully into my old armchair and Holmes went to the mantelpiece. He looked casually at his latest letters transfixed in the middle of it with a large jack-knife, and filled his pipe from an old tin box he had been using ever since Mrs. Hudson threw away his Persian slippers while he was in Sumatra.

"I'm expecting someone to call at any moment," he said, striking a match. "Someone who, if I'm not mistaken, will tell us a tale of the greatest interest. Meanwhile, my dear fellow, do help yourself to a cigar from the coal-scuttle."

At that moment I was aware of a light step on the stairs. My old friend was at the door an instant before the knock came, and ushered in a young woman. I had almost said a young lady, only a quick glance at her clothes revealed her to be of the servant class.

She was rather above the middle height, slim, with dark hair and eyes, which seemed the darker against the absolute pallor of her skin. I do not think that I have ever seen such deadly paleness in a woman's face. Her lips too were bloodless, but her eyes were flushed with crying. Holmes led her gently to a chair by the fire. "Now," he said, "when you are settled you can tell us about your problem with your master."

The girl started, her face suffused by a deep blush which entirely overcame its former whiteness. I saw that in spite of the clothes and unfashionable hat she was really rather comely. *At first I suspected a mere vulgar intrigue,* but a glance at Sherlock Holmes' grave face rapidly dispelled that thought. "You are wondering how I know," he said, looking at her closely. "Before coming here you have put your hat on back to front. Also, it is rather late for a youthful person, and of the female sex, to be out." He took a draw on his pipe. "But I suppose as your mistress is away for the day you have been at the beck and call of your master and until now have had little chance to consult me."

Not knowing Holmes' methods as well as I do, the girl was listening to all this with the utmost amazement. So surprised was she that she even neglected to adjust her hat which, now my old friend mentioned it, did look somewhat odd. "How did you know my mistress had gone to Surbiton?" she gasped.

"I didn't. That is to say, I was unaware of the precise location of her destination. Let me ask you, did you take a cab in order to get here?" the young person nodded dumbly. "Then the few spots on your shoes must have come from the house. Perhaps when you waited at table?"

I thought our young visitor would faint and sprang to her aid, all my medical instincts rushing to the fore. She had jumped to her feet and now swung in the direction of the door, looking as if she would hurl herself through it if we tried to stop her. "How do you know I waited at table today?" she cried. "I never do normally."

"No," said Holmes. "That large blister you have between the finger and thumb of your right hand shows that you are unused to handling hot plates; and if your mistress had been at home she would never have allowed you to continue going about your duties with shoes made dirty by drops of gravy. Also, of course, if she planned to be away for more than a day she would have taken you with her. No doubt she left you some sewing to do." He smiled. "You really ought always to use a thimble, you know!"

The poor girl put her pricked fingers to her head. *"Forgive this weakness, Mr. Holmes. I have been a little overwrought...if I might have a glass of milk and a biscuit, I have no doubt I should be better."*

"When you are quite restored..."

"I am quite well again. I cannot imagine how I came to be so weak."

Seeing the servant was now calmer, I invited her to sit down again. "That's right," said Sherlock Holmes kindly. "There is really nothing to be afraid of. Putting your hat on like that was the natural act of someone not used to coming out at night to consult a gentleman about the irrational behaviour of her employer's husband."

To my great consternation our visitor suddenly burst into tears. "I am at my wits end what to do," she sobbed. "It's such a good place, sir."

Holmes began restlessly pacing the room. "And you naturally want to keep it," he said. "Something which is becoming increasingly difficult with your master's seemingly inexplicable changes of mood." He suddenly *pushed back the frill of black lace which fringed the hand that lay on our visitor's knee. Five little livid spots, the marks of four fingers and a thumb, were printed upon the white wrist.* "One day he is quite rough with you and the next gives his footman the night off so he can sup with you, making sure you place the plates first as we have seen. Quite extraordinary. You blushed at the remembrance of it."

The girl looked steadily at Holmes. "He has been trying to persuade the mistress to sell her ornaments and asked me to help him. He's quite kind to me when he thinks I'm about to succeed with her, and very violent if she seems to be changing her mind. *Indeed, he* [has] *drifted into the habit of winding up every meal by taking out his false teeth and hurling them at his wife.*"

55

I found it hard to suppress a smile at this. However, Holmes' continuing gravity caused me to check instantly a natural inclination to laugh.

"This appears to be a most serious case, as I suspected when you first asked for an appointment," he said. "But it grows very late. Put on your cloak and Doctor Watson will see you safely to a cab. Rest assured I shall solve this case, and in such a way that you won't lose your employment."

The servant girl smiled gratefully and we left the room together. When I returned a few minutes later, having blown my whistle for a cab and settled the girl into it, Holmes was in his dressing gown and slippers, a violin on his knees. "Anything but that," I said to myself. He was inclined to scrape away at the catgut when considering a case, although he could play the instrument well enough when he chose. As usual he read my unspoken thoughts. "Don't worry, Watson. I've finished for tonight. Now, what do you think of that little episode?"

"I am intrigued to know what ornaments were meant, or why the husband hates them so much."

"Impossible to answer those questions at present. What did you think of the girl?"

I glanced at him in some surprise. I had seen earlier how *my friend took the lady's ungloved hand and examined it with as close an attention and as little sentiment as a scientist would show to a specimen.*

"Charming," I replied in a puzzled tone. "But why were you so certain her mistress would wish to have her company on a longer stay away from home?"

"Come, my dear fellow, she is no ordinary servant but a superior lady's maid. Now, since it is so late I assume you will want your old room for the night. Tomorrow we will have to get to work in earnest."

Little did I guess then what dens we would visit, or how many cabmen we would solicit for information during the next fortnight. As always, when Holmes was on a case he shook off his drug-induced lethargy and became indefatigable.

He adopted a number of disguises such as the one when, having sent me back to Baker Street early, he made a pretence at being *a drunken-looking groom, ill-kempt and side-whiskered with an inflamed face and disreputable clothes* [who] *lent the ostlers a hand in rubbing down their horses* [for] *"twopence, a glass of half-and-half, two fills of shag tobacco, and as much information as I could desire."*

But I was used to exhibitions of his skill as an actor, and reflected on what I had once been told during another case by the young boy who acted as page after it became clear that I was intending to leave Baker Street: *"He's following someone. Yesterday he was out as a workman looking for a job. Today he*

57

was an old woman. Fair took me in, he did, and I ought to know his ways by now. "

One morning, when the leg wound I had sustained at the battle of Maiwand in July 1880 was particularly troublesome, I left Holmes to visit a noisome place down by the docks while I spent the day in my old lodgings. *The jezail bullet which I had brought back as a relic of my Afghan campaign throbbed with dull persistency. With my body in one easy chair and my legs in another, I had surrounded myself with a cloud of newspapers, until at last, saturated with the news of the day, I tossed them all aside.*

Suddenly I became aware that Holmes had entered the house and was slowly mounting the stairs. Knowing the quick step he adopted when engaged in solving a crime, I feared that he had been hurt and sprang out of the chair just in time to see him struggling through the door with two bulky objects which he endeavoured to place on a nearby table.

"You'll have to help me Watson," he gasped. "I've carried this fiendish burden all the way from Shoreditch and I'm absolutely done in."

"Good gracious, Holmes!" I cried. "You don't mean to say that you have been walking about London with that thing? Why on earth didn't you take a cab?"

"Because I wished to be followed," said my friend cryptically, "on foot." He ran to the window, pulled back the blind and peered out into the street. "You see, Watson?" He waved his pipe excitedly. "There's our man. Anxious, if I am not mistaken, to get back his property. The question is, will he be brave enough to come up here and ask for it?"

Full of curiosity, I looked over his shoulder. All I could see was a poor down-at-heel costermonger. Not even that. More like a rag-and-bone man, whose unsightly cargo was covered by a filthy blanket.

"What property of his could we possibly have?" I asked.

"Why what I have just brought in, my boy!" Holmes strode over to the table, where there sat two large brass monkeys with their hands covering what must have been, if fully visible, the ugliest faces I ever saw in my life. "Why two?" I asked curiously from the window. After all, even I was aware that brass monkeys usually came in threes.

"One for each end of the mantelpiece," cried Holmes. "That wretch you can see arrives in a respectable neighbourhood with his wares and persuades the housemaid to replace whatever is above the fire-irons with what he has in his cart. All she knows is that her mistress is tired of looking at the usual ornaments so she gladly makes the change, hoping to get into her employer's good books."

"By Jove," I chuckled. "It's like one of those stories that poor woman has to keep telling to avoid having her head cut off!"

"Lane's *Arabian Nights*" replied Holmes laconically. "New Lamps for Old. What neither the maid nor the mistress knows is that the master has arranged for that fiend lounging out there to call."

"I confess I am in the dark," I said. "Why on earth should a respectable man want someone like that hanging about outside his house and knocking at his door?"

For answer, Sherlock Holmes began gently unscrewing the head of one of the monkeys. I gave over scrutinising the man with the barrow and strolled towards the table, where I saw that the body cavity of the brass ornament was filled with tiny packets. Round the inside rim of the neck were faint traces of brownish white dust, which defied all my medical knowledge to identify. I stretched out an exploratory finger meaning to taste, or at least smell, the deposit.

"No, Watson!" Holmes pushed my hand away before I could touch anything. I gazed at him in horror. "Whatever is it?" I demanded, unused to seeing him make such violent gestures.

"Cannabis."

The word hung in the air between us. I recalled the vast number of brass monkeys I had seen in so many London drawing-rooms and shuddered.

"Yes," said Sherlock Holmes in reply to my unspoken

thought. "Now you realise why it is so important to solve this case. Things have already gone too far. This is the answer to one man's moodiness and his expertise with the false teeth. His wife's maid must have opened the door to that wretch when she went for her morning walk. Being close to her mistress, she would know that certain ornaments were too highly prized by her to take anything else in exchange. Imagine the plight of the husband when he found his ruse continually foiled."

"They say it's not addictive," I murmured, remembering his own psychological dependence on cocaine, and wondering why so many appearances at the door by our friend outside should go unremarked by the lady's-maid or her mistress. But Holmes had dashed down the stairs. He came back minutes later with a loudly protesting runt of a man who he gripped firmly by the collar. I beheld *a middle-sized man, coarsely clad and extremely dirty, but the grime which covered his face could not conceal its repulsive ugliness. A broad weal from an old scar ran across it from eye to chin, and by its contraction had turned up one side of the upper lip, so that three teeth were exposed in a perpetual snarl. A shock of very bright red hair grew low over his eyes and forehead.*

"Well, Watson, what can you tell me about him?" he asked, flinging the miscreant into a chair.

"His clothes are remarkably seedy. His boots need mending,

and by the look of the dirt on them I would say he comes from Hoxton."

"Overlaid by other dust after his forced tramp from Shoreditch, of course." *Sherlock Holmes clapped his hands softly together and chuckled. "'Pon my word, Watson, you are coming along wonderfully. You have done very well indeed.* There is no mistaking the heavy clay of the London Basin, and Hoxton soil is always easy to spot. What about the ash on his waistcoat?"

I looked, but confessed I could make nothing of it. To tell the truth I was rather miffed at having my efforts interrupted. The fact that the man wore a very old pair of trousers, an open-necked shirt and a dirty red choker, and that his sleeves were rolled up to show scrawny forearms as filthy as his face were matters I would have commented on next, given a chance.

Holmes spoke again. "*It is the ash of a cigar, which my special knowledge of tobacco ashes enabled me to pronounce as an Indian cigar. I have as you know devoted some attention to this, and written a little monograph on the ashes of 140 of pipe, cigar and cigarette tobacco. It was an Indian cigar of the variety which are rolled in Rotterdam.* Now where would such a creature get a cigar? It is unlikely he was ever in Rotterdam."

Knowing nothing of imports and exports, I owned myself baffled.

"Never mind," said Holmes kindly. "What do you make of the tattoos on his arms? I would say definitely Chinese."

As I was so familiar with his love of praise, even though he tried to hide it, I decided to humour him and said heartily, "Wonderful. I don't know how you do it."

"Commonplace," he replied smugly. "You know my methods by now, Watson. After all, you've written about them often enough in that irritatingly unscientific way of yours." Taking a small, damp sponge, he began scrubbing vigorously away at our captive while I glowered in the background, hurt at having my well-meant attempts to bring his talents before the public slighted in such a way.

"The fish you see more clearly now on the right forearm could only have been done in the East," said Sherlock Holmes, flinging away the sponge. *"I have made a small study of tattoo marks, and have even contributed to the literature on the subject. That trick of staining the fishes' scales of a delicate pink is quite peculiar to China."*

I suddenly remembered something. "You have been down at the docks all day!"

"Exactly. I will send a telegram to Lestrade suggesting he impound this fellow's cart and its contents and then we will all three be on the way to Hoxton before daylight goes. This time we will take a cab. Meanwhile, it would be as well to put these beauties in the safe."

"Such brass ornaments come into Rotterdam from the Dutch overseas possessions," remarked Holmes complacently when we were all seated safely in a four-wheeler and bowling towards Hoxton. "It's very easy to bring them to London, along with a cargo of cigars, aboard a regular packet boat. I discovered that most of the crew are Chinese, and one of them is a tattooist."

"So that's how he got any cigars, from a sailor," I cried, staring at the cowed man opposite. "He didn't go to Rotterdam. "Yes," said my friend in answer to my first observation, "*cigars of the peculiar sort which are imported by the Dutch from their East Indian colonies. They are usually wrapped in straw, you know, and are thinner for their length than any other brand.*"

"But what about the cannabis?" said I.

"I'm afraid you will have to wait for an answer to that. *Now here is my pocket Petrarch, and not another word shall I say of this case until we are on the scene of action.*"

The cab took us to one of the meanest streets in Hoxton and to one of its meanest houses, set well back from the road and screened by a high, untrimmed hedge. This address was evidently a blind since, unless our friend proved to be just a go-between, he must be very wealthy. As we went through the gate, I saw that the one thing that might redeem such a place was the huge number of plants, belonging to the *Moraceae* family, which covered the garden. The coarse-toothed grey-green leaves and drooping stamens combined to produce some magnificent shrubs.

Holmes, however, has no eye for the beauties of nature, in spite of his once rhapsodising about a rose when he helped my old school friend Percy Phelps to prove his innocence over a stolen Naval Treaty. He hurried our prisoner up the path. "Do you deny that you process the drug in a derelict Shoreditch warehouse, where I've no doubt we'll find your vats and paddles as well as your drying agents? I tell you, you can't deny it. The raw material is growing everywhere...'

"I see you've remarked on the fact that brass monkeys normally come in threes," I said, putting the manuscript back on the table. "But cannabis can't be grown outdoors in Britain. Did you mistake the powder for some other drug? Morning Glory often appears accidentally in suburban gardens and, by the way, this isn't your best effort. Not by a long chalk. For example, everyone already knows about the jack-knife in the middle of the mantelpiece. I saw it myself when I first came to Baker Street. As for the page, surely he was with you both sometime before we got married?"

"No, it isn't," he replied wearily. "My best effort, I mean. "But because anything about Holmes always increases sales at least ten-fold the Editor may take it."

65

"There's also something odd about the text. It makes me wonder if I've read these sentences before."

"Not all of them," he said defensively, "only the ones in italics."

"Any Editor would recognise them immediately!"

Watson came over from the window, placed his hands heavily on the table and said in a loud deliberate tone, at the same time as he gazed intently at me with eyes which were beginning to look half-crazed, "If I'm to have any chance of success with something new, I'll have to kill you off."

"Not on your life," I said, picking up a weighty cruet and preparing either to use it or run.

"Not literally," he yelled as I raised my arm. "But you've no idea what a tremendous strain it's been, having to make a passing, and usually totally inadequate, reference to you now and again just to show you were still around. I'm surprised the readers swallowed it."

"They swallowed all the rest of it, didn't they? If you are not really going to polish me off (for which information, thank you very much) what *are* you going to do?"

"I thought you could stay with Arthur's mother. She lives on someone's estate in a small village called Masongill. It's in Yorkshire, I believe. Then all that needs to be said is you've nobly gone to take care of her in her old age and won't appear in these pages again for some time, if ever. Then that would be that. I'd be saved the trouble of sending you off to a mother and an aunt, both of whom you haven't got, or on visits that could never reasonably have taken place. Not, anyway, without more explanation than anybody was able to think of under as much pressure as I was to produce results for an impatient Editor."

I made a great effort and managed to remember that Arthur was his literary agent. But if he thought I was going to live with a woman of advanced age at the back of beyond, in a place I'd never heard of, he had another think coming. Anyway, since it was *all* going to be what Watson had called eye-wash from now on with both Holmes and Moriarty gone, why did I need to go away from home in the first place?

"I've a much better idea," I said, carefully setting down the cruet. "Forget Holmes. Write about the mystery we're going to solve together."

"What mystery?"

"We haven't found one yet," I said airily, walking towards the kitchen with a spring in my step. "But, mark my words, something will turn up."

Chapter Four

Well something did turn up, and even sooner than I anticipated. The next morning at breakfast John showed me a letter he'd just received. "It's from Tadpole Phelps, an acquaintance of mine. He's of excellent family, you know. We met when Holmes was supposed to be investigating the theft of a naval treaty."

"Yes, yes," I said impatiently. "You mentioned it in that silly story you showed me recently. And didn't you tell the *Strand* readers he was an old school friend, along with a whole lot of nonsense about cricket stumps and so forth?"

"You must admit it made a good introduction. It was always a problem trying to fill the space allotted to me in the magazine, which got larger as Holmes became more popular. If you read this letter you'll see Tadpole's been invited for the weekend to the Duke and Duchess of Loamshire's Country House. He can't go because his wife's expecting a little stranger very shortly, so he's passed the invitation on to us."

"He can't know much about heredity otherwise he would never have married that woman. You painted her whiter than white. But how could she be, with such a brother? A man who had no scruples about letting his sister's fiancé be wrongly suspected of theft: and would have seen him die of brain fever without turning a hair so long as his own hide was safe."

"Never mind that now," John said hurriedly. "The point is, are we going?"

It was a bit worrying. Would the Duchess recognise me? I had been wearing a veil. I decided to risk it, and Watson said in a tight voice, "Remember not to make our bed, or put anything that might embarrass you in your valise. At these great houses a valet will unpack for us and lay out our things every morning and evening."

"I," I said, drawing myself up to my full height of five foot three, "am a Lady." How could there be anything embarrassing in my luggage?

"A Lady my eye!" said John derisively, and we danced merrily round the room together. Really, since poor old Holmes went into the water, Watson has become quite human.

The first thing the Duke did when we arrived was pinch my behind. But I soon put paid to that kind of behaviour by kicking him in the shins, accidently on purpose, with the heel of my shoe under cover of rearranging the flounce on my travelling outfit. That evening, while we were dressing for dinner, I showed John a bruise the size of a shilling and he threatened to go straightaway and punch His Grace on his aristocratic nose.

"Not before we've had something to eat," I said, gathering up my train and sweeping out of the room. The sale of yet another of the Agra pearls had provided us with very creditable togs, and we had nothing to be ashamed of as we took our places at table among the glittering cutlery and delicate epergnes. John and I, of course, had relatively low places (Tadpole wasn't of that good a family, it turned out). But from where we sat I had a very good view of the Duchess's rope of diamonds. She must have got them back when John Clay was caught robbing that bank in Coburg Square. And it wasn't difficult to guess who got them back for her either.

The next evening there was no great dinner, only sandwiches and cold meats in the little sitting-room adjoining our bedroom. The house was in an uproar. There was panic everywhere and the Duke was racing round the grounds with a pair of pistols. The Duchess had had her diamonds stolen again. Really, that woman was very careless. Scotland Yard had been called in, of course, and when we at last ventured out of our rooms who should we bump into but John's old acquaintance, Inspector Lestrade. He was wearing a black arm band and looking very disconsolate. "I had many a skirmish with Mr. Holmes," he said sadly. "But I'm sorry he's gone. Mind you, since we've also seen the good riddance of 'The Napoleon of Crime' as Mr. Holmes used to like to call him, the Yard has had a great deal less work to do."

"It's an ill wind blows nobody any good," said my husband. "But remember, my wife and I are fortunately here to help you.

70

Might I suggest you search the house while we go over the grounds?"

"In the dark?" asked Lestrade.

"A good point," conceded John. "It will have to be done in the morning."

"The Duke's still out there," I said, "making a fool of himself. There's no need for you to do the same."

"Excuse me, madam," said Lestrade gravely, "but if His Grace went out immediately the alarm was raised he'd have a good chance of catching the thief red-handed."

Seeing from the expression on my face that this difference of opinion might grow to such proportions it would hinder the investigation, John said soothingly that this time we would be on the Inspector's side and co-operate with him fully. "There will be a pooling of information, and I think you should meet us at eleven o'clock tomorrow morning in our little sitting-room to discuss a plan of action."

When the Inspector put in an appearance the next day he looked worn out, and more sallow than ever. He'd been instructed to take his meals below stairs and given an uncomfortable bed in one of the attics. Sighing heavily, he said he hadn't been able to sleep a wink because of the noise from the bats in the eaves.

"Better than bats in the belfry," said John, who since he lost

71

Sherlock is prone to making quite terrible jokes. "My wife will interview all the valets and the footmen while you and I comb the grounds for clues. I've got Holmes' spy glass here. I kept it for a souvenir. You never know, it might bring us luck."

The first footman to whom I spoke had a good leg, and a pair of bright blue eyes. If I wasn't careful he could tell me anything. Making a mental note for us to get better acquainted, I asked him if he had waited at table the night the Duchess of Loamshire lost her diamonds. No, he said, it was his turn to stand on one side of the double doors to the dining salon and keep as still as a stature. What about the other footman on duty with him? "The same," he said briefly.

But wasn't it possible for someone to pass the jewels to him as he (or she) went out of the dining-room and along the covered way which separated the kitchen quarters from the main house? The look he gave me showed as plainly as possible that I'd betrayed myself as a *parvenu*. There wouldn't be any women in the dining-room apart from the hostess and her guests, and if it was an inside job any of the other male servants could have put the diamonds in one of the serving hatches with the dirty plates. An extra tug on the ropes would alert an accomplice –of either sex – in the kitchen, who could then secrete them where they liked.

The next thing, therefore, was to interrogate the Cook. Once again, I gave myself away. There was an army of cooks milling about the kitchen, along with maids, boot blacks, scullery hands, skivvies who kept the fires going and a hundred other people following a number of indiscriminate tasks. I collared a wizened little man in a frock coat who was doing something with a white powder in one corner of the room and occasionally uttering little yelps of frustration. Walking boldly up to him, I asked in a low voice, "Do you know anything about some diamonds which have been stolen?"

"Certainly not," he said, turning his rheumy old eyes on me. "I'm an artist in sugar craft, and am always called in whenever His Grace has important guests. But this particular edifice, which the Duchess insisted on, is giving me gyp. I've no time to discuss diamonds. Ask that little girl over there in charge of the butter."

The Duke's Family Seat was, at least in its earliest architecture, decidedly medieval. I felt like I'd strayed into a kitchen more suited to the Tudors, and half expected a large boar's head stuffed with truffles to stare me suddenly in the face. Also, I wasn't sure if the old man meant me to check his credentials or ask the girl about the disappearing jewels. As it turned out she was too frightened at seeing a female guest below stairs to tell me anything, so I went off in a huff to interview the butler. Hurrying towards his pantry I suddenly heard a terrific scream, and a few seconds later a great clatter of knives and forks falling onto slate slabs. The butler rushed out of the pantry, colliding full-tilt with the Duchess, who was rushing equally madly out of the conservatory.

"Help, murder!" she screamed again, and fell in a large heap to the floor. Stepping carefully over her, I walked calmly into the place she'd come from so precipitately –with the feeling that I presented a most lady-like contrast to the entire clamour. There among the camellias, on a secluded bench more often used for dalliance by bored young fellows just down from Oxford, sat a very dead Duke. A small pair of scissors with delicately jewelled handles was stuck in his chest, and blood disfigured his shirt front. I learned later that, worn out by his perambulations of the evening before, he'd gone for a snooze among the plants: where he thought no-one would disturb him, at least until the Duchess came to choose the flowers for that evening's table, always supposing the diamonds had been recovered by then. However, having as usual not very much to do, apart that is from sitting on a sofa in the drawing-room lamenting yet again the loss of her jewels, Her Grace had come into the conservatory early, found the Duke with his collar awry and his mouth open and then screamed the place down. Well, robbery had now been aggravated by murder. Lestrade was sent for, and he immediately wired for Inspectors Athelney Jones and Tobias

Gregson to come down at once from the Yard.

I sent John to interview the ancient housekeeper and went in search of the Head Gardener. It was a most pleasant surprise to find he wasn't the faithful, gnarled old retainer I'd expected, but a tall young man with an eye on the main chance who obviously knew how to take care of himself. "Were you with the Duchess when she went to choose the flowers for this evening?" I asked sternly.

"Yes and no," he said. "She was inside the conservatory. I was outside." Well, that could be easily checked once the Duchess was fit to be spoken to. The stalwart young man glanced down at his dirty boots as if to say I should have known he wouldn't be allowed into any part of the house wearing them. But I was determined to give him his come-uppance. "You may call yourself Head Gardener, but I don't think you've been in the Duke's service very long," I said shrewdly. I saw him framing as if to say, "What business of it of yours?" But he suddenly thought better of it. Instead he answered pertly, "That's as maybe, but I'm country-bred and know a plant when I see one." For some obscure reason this made him laugh and I could hardly restrain myself from boxing his ears.

"Who engaged you, the Duke or the Duchess?" I snapped. It was unlikely to be either. They were far too exalted to be bothered by such a mundane thing as interviewing a would-be servant. But to my surprise the Head Gardener moved a step nearer and said, "The Duke's a ratting man. He engaged me."

"An illegal pastime," I thought, "even for Dukes." It involved going in secret, and probably in disguise, to upstairs rooms in low-class public houses where a large pit, newly white-washed after each session, would be used for ferocious fights between 'made' dogs and any number of rats. Bets were taken on how many rats could be killed in a given time by a particular animal, and respectable men played the game cheek by jowl with the lowest of the low, drinking the same hot gin and sitting in the same tawdry surroundings.

The Head Gardener was obviously familiar with such things; and also, until New Oxford Street cut a great swathe through the Holy Land more than forty years earlier, with the largest and worst rookery in the whole of London. The remnants of it were not far from the Loamshire's Town House. How easy for an insider to fence the diamonds at top speed in such a place. As if reading my mind the young man said, "If it's diamonds you're thinking of, or a murder weapon, you can search me if you've a mind. Or my lodging."

"I'll forego that for the time being," I said sarcastically, and swept back into the house. John had had no luck with the housekeeper, who was as deaf as a post and had the greatest difficulty in understanding what had happened to the diamonds or the Duke. I told him about the gardener, and said I hadn't made any searches because surely he wouldn't have mentioned such a thing if he hadn't been confident about my not finding anything.

"Could it have already been hocked down here," said my husband, meaning the necklace. "Even though it's much too valuable and distinctive to suit an ordinary 'uncle'? As for the murder, if the gardener did it he'd know the knife is still in the victim."

"Which is something pointing to the murderer being in a terrific hurry, as he would be if the Duchess suddenly showed up in the conservatory. Unless, of course he (or she) wants to incriminate somebody. It's extremely difficult to investigate a theft *and* a murder. They may be connected but, on the other hand, we could be dealing with two sets of people with two sets of motives. One, the jewels have been stolen for money. Two, a different person had a grudge against the Duke."

"Money could come into it on both counts. 'A' steals the diamonds to sell. 'B' inherits the title and all that goes with it on the death of the Duke. Who is the heir, by the way?"

"The Duke's nephew, the young Lord Saltire. He's a boy of ten and lives with his widowed mother in France. The Duke's Secretary, the late Duke's that is, has already sent a cable."

"Have you spoken to him?"

"Not yet, but I'm on my way. How did you and Lestrade get on?"

"I've been on my hands and knees for hours, trying to employ Holmes' methods. There's no cigar ash, no depressions formed by a wooden leg, no wheel marks from any vehicles, not so much as a bent blade of grass. It's hopeless; and the coppers Lestrade called in are trampling all over everything."

The Secretary, when I finally ran him to ground, proved to be a very astute young man, not given to wasting words. I asked him how long he'd been with His Grace and if he'd ever had cause for complaint. After a long pause, and just before I was going to repeat myself, he told me he'd been with this particular employer for ten years and had never had anything to complain about. "That is, allowing for the naturally high-handed manner of the aristocracy." The Duke trusted him implicitly, and he hoped he'd always performed his duties well and to the best of his ability. The Duchess...I pricked up my ears and gave him an encouraging smile.

"I'm afraid Her Grace is a little highly strung. She's inclined to make a fuss over small things, and at present is utterly prostrated and in the hands of her personal maid. I have no idea when you will be able to see her."

That was no surprise. I wouldn't call the stabbing to death of a husband with a pair of ornamental scissors in my own conservatory, and with a house full of guests, a small thing. Even if he did go round habitually pinching a certain part of his female guests' anatomy. Had anyone sent for a doctor? "Yes," replied the young man. "We were hoping he would have arrived by now. But what a blessing your husband is staying with us. We can make use of his medical expertise until the Duchess's own medical man gets here."

Telling him hastily that I hoped we would soon have the chance of more conversation, I almost ran out of the room. My object was to find John and tell him to keep out of the way at all costs, especially of the old Duke's Amanuensis, at least until the Duchess's personal physician arrived. When he learned the reason for my concern he said testily that he could wield a bottle of smelling salts with the best of them, and not to be so jumpy. Once the family doctor came he might be forced to resume his old role temporarily, especially if anyone found out he was the 'doctor' who once worked with Holmes.

"You said something earlier about the murder weapon being left in the body to incriminate somebody," I said, intent on calming him down. "Do we know whose knife it is?"

"Not until the doctor prises it out and we can check it for fingerprints. I thought you told me the deed was done with ornamental scissors."

"Scissors or knives," I said crossly. "It's all the same to a

79

dead Duke."

"Lestrade will want to know the time of death."

"You told me Holmes allowed you to let rip on the subject of rigor mortis once. Have you examined the body?"

"If you recall, I've not had a moment to spare from examining the grounds. You're the one who's been closest to it. Apart, I assume, from the Duchess –who may simply have seen her husband's body from the doorway. Did it look to you as if some kind of stiffening had set in?"

"No," I said soberly, suddenly thinking the murderer might have been hiding behind the orchids at the same time as I was in the conservatory staring at the recumbent Duke. "But do you remember the dinner we had when we first arrived?"

"I certainly do. The turbot..."

"Forget the food for a moment," I said peevishly. "There was a man seated two or three places to your left who looked awfully like Raffles."

"You mean the chap they privately call, in certain circles, the amateur cracksman?"

I nodded. "Of course he had that boy, Bunny, with him."

"You think he may have stolen the necklace and passed it on to Manders. Is that it? It would be easy for the lad to go down to the village post office and..."

"Send the diamonds to Raffles' London address by registered

post," I finished.

"By Jove!" Watson went to the nearest window. "I notice that the two of them are strolling together in the kitchen garden at this very moment. Run down and try what you can get out of them."

Seeing Raffles close up was even more devastating than seeing him at a distance in the dining-room. His dark eyes and hair, along with an aquiline nose and a neat newly grown toothbrush moustache, made him the handsomest man I'd met in years; and his superbly cut clothes, perfectly styled for a country weekend, set off his lithe figure to perfection. There was no denying the predatory glint in his eye as I came towards him. But Bunny looked daggers.

Later, in the privacy of our bedroom, I told John I wasn't able to make much progress. "You could hardly ask him outright if he'd pinched the gewgaws," he said, turning over and beginning to snore. Shaking him by the shoulder, I said in a stage whisper, "Raffles gave me the distinct impression he was off duty, so to speak. Taking a holiday."

"Maybe a busman's holiday. We'll have to keep a sharp eye on him, I can tell you."

"Bunny's very protective. He'd like to make everybody think Raffles is perfectly honest, even while he's secretly full of admiration for his daring robberies. One other thing, Mr.

Manders hates women."

"Well he would, wouldn't he?" mumbled Watson, dropping off in spite of all my efforts to keep him awake.

As time went on it became obvious that everyone was extremely irked at being kept in the country. But Lestrade insisted no-one could leave for home until the diamonds were found and, more importantly, the Duke's murderer been apprehended. "But they may never be found," I wailed, "and the Duke's killer may already have fled the country."

"You wanted a mystery to solve," said my husband, "so it's up to you to solve it. Me, I keep trying to use Sherlock's methods."

"Yes," I said sarcastically. "Sitting on a pile of cushions all night and refusing to come to bed, mumbling about 'a three-pipe problem' and smoking them one after the other. All it does is make you ill."

John stroked his moustache complacently. "The only thing we can be sure of," he said, "is that Lestrade will suspect the wrong person."

This turned out to be perfectly true. The next morning the Inspector arrested one of the kitchen maids. But whether this was for the theft of the diamonds or the murder of the Duke wasn't made clear until much later.

The following morning I told John I was going to the village for a few necessities. It was as I strolled down the High Street that a familiar voice assailed me. Turning round, I saw Emily walking determinedly over the pavement. What on earth was she doing here?

"I might ask you the same question," she said. "As for me, I'm staying at the Hammer & Pincers."

"Alone?"

"Yes. Don't look so shocked. I have my maid with me, and my coachman. Come up and have some tea."

She asked me over the tea cups how things were going on at the Big House. I couldn't help wondering if she wanted to muscle in on my murder mystery, or how she had heard of the bizarre happenings at the Loamshires' Country Estate. I must have looked slightly miffed because she said airily, "Don't worry. I've plenty of other fish to fry. It sounds to me as though you and Dr. Watson are exhausting yourselves interviewing too many people. Surely you should employ a process of elimination? Could 'A' have been where he said he was? How could 'B' not be where she said she wasn't?"

I stared at her blankly, thinking she suddenly sounded like Sherlock Holmes. "In a house of that size and degree of organisation," she continued, "it would be difficult for all but a very small number of people to be out of place. But they alibi each other, singly or in groups." It all sounded very learned.

"It depends whether we're talking about a theft or a murder," I said. "Elements of upstairs and downstairs could be involved in either, together or separately. But now that Lestrade's arrested somebody it looks as if we can at least go home."

"What, and leave everything in mid-air? If you ask me, the Duchess did it. I understand they were her scissors, the ones she always uses for snipping off itsy-bitzy pieces of greenery. She was at the scene of the crime..."

"But she raised the alarm," I said feebly, "and what about motive?"

"*Does* one have to have a motive for killing one's husband?" asked Emily with a laugh. She picked up the teapot and began pouring out more tea. As I watched her, there was a terrific bang. The window shattered, and something embedded itself in the side of a battered chiffonier standing against the opposite wall. Emily dropped the teapot with a crash and screamed inexplicably, "Hell's teeth, he's found me already."

Before I could stop her she'd wrenched open the door of the little sitting-room and rushed out into the inn yard. I heard the babble of voices, the tramp of feet and a few screeches. I didn't think the screeches came from Emily but, leaning out of the broken window and carefully avoiding very sharp shards of glass, I heard her tell the landlord she'd pay for the damage, but that she would have to leave at once.

Slowly wending my way back to the Duke's residence, I found the blinds down and one of the valets busy packing our belongings. John looked crestfallen. He didn't trust Lestrade's judgement, but we hadn't managed to come up with any other solution. When we finally reached home I left Watson looking through some manuscripts in his old tin trunk and re-reading back copies of *The Strand Magazine*. He was searching for ways in which Sherlock would have tackled the theft of the jewels and the murder of the Duke of Loamshire. I told him all about Mrs. St. Clair's theory, and the pistol shot through the inn window. He said he didn't have a clue about *that,* but the idea of the Duchess killing the Duke was not only ludicrous but far too obvious for a detective to contemplate.

"The most likely suspect always turns out to be the most innocent," he said. Obviously he'd been reading the account of the murderous builder from Norwood again, as well as *The Five Orange Pips.* "But why did Mrs. St. Clair call out 'He's found me *already'* after the shot was fired?" he asked.

"I've no idea. Obviously she knew someone was on her trail and was planning to escape immediately after tea."

"And because she went for a walk, bumped into an old friend and invited you to join her, left it too late. But why should anyone be after Mrs. St. Clair?"

"The capers she gets up to, the whole world could be after

her."

"I'll bet money on it that it was a man: and the man most interested in getting to her would be A. J. Raffles, if he suspected for a second that she had the diamonds."

"Is he a good horseman?" I'd heard the sound of hooves above Emily's scream, and whoever it was must have moved like lightning considering the speed with which she left the room and reached the inn yard.

"Brilliant," said Watson, who betted on horses but had never ridden one –in spite of convincing certain people he'd been an assistant surgeon in Afghanistan. Where nearly everyone rode something, even a camel. "And an even better cricketer," continued John. "But the woman couldn't have had the necklace. She wasn't anywhere near the House."

"She was as near as The Hammer & Pincers," I retorted. "In other words, within walking distance."

"Are you suggesting someone from the House gave them to her?" Watson began rummaging frantically through his tin box. "I knew Sherlock would come up trumps," he shouted. "Here it is: 'His footmarks had pressed right through the snow, so long he had stood there.' Well it wasn't snowing, but I've only got to ask Lestrade to check under a window for a deep footprint..."

"All the windows?"

"No," he said triumphantly. "Dalliance, that's what it was.

The Head Gardener making love through the butler's pantry window late at night to the girl Lestrade's already arrested. She's so smitten, he easily persuades her to hand over the necklace. There's always been so much talk of the damned thing she knows where to find it. Even if it means running the risk of being seen in a part of the house where she hasn't any right to be. Or any reason, either."

"But you seem to forget the Duchess was wearing the diamonds," I protested.

"We probably only thought she was."

"Are you asking me to doubt the evidence of my own eyes?"

"Of course not. But as she was dining in her own house the necklace could have been a paste replica."

"And in spite of saying he was off-duty, Raffles was also after the real diamonds," I breathed. "Do you think he persuaded Lestrade to make an arrest out of chagrin?"

"Who knows?" said John carelessly. "He may have known something about what was going on between the kitchen maid and the gardener and decided to wait until one or other of them had removed the loot from the house. Raffles has been heard to say that as a general rule he would never abuse his position as a guest, but I must say that didn't stop him pinching old Lady Melrose's necklace of diamonds and sapphires when he and Bunny were both invited to Milchester Abbey. She's very similar to the Duchess of Loamshire," John went on. "You know, insisted on wearing her wonderful necklace every night during the house party. Only she wasn't content with paste." He walked to the window and stood for some moments looking up at the sky. "Let's hope there's been no rain, and the Head Gardener's been too busy to instruct anyone to rake over the flower beds."

"Flower beds? You had him standing outside the butler's pantry a minute ago. Do you think he passed the diamonds to Emily?"

"Undoubtedly. Got them from the gulled maid and walked down to the inn later that morning: where he handed the jewel over on the promise of a cut immediately the necklace was sold. No-one would notice his absence in all the uproar once the Duchess discovered her diamonds were missing. No wonder he was so cocky when he suggested you have him and his room searched."

"And Raffles knew?"

"Knew what?"

"Where the necklace had been taken."

"Perhaps not immediately, but he obviously got some kind of clue later."

"It still leaves us with the murder," I said thoughtfully. "I can't see a young kitchen maid doing that."

"She'd have access to plenty of weapons," said Watson flippantly. "But, no, it's not likely."

I stared at his old tin box and the manuscripts spilling out of it all over the floor. "Your precious Sherlock was rarely rude to women," I said. "But according to you he didn't like us much. If you want my opinion it's because he didn't have a clue how our minds work." I couldn't tell him I knew how careless the Duchess was with her diamonds, or that she absolutely insisted on wearing them on every public occasion. But I guessed the Duke was thoroughly sick of the ever increasing insurance premiums; and of the terrible fuss that ensued every time the necklace was mislaid. He must have threatened to sell them himself. Well, no red-blooded woman was going to stand for losing her status by having her most spectacular ornament taken away from her. The Duchess must have, as Emily said, murdered her husband, and then fainted, or pretended to faint, at the thought of what she had done.

John's theory, that the Head Gardener had murdered his master as well as stealing the diamonds, wouldn't hold water. There'd been no great muddy footprints inside the conservatory; and the Duke's hobby meant plenty of money coming the young man's way. To kill him would be like killing the golden goose.

"Get in touch with Lestrade before he's silly enough to let that girl is hanged," I said. "Ask him to interview the Duchess even if her doctor does say she still hasn't recovered from the shock of her husband's death. I'll bet you twenty to one she confesses."

Which was exactly how it turned out.

Chapter Five

A week or so later, when Watson was in bed with a cold and I was busy cosseting him with hot cocoa and the occasional mustard plaster, he suddenly said, "Sherlock Holmes once told me how he knew I'd been laid up with a cold, said that he could easily tell from the state of my slippers!"

"Wouldn't he just," I said sarcastically. "Ordinary mortals see a runny nose and a well-plied pocket handkerchief before coming to such conclusions."

"You can read all about it in the account of the Stockbroker's Clerk if you like," said John weakly, blowing his nose like a trumpet.

"I remember that occasion for other reasons," I retorted. "There was I, getting dressed for the day and ready to come down to breakfast when, early as it was, you rushed upstairs in a lather to say you were off to Birmingham at a moment's notice – with not the faintest idea when you'd be back."

"What else could I do, with Holmes sitting downstairs in the best armchair and a cab already at the door?"

"Stop letting yourself be taken for granted for one thing," I said, plumping up his pillows and running downstairs to answer the door bell. We had both thought it safer to get rid of the servants, and even the slavey had been given her marching orders. You can imagine my surprise when I saw a disreputable old cockney shuffling his feet on the step. Fixing his face in what I'm sure he thought was an ingratiating leer he said hoarsely, "Could you fix me up, Missus, wiv a pair of ol' boots?"

"No I could not," I said, attempting to close the door. Wondering why it wouldn't shut, I saw that the old wretch had his foot in it. White with temper, I told the man in no uncertain terms to clear off or I'd call the police.

"I don't think so," said a cultured voice in a whisper, making me stare at the cove as if I'd taken leave of my senses. Those steely blue eyes could only belong to one person. Without a word, I opened the door wide enough for him to slip into the hall. In the few seconds it took me to close it Raffles had regained his youthful athletic figure and now stood looking down at me with a sarcastic smile on his handsome face. "Well, where are they?" he asked.

"What?" I replied, stalling.

"The diamonds, of course." There was no change in his manner, but his tone suddenly had a nasty edge to it.

"If you mean the Duchess of Loamshire's necklace, well I haven't got it."

"But you may know who has. She escaped me the first time from the Hammer & Pincers. But I won't be foiled a second time."

"If you mean Emily Fanshaw, with whom I was taking tea on the afternoon you fired so indiscriminately through the window of the inn, even if you are right and she still has the diamonds what makes you think she'll give them to you, or even to me?"

"There are ways of making a woman part with things, even her jewels; and if you won't tell me voluntarily where this Miss Fanshaw, as she calls herself, is I can always do something to make you."

Well, John was ill upstairs and there was no-one else in the house to protect me. Taking a step back from him, I said tremulously, "If I tell you where Emily lives will you promise not to kill her?"

"I'd like to," said Raffles. "That is, I'd like to promise not to do her in. After all, I only carry a shooter for my own protection and got rather carried away that time in the country. But I won't hesitate to murder her if she refuses to part up with the goods."

"I'll risk it," I said, scribbling away for dear life and handing him a piece of paper with her address on it. At the same time I hoped Emily would be able to take care of herself more successfully than when we were in Whitechapel together.

With that Raffles went away, once more adopting his old man's gait and, I supposed, his almost convincing cockney accent. No sooner had I mounted the stairs to our bedroom to see if John wanted any more whisky and water when there was another ring at the door bell. I ran to open it and almost fainted when I saw who it was on the step.

"Professor Moriarty!"

"The very same, dear lady," he said, sidling into the hall.

"But you're dead," said a familiar voice close by my left ear. I turned to see John standing at the bottom of the stairs in his dressing-gown and the famous slippers. The ones he said he would keep forever in memory of Sherlock. Moriarty turned to him with a furious snarl, and with such a venomous look I got between them in case he suddenly sprang at my husband's throat.

"Dead?" he screamed. "You pretended to the benighted readers of your lying prose that Holmes escaped from those infernal waters, whereas obviously it would be me, Moriarty, who was clever enough to get away."

Full of the most insane fury, the old man executed a little dance on the two nail marks left in our hall linoleum by a workman we had recently had in the house to repair the gas and shook his fist in the air as if he would have liked to bring down the whole ceiling about our heads. "Thanks to that idiotic, over-rated friend of yours my whole organisation has collapsed. I've had to sell my Greuze, and the best Lieutenant I ever had is languishing in some filthy goal. If only Moran had had the decency and good sense to shoot Holmes with his dratted air gun when he was tailing him at Reichenbach instead of letting him mess about later with a ridiculous bust which wouldn't have deceived a child. As for Mrs. Hudson and all the help she gave to her dear lodger on that occasion..." Professor Moriarty suddenly stopped from sheer want of breath and I found myself thanking my stars I wasn't Holmes' housekeeper. Not for all the tea in China would I have been in her shoes.

"Well, what do you want us to do about all this?" asked John with unexpected firmness.

"Give me the necklace, you fool."

"I just heard my wife tell somebody else we haven't got it. In any case," said Watson, drawing himself up to his full height, "since we are now detectives following in my friend's footsteps ourselves our job is to recover stolen goods not give them to other crooks."

Moriarty's sibilant voice had sunk to its usual whisper and sounded more snake-like than ever. "You'll live to regret this Doctor," he said. "I haven't a cent to my name now and must get money from somewhere if I'm to rise again to my former heights."

"Sink to your former depths you mean," said John, looking rather proud of this riposte. "After all, you can always go back to cramming young duffers who want to get into Sandhurst."

The slam of the door as Moriarty left shook the house. But,

"Put the kettle on," was all John said as he marched stalwartly back upstairs. "Make me another mustard plaster and yourself a good strong cup of tea."

"Thanks for the prescription," I said weakly, and walked slowly into the kitchen wondering how we'd ever escape James Moriarty —to say nothing of A. J. Raffles. I decided that as soon as Watson was better I'd get in touch with Emily, to warn her and ask for help. Meanwhile, the kettle was singing on the hob and the gasogene needed attending to in case Watson got tired of beef tea and fancied a whisky and soda. In a dream that was slowly turning into a nightmare, I reached into the cupboard for a cup and saucer and bent down to retrieve the tin of mustard I'd left under the sink. Watson may not have been the best of doctors but he was a model patient, and I must look after him. That was why I almost ignored the telegram that came that afternoon. It was addressed to John and when I took it up to him he tore it open and then jumped out of bed. "It's from the Norwegian Embassy. They've lost their most famous explorer!"

Deciding he was rambling and that I'd have to call in Anstruther, I moved swiftly towards the door. Explorers were meant to find not lose things —especially themselves. And why should the Embassy contact Watson? But he shouted to me to come back to the bedside and read the telegram for myself. I picked up the yellow piece of paper resting on the counterpane and saw the words 'Deeply distressed at death of Holmes. As his closest friend hope you learned enough from him to help us. We can't find Sigerson.'

By this time John was struggling into his clothes and pulling his old valise out from under the bed. "I'm off to borrow a pair of skis from Arthur," he said. "Ring the Embassy and then find out the time of the boat train from King's Cross to Newcastle." Well, he'd said in one of his literary effusions that he was 'a prompt and ready traveller', and this was certainly a good example of it.

It turned out that the boat train left twice a week at nine o'clock in the morning, so Watson had to contain himself until the following day. Even then, we had barely time to get to the station and take a hurried farewell. My excited husband waved to me from his third class carriage as it moved out of King's Cross, and I stood on the platform waving my handkerchief until the train was out of sight. He would be at the Tyne Commission Quay some time that afternoon and arrive in Oslo after a two day journey by steamer. He'd promised to write to me, and I'd said I hoped he wouldn't be too seasick. After all, never having travelled to Afghanistan in spite of what everybody thought, he had little experience of a rough sea.

The first letter wasn't long in coming. It began 'Dearest Mary'. Well, that was nice. John had already met the King of

97

Scandinavia, and been offered a large reward if he succeeded in his mission. I was not to worry if I didn't hear from him for a bit as he was off to Spitzbergen hoping, but in some doubt, that the journey would make him less ill than the one he'd already undertaken. Poor Watson. He would find it so humiliating continually vomiting over the side while the other passengers strolled about on deck chattering away nineteen to the dozen. But I had no time to waste on his woes since I had already decided to do some sleuthing of my own while he was away.

Ever since my adventure with Emily Fanshaw in the Whitechapel shambles I'd hated going to the butcher's. The cuts of meat on the white slabs in the window reminded me too much of the heartless slaughter that had gone on there. But like any typical British bulldog type John loved his roast beef, and it was high time I settled my monthly account. Unusually for the trade, our butcher was an Irishman, full of a robbery which had recently taken place across the water and dying to tell me all about it. At first I thought he meant the Ardagh Chalice had been pinched. A Celtic Communion Cup made of silver and decorated with precious stones, it had been discovered hidden under a thorn bush in a small village in County Limerick some years ago and was now in the National Museum of Ireland. It reminded me of the so-called Ardagh emeralds stolen by Raffles and Bunny, although I didn't find out until much later which of their many pawnbrokers, fences and money-lenders disposed of them and how much the rascally pair got. But my meat merchant said no, it wasn't the Chalice, and he'd never heard of any Irish emeralds. "There's been a daring raid on some bullion being sent to Dublin from Belfast by an Irish Bank."

Well, here was something for me. Leaving a note for John with the young man who still occupied our front parlour and packing a small case, I left Euston that evening by the Irish Mail for Holyhead. The train was jam-packed. But I managed to find a seat opposite an elderly woman dressed in black, like our widowed Queen. She had an unbecoming bonnet perched on top of her head and kept in place by a white ribbon tied under her chin. Altogether a museum piece. But she seemed friendly. When it came to exchanging names she said cheerily, "I'm Mrs. Marple, travelling to Holyhead."

"Mrs. Watson," I said briefly. She was immediately interested.

"Not married to that wonderful man who writes such sensational stories for *The Strand Magazine*?"

"No, no," I said hurriedly. "In any case, I'm a widow."

"So am I, my dear. But I have a daughter. In fact, I have several daughters. However, Jane is the cleverest. She's always finding out things and often says 'That was the point, you see'. Trouble is, none of us do see. Until she explains everything, that is."

I asked Mrs. Marple why she was travelling to Holyhead. It was to get to Ireland, she said. The up-train from Belfast to Dublin had been robbed at Dundalk of a considerable sum of money in gold destined to pay the officers and men at the Curragh. "Nobody knows who did it, or where the money is now. I thought I'd try my hand at solving the mystery, just like Jane. Though she confines her efforts at present to how many jam tarts the kitchen boy has stolen or where cook keeps her tipple. That's the trouble with cooks these days. So difficult to get, you have to allow them their little foibles. Jane's cost me two already. She does seem to take rather an *unforgiving* view of human frailty. I remember how cross she was when I decided to redecorate the nursery. I was so tired of those anaemic irises. But she said she loved mauve. She made an awful fuss. And to think my dear," continued Mrs. Marple, "she was only three at the time!"

So, there were going to be two of us on the job. I looked at Mrs. Marple and decided it could be worse. She had a sharp look in her eye for all her cheerfulness, and may have learned something from this frightful daughter of hers. If I could keep her off 'Jane' we might get on very well together. A thought struck me that if she was doing this for 'fun' the reward wouldn't mean much to her. If I had a hard-luck story ready I could collar nearly all of it.

The overnight ferry reached Kingstown Pier early next morning. Mrs. Marple and I caught a connection to Westland Row and from there asked a jarvey to convey us to Amiens Street Station for the train to Dundalk. I have to admit that he did this very cheerfully. But in the most broken down gig, and the most jaded horse I ever encountered outside a glue factory. The plan was for us to catch the down-train with as little delay as possible.

I noticed that, instead of having her belongings packed conveniently in a valise, Mrs. M. carried her possessions in a number of large bags which she was always dropping. I noticed, too, quite a lot of wool whenever I helped her to pick things up. But I said nothing. We all have our little eccentricities.

At Drogheda, the signal box was a most imposing sight. On two floors, with four gothic windows below the room where the levers were worked, it looked as if it should belong to a much busier station. As our train swept through, a most handsome young man in full railway rig opened the door of this room and stepped out onto a balcony. I waved very discreetly so that Mrs. Marple didn't notice but it wouldn't have taken much to make me change my mind, leave the train and stay in the town for a week on the chance of meeting up with him. However, the ride to Dundalk was quick and smooth owing to the easy gradients –

except for a four mile rise after Drogheda, followed by a steepish descent of just over seven miles. This last was quite thrilling, although it made my travelling companion nervous. The first thing to do when we arrived at Dundalk was to find a hotel and, after we'd inspected the room, sally forth to look at the Bay. "I wonder why Dundalk?" mused Mrs. Marple. "There are other stops between Belfast and Dublin."

"Perhaps they intended to escape by sea," I said, "in a private boat. A yacht or something." The sea lay calm before us and there was a beautiful blue sky: with small fluffy white clouds edged a delicate shade of pink sailing lazily across it. I wondered how long such weather would last. I'd heard it nearly always rained in Ireland.

"The first step is to go back to the station and find out as much as we can about what happened," said Mrs. Marple dragging her gaze away from the water. She picked up her bags and stuck a couple of long grey needles back inside one of them. "Goodness knows when I'll get this matinee jacket finished with all this junketing about."

Well, it was either fighting crime or sitting in a rocking chair with her feet up and her fingers busy counting stitches. She'd made her choice. I didn't feel it incumbent on me to say anything so she'd have to put up with it. I strode purposefully into the station with her close behind me, that ridiculous bonnet bobbing from side to side in time with her tiny, almost mincing, steps.

The stationmaster was just coming out of his office when we walked onto the main platform. A big, bluff man in a smart uniform, his face glowed with health even though he had a worried look in his eye. "Thinking about the robbery," I said to myself. So was I, and dying to know if we'd find the gold. It was when I asked for particulars of the theft that I hit the first snag. Although he was extremely polite the man wouldn't be drawn. I realised that, by telling Mrs. Marple I had no connection with the Watson who wrote for *The Strand* and consequently no connection with Holmes, I had forfeited what ought to have been a great advantage. There was only one thing to do and that was to get rid of her for a bit. Just as I was wondering how to do this without being too obvious she suddenly said, "If you don't mind, my dear, I'll make my way to the main street and meet you in a tea-shop. Who knows, I may be able to find some nice knitting patterns on the way."

"And some more wool," I said to myself. "Green for old Ireland." Aloud I said, "Very well, Ellen. But don't tire yourself." We were already on first name terms. She'd told me her proper name was Helen but Jane thought that was altogether too pretentious. "I can't think why," said Mrs. Marple wistfully as she went off festooned with carrier bags. "It's not as if I've ever been in service, where no domestic would be allowed to call herself Helen or anything else half so high-sounding."

As soon as she was out of sight I turned my attention back to the stationmaster and told him of my connection with the art of solving crime. He immediately invited me into his office, asked me to make myself comfortable in the only chair with a cushion on it and enquired if I'd like a pint of porter "to refresh yourself after your journey." He then sat staring at me like a hopeful dog after a bone. It was as if he expected me to produce the gold straightaway out of my reticule, along with the names and addresses of all the people who were concerned in the stealing of it.

The first thing I wanted to know, of course, was exactly when and where the robbery had taken place. I was astounded to hear the stationmaster say he had no idea. "When the train arrived at Dundalk the guard's van had been broken into. The man himself was trussed up in the corner unconscious, the safe blown and the gold nowhere to be seen."

"Where would the train stop between Belfast and Dundalk?"

The harassed man scratched his head. "Do you mean the official stops to take on passengers and water, or the unofficial ones when there's a cow or a sheep on the line? Or do you mean the times when there's trouble with the Fenians, who wouldn't hesitate to hold up half-a-dozen trains if they were short of funds? Except that those scalpeens would rob all the passengers as well."

I'd forgotten about that murderous bunch. But by the sound of it the gold could have been lifted anywhere along the route. No, said my informant. "The guard was seen leaning out of his cab and waving to some children standing on the platform as the train passed through the station at Goraghwood."

This was the final station before Dundalk. So the station - master, in spite of what he had just said, had a very good idea when and where the robbery could have occurred. "Do you think the thieves have been on the train?" I asked.

"Everybody was searched as soon as we discovered what had happened, even the women. But nothing came of it."

"Was the bag containing the gold thrown out of the train window, do you suppose?"

"It's not impossible. But the line was searched from here to Dublin and nothing came of that either."

My mind was occupied with the notion of how a safe could be blown, perhaps as the result of an explosion from a Fenian bomb, without alerting the whole lot of them that something highly undesirable was going on, and why the police hadn't acted faster than they did.

"But," said the railway official in a strangled voice, "it was two days before the company released the news. The managers wanted to cover it up you see, although that eventually proved impossible. The money had gone, and the soldiers were anxious for their pay. As for the noise from the bomb, that would be lost in the racket of the train."

It was evidently a very small bomb then, like the cook's baby. A small bomb and a small safe. My butcher had exaggerated. "Did the company want to replace the gold from its own funds and no-one be the wiser?" I asked.

"Yes. But the shareholders wouldn't hear of it. Even a relatively small amount of gold is worth stealing. They wanted the thieves caught and made an example of."

"But they have had no luck so far?"

The stationmaster shook his head glumly. "If something isn't done soon to recover the money it won't only be the train which will be on the line." I had to laugh, but naturally did it to myself to save offending his finer feelings But did he mean his job would be on the line or that he'd top himself by jumping off his own bridge? Promising to do what I could, I went in search of Ellen. I didn't find her in a teashop for the simple reason that there weren't any teashops in Dundalk. Not such as the ones we knew in London thanks to the Aerated Bread Company. Instead, a little rosy-cheeked woman wearing a long black skirt waved to me from a shop doorway and indicated with her other hand that I should go round to a side entrance. When I went in I saw

Ellen, with a pint of porter in front of her, busy knitting a baby's bonnet.

"They say it's medicinal," she said with a smile, indicating her glass. "I told the woman that as soon as you arrived she was to bring some for you too." I noticed the drink was making her cheeks red, and that she seemed rather out of breath. "Strong stuff," I thought and waited eagerly for a glass.

The only place for us to sit was on a bench opposite the door through which I had entered; and there was another, tightly closed, door at the end of this long narrow room separating it from the rest of the outfit. When rosy-face brought me my drink I was able to see through the open door that her 'shop' was nothing more than a front parlour filled with as many different kinds of goods as could be crammed into it. The sill of a bow window was piled higgledy-piggledy with tins of tobacco, curling papers, flat irons and shoe-horns, all looking as if they'd been there for centuries. This window, so cluttered it was difficult to see through the panes, looked out onto the street and was obviously meant to tempt passersby to come in and sample the other delights of the dwelling.

Taking a seat beside Ellen and narrowly missing the knobs on her flying knitting needles, I sipped the creamy brown liquid gratefully. "The natives call this a snug," she said merrily, "where respectable matrons can drink in private without anybody knowing anything about it." She asked me how I'd got on with the stationmaster, looking at me shrewdly through her *pince-nez* all the while. I told her that the Irish police had been busy but hadn't found out much. Was there a satisfied gleam in her eye? Was she hoping to do better than the Garda? I know I certainly was.

"And you, my dear?" she said, as if reading my thoughts.

"I haven't much to go on at the moment."

She settled herself comfortably on the bench and resumed her knitting, saying there was still plenty of time and suggesting I might like to take a stroll round the town before dinner. "I won't accompany you if you don't mind. I'm not getting any younger and am feeling rather tired after our journey. It would be wiser if I went back to our hotel for a rest. But you might find there are clues everywhere."

"More knitting," I thought sourly. "She'll be sitting in the hotel lounge with her little beady eyes on everybody and the needles going like mad. As if that would help." Crooks and gold could be miles away by now. I watched her walk very slowly away from the snug. It was true she was tired. The bags of knitting and anything else she'd brought with her seemed to weigh her down more than ever. I wondered if I ought to go back to the hotel with the woman as an act of kindness and maybe offer to carry her stuff. But I decided against it, anxious to pursue my idea of a private vessel escaping by sea to Liverpool. Somebody must surely have seen something.

It was quite late when I returned to the hotel only to find Ellen not in the lounge but fast asleep in our room. She was breathing gently, with her mouth wide open. Really, it was pitiful that women of her age and stamp should imagine they'd be the slightest use when it came to solving crime. After creaming my face, I climbed into bed and was soon fast asleep myself –only I hoped a little more elegantly.

I have no idea what woke me, but in the faint light coming through the bedroom curtains I saw Ellen fiddling about with one of her bags. Wool, needles and bits of knitting littered the floor, and to my surprise she was fully dressed in her travelling cloak and sensible brogues. Something made me lie quite still for a few minutes. But when I saw her through the gloom trying to tiptoe to the door half carrying, half dragging a bag which was obviously almost too much for her, I asked in a whisper where she thought she was going. "To join Angelo," she said calmly.

"Angelo?"

"My lover."

Her what?

"It's so much nicer than 'paramour'. Paramour is *not* a respectable word for a Lady to use."

"And 'lover' is?" I thought, stupefied. The idea flashed through my mind that I was having some sort of nightmare. "Is there any particular reason why you should see Angelo tonight?" I asked carefully.

"Why, to give him back the gold."

I sat bolt upright in the bed and stared at her goggle-eyed. This was nightmare with a vengeance. "It's in that bag you're trying to carry isn't it? But how did you get it?"

"Angelo gave it to me."

"When?"

"This morning. I only just got to that snug in time and was quite out of breath when you came in."

"And why did he give it to you?"

She shifted the weight of the bag from one hand to the other, still dragging it along the floor. "He was sure the police were after him. But he didn't think they would search me."

"And where did your precious Angelo get it from?"

"The gold?"

"Yes, the gold."

"The guard's van, you goose. He took a prize pig to the station in Dublin. Of course, it had to be put in the guard's van. But as the train approached Dundalk Angelo made an excuse to leave his carriage to find out how the animal was getting on. Naturally he was careful to have the neddy up his sleeve and the bettys in his pocket."

"Neddy? Bettys?" I sounded like a complete idiot.

"An iron bar and a set of pick locks," said Ellen patiently. "He was going to use them to cosh the guard and open the safe."

"What about the bomb? And what happened when he was searched along with all the other passengers?" I added cunningly.

"There was no bomb, silly. We both agreed it would be much too dangerous for dear Angelo. I'm afraid I can't answer about the search. On such a crowded train he must have managed to dodge it somehow. Perhaps by going up and down the corridor or in and out of the lavatory. He's very clever, you know."

He'd have to be damned clever to dodge anything while loaded down with sovereigns. "Clever enough to find neddys and bettys," I said sarcastically. "I doubt if they sell them in Whiteleys."

Mrs. Marple giggled. "They certainly don't, my dear. And they don't sell them in the ironmonger's in our village either. He's much too law abiding." She sounded as if she regretted this. "No, Angelo went up to London to an eel-skinner in Pinchin Lane."

I was too far gone to ask her to explain an eel-skinner. I just hoped it wasn't what it sounded like. And not done while they were still alive. By the time I'd recovered what wits I had she'd

111

staggered out of the room under the immense weight of the gold and I heard the sound of a horse and trap being driven away at a furious pace, no doubt by the ever resourceful Angelo. Cursing myself for a fool, I got up and ran to the window. Outside it was like the city of the dead. Why hadn't I yelled blue murder and roused the whole hotel? Mrs. Marple would be apprehended immediately, the gold recovered and Angelo not have time to get himself and his horse off the premises before the police were all over him.

After a very restless three hours, which I spent trying to understand why the Marple woman had taken up with me in the first place, I dressed, packed, went down to an early breakfast and tucked into some ham and eggs, drank two cups of hot coffee and finally made up my mind what to do next. Angelo and Ellen would be too far away by now for me to do anything about them and their stolen gold. She had spoken of 'our village'. Did they intend to go straight back there with the money? But how would they travel? Not by train surely?

After paying my bill and leaving my valise in the lobby, I went outside and surveyed the terrain. Would there be any harm in following Holmes' methods? In his words, "I approached the house on foot, and with my mind entirely free from all impressions. I naturally began by examining the roadway, and there I saw clearly the marks of a cab, which, I ascertained by enquiry, must have been there during the night." Well I was certain Angelo hadn't been driving a cab and, by dint of looking carefully at the marks on the grass verge alongside the hotel, I confirmed that what I'd heard in the early hours of the morning was indeed a pony and trap. The surprise was it hadn't turned towards the railway station. That would, as I had already surmised, be a mite too risky probably. But in that case which way had the pony and trap gone?

I couldn't wait to tell Watson what had happened to me in Ireland, and welcomed him back home more effusively than usual. He hadn't managed to nail Sigerson and so forfeited his fee. "But the King was kind enough to give me this," he said, holding out a most beautiful snuff box decorated with fine filigree work. "I'll take it round to old Abrahams tomorrow. He'll give me a good price for it."

"A better one than Sherlock gave him for the Stradivarius I hope," said I, examining the box again and thinking what a great help the value of it would be when it came to paying the household bills. "By the way, is that the Abrahams Holmes had to stay in London for, the one he said was in mortal terror of his life?"

"You remember that investigation," said John, pleased. "Lady Frances Carfax of the coffin case. You know," he continued proudly, "Sherlock actually asked *me* if there was a spark of life left in her. But before that I had to travel to Lausanne on my own to carry out some preliminary researches into the business on his behalf."

I asked about Sigerson and Watson said, "I traced him from Spitzbergen to the Lofoten Islands. Harstad to be exact, and then up a gigantic ice-covered mountain which overlooks the town. A fine old time I had of it I can tell you. Those things of Arthur's…"

"Then what?" I asked, busy filling his pipe with 'Ship's' for him.

"Everything went well until he spotted me some way behind him. Once that happened he moved like mad, uphill through the snow. Sigerson's a tall, thin man, with an emaciated figure which even the furs he wore couldn't disguise, so naturally he was able to get a head start. He disappeared for a while and the last I saw of him he was waving to me from a balloon sailing over the open sea, with his discarded skis sticking up in the basket like two curved scimitars, and yelling that he was off to Tibet to meet the Dalai Lama. Or perhaps he said the Khedive at Khartoum. It was difficult to make out at that height, and with all that wind. Besides, those skis…"

"Some climb," I said, "and the Khedive's moved his capital to Omdurman."

"No wonder the man gets lost," said Watson, meaning

Sigerson. Puffing hard at his pipe, he continued meditatively "You know, Mary, although Sigerson was wearing goggles his face seemed awfully familiar. That hawk-like nose…"

"Never mind Norwegian explorers," I said hurriedly. "I've something much more interesting to tell you, something which should net us a fat fee if we're successful."

When I got to that part of my story which involved Mrs. Marple, Angelo and their flight with the Curragh gold, John had his own ideas about why she'd made my acquaintance. "As soon as she realised you were going in the same direction as herself she probably thought she'd be safer keeping an eye on you. What could be better than two ladies sharing a hotel room, especially if one were much younger than the other? It would give a very good impression of a fluffy old besom being kindly looked after by her daughter, or perhaps a penniless niece. What interests me is this fellow Angelo. Do you think they live together in the same village? That should cause some talk."

"Probably passes him off as her odd job man or her gardener," I said dryly. "But until we find out which village, the money's as good as gone."

"That may not be as difficult as it sounds. If we put our heads together we might come up with one or two possibilities. She travelled from Euston, so my guess is she lives south rather than north. What about her luggage labels?"

"She kept her things in bags for some mad reason, and in my opinion she would have removed all labels from a case if she had carried one."

"But, surely, arriving at a respectable hotel with unlabelled luggage would be bound to excite suspicion, even if it was less conspicuous than lugging all those bags about?"

"I don't think the gold coins could have been carried so easily in a case, and a hotel receptionist might wonder why a middle-aged woman had packed such heavy luggage for so short a stay." As it was, I recalled the struggle she'd had in the bedroom in Dundalk: and of course all that knitting poking out of the top of her bag as she trotted through the town had been designed to give her the appearance of such an innocent old tabby!

"Accent?" asked John.

"Well, she wasn't Welsh, Cornish, Irish or Scottish. In fact she didn't have a pronounced accent of any kind."

"That points to the Home Counties or the Cotswolds. It could be Hampshire, I suppose, but I wonder where?" John went into his study to fetch a gazetteer and by dint of hard guesswork, lots of cups of tea and a few arguments we finally decided to try the Cotswolds, travelling down by train to a small village just outside Chipping Norton. Enquiries revealed that a Mrs. Marple did indeed live there and that "That youngest daughter of hers is a terror, always poking her nose into things that don't concern her and minding other people's business instead of her own."

John and I booked into a small hostelry and I sent a pot-boy with a note to ask if our quarry would receive us. He was back almost immediately to say Mrs. Marple would be delighted to see us. She would also be sure to have tea, with home-made scones, ready for four o'clock tomorrow afternoon.

"My, but the old girl takes some risks," said Watson, "especially after what you saw in Dundalk, and with that girl of hers in the house."

"You've forgotten the resourceful Angelo," I said, "and believe me I intend to be there on the dot."

The house was small, but neat and well-appointed and surrounded by a fine garden. It was also positioned so that the occupants could see the coming and going of almost everybody in the village. Some windows overlooked the church and others overlooked the High Street. Anyone going to visit the vicar, the butcher, the bakery, the chemist or the tiny wool shop was easily spotted, and a doctor's surgery stood within sight of the front door.

Mrs. Marple was all smiles as we approached and said it was such a pity that dear Jane had just left for a finishing school in Switzerland. She trusted, however, that we could entertain each other and looked hard at John. I told her with a very brazen look that I wasn't a widow, in spite of what I had told her on the way to Holyhead, but all she said was, "He looks the image of those drawings in *The Strand Magazine*."

Angelo –or someone I took to be Angelo, though I'd never actually seen him of course – came in looking like an old and wizened gnome, carrying the tea things and a tray of sandwiches and cakes. He placed the tray before his mistress ("In every sense of the word," I whispered to Watson, making him almost choke on a cucumber sandwich) in a very deferential manner, and Mrs. Marple calmly proceeded to do the honours of the tea-table. Angelo, however, gave no sign of knowing who we were, and sidled out once he'd delivered the goods, like any well-trained servant. I wondered idly what had become of the kitchen boy who stole jam tarts and the cook who liked a tipple, and looked carefully round the room over the top of my tea-cup, marvelling at all the things that were in it. Framed paintings which Watson later told me weren't copies but highly expensive originals, "Including one by Greuze of 'a young woman keeking at you side-ways' as Inspector MacDonald once said."

Could she have bought it from Moriarty? It would be a dangerous thing to do if ever he wanted it back. There were several side-tables loaded with all kinds of bibelots. Expensive glass crowded the mantelpiece, and the silver tea things seemed fit for a Queen. Mrs. Marple's day dress, though certainly not modish, had obviously come from one of the best dressmakers.

Muted though it may have been, the whole room shrieked money. "And finishing schools aren't cheap either," I thought, wondering if Mrs. Marple had sent all her daughters to one at some time or other. I also speculated on whether or not Jane had been sent away for reasons other than to further her education.

Of course it was impossible to ask to see over the rest of the house, although a wicked look in our hostess's eye hinted that she would have liked to tell us to wander round at our leisure. But I guessed the rest of the place looked much the same, loaded with expensive goodies and with all the latest gadgets in the kitchen, as well as running water in the bathroom. What did she tell all the other village tabbies when they made their early morning calls? I soon found out. John had asked permission to smoke in the garden and on the way back to our lodgings said he had spotted all kinds of hideous artefacts from foreign parts lurking in a conservatory. "Mrs. M. must be passing herself off as a soldier's widow, someone very high up in the service. Or perhaps she says her husband was ambassador to Haiti or some other such God-forsaken place; where they paid men a lot of money to get on with the job without complaining too much, or demanding to be recalled."

"He must have died while Jane was a baby," I said. "Otherwise she would have given her mother away. My guess is the Irish sovereigns are still in the house. If so, we'll have to get after them."

"Break in, you mean?" Watson sounded quite excited. "I wonder where I can find some more black silk. I used it when we broke into that blackmailer's house I told you about."

"Never mind that. Just be ready as soon as it gets dark."

After waiting for what seemed an age for the sun to go down, we crept from the hostelry and ran rapidly towards the High Street. The moon was high and gleamed palely on the church tower, lighting up the so-called 'Hertfordshire Spike' rising from its centre, an architectural feature which (despite its origin) had spread everywhere. While I kept a look-out, Watson walked round the outside of the Marple ménage looking for an entry point. After what seemed like a very long time, but was probably just a few minutes, he beckoned me over to a back downstairs window. He had found a faulty catch and, with his penknife, managed to open it. Giving me a leg-up, he followed my retreating figure into what I already realised was a kitchen. I'd been right about the gadgets. They were everywhere. But there was no sign of any sovereigns. Still, one couldn't expect to see them displayed on the dresser.

We tiptoed through all the rooms, upstairs and downstairs, without finding a thing. I even went into Ellen's room and reached under the mattress. She was sleeping as inelegantly as usual, and there was no sign of Angelo. In the end we had to give it up. John had nearly tripped over the fire-irons in the hearth and frightened me to death. We'd be caught napping if we didn't scarper.

The next morning at breakfast, while I was on my second cup of not very good coffee, John said, "There's nothing for it but a telegram to Raffles." We didn't have to wait long for an answer. As soon as the boy had gone out of the room Watson tore open the envelope and said, "Ingot" in a loud voice.

"Ingot?"

"That's what this telegram says. One word, 'Ingot'." He waved the paper in the air. "Now what on earth would he mean by that?"

"Just a minute," I said. "That crafty gentleman told me in the kitchen garden at the Loamshires that if he and that Bunny of his had stolen something very valuable, say a gold ornament or statue, something which might easily be recognised, he'd melt it down into a nugget and tell the Bank of England to exchange it for sovereigns. So why shouldn't sovereigns be melted down to make a nugget, an ingot as he calls it in the telegram?"

Watson scratched his head. "Depends how easy it is, and if they had time. The butcher here said nobody left the house for several days after Mrs. Marple's return from Ireland. She didn't even go to the station to see Jane off. But, if you remember, we found no sovereigns, and also no ingot. Come to that, I'm not so sure I'd recognise one if I did see it. Of course, it could be being used as a doorstop. Nobody would notice what it really was in that crowded house."

I gazed out of the inn window deep in thought. People were passing to and fro across the yard and I could hear the rattle of harness and the lazy clip-clop of several horses. Stable boys ran back and forth with buckets. It looked like a scene out of the eighteenth rather than the late nineteenth century. Farm carts rattled over the cobbles and farmers stopped to chat to each other under a bright sun at the top end of the High Street. There had been an awful lot of ornaments in that house. Who was to say one of them wasn't made of solid gold? And if we were successful in finding it the police would be the ones to go to the Bank to exchange it for sovereigns, and we would receive a just reward.

But it would mean a repeat performance of last night's adventure.

Chapter Six

That was how we found ourselves once again going, at dead of night, in the direction of the Marple residence.

"This time I'll take a bull's-eye lantern," said Watson.

I didn't bother to enquire where he'd got it from, probably one of the stable boys. But it would help us to see what we were looking for, and we could shut off the beam if we were disturbed. John was muffled up to the eyes in a thick scarf and I had put on a warm cloak. There was no moon. But we knew the way, and very soon saw the shadow of the church tower looming before us, Mrs. Marple's outwardly respectable place nestling in front of it as innocent-looking as a new-born babe. John found the faulty catch once more, climbed through the window, crept round to the front door, released the bolts remarkably quietly and let me into the hall.

"You try the dining-room," he hissed, "while I search the kitchen."

But would Ellen be brazen enough to display her ill-gotten goods on the ground floor? The answer was yes, she would. No sooner had I entered the dining-room than I saw two monkeys gleaming one on each end of the mantel-piece, with a fantastic amount of bric-a-brac in between. They reminded me of the story Watson said he was going to try to palm off on the Editor of *The Strand Magazine.* Only those monkeys, as far as I remembered, were made of brass. I stretched out my hand to check if my theory was right, that the sovereigns stolen from the Belfast to Dublin train were no longer in existence but had not been melted down to form a nugget. Instead they'd been fashioned into something which, as I had thought, would go unnoticed in a house crammed full of so many other decorative objects. The reason why we had failed to see them on our first nocturnal foray was because we had been looking for gold coins.

But just as I reached up to test the weight of one of the monkeys a voice said angrily, "Put your hands up!"

I spun round to see the little old manservant glaring at me from behind Watson's broad back. "Don't make a sound unless you want to be a widow," he said viciously.

It was then that I realised there was a gun pressed against John's jacket: and saw a face which showed the man holding it wouldn't hesitate to murder anybody who got in his way. I put up my hands and Angelo (for who else could it be?) gestured that I should stand beside my husband so that he would have us both covered.

"Right, now march," he growled.

I reached for John's hand. Apart from the fact that it was icy cold, he showed no other sign of perturbation, and we turned and went out of the dining-room towards Mrs. Marple's kitchen. The first time we'd been in there I had been unaware that there was a door into the cellar. Now it was open, and Angelo forced us to go down a flight of steep steps into a large room full of all kinds of apparatus including an anvil stowed under a table loaded with coiners' tools, dyes and a heavy smelting iron.

There were various other artefacts very much in evidence, but I couldn't name any of them –and everything was bathed in a very bright light which came from a lamp hanging from the ceiling. It was obvious that someone's work had been rudely interrupted.

To the left as we entered the cellar was a strong-room which took up half the available space. The heavy door looked shut fast, and there was a gas pipe leading to it along the skirting board. This then rose from the floor in line with the angle of the wall and I saw a tap half-way up. Just underneath the coving there was a short bend in the pipe where it entered the strong-room. But the strangest thing of all was that both the piping and the tap looked brand new, at odds with the rest of the house. It could almost have been put in the day before. But there was no time for any more speculation. Angelo produced some stout rope and, still keeping Watson covered, ordered me to tie him up. This done he tested the rope, opened the strong-room door and pushed John inside so hard he fell heavily to the floor. Before I could protest, Angelo trussed me up like a chicken and gave me the same treatment so that, worried as I was, I wondered where such a little man could have got so much muscle. He closed the door on the pair of us, but not before I'd heard him snarl in a thick foreign accent, "I 'ave been waiting for you, ever since Ellen told me you were in Dundalk."

It wasn't long before we both smelled gas. Looking up, I saw it was coming from the ceiling rose. Evidently our prison hadn't always been a strong-room. I had put in several slip knots when I tied John up. I hadn't been able to do the thing too brown as I guessed Angelo would test my handiwork. But I had hopes Watson would be able to wriggle out of his bonds before the fumes overcame us. However, it took far longer than I bargained for, and by the time he was untying his legs I began to feel it was too late. But, coughing and spluttering, he eventually crept over to me, made several attempts to loose my arms and then suddenly keeled over in a dead faint. The few seconds he was out seemed like hours, but he came round eventually and managed to pull his pen-knife out of his trouser pocket by tearing the lining. With trembling fingers he cut hurriedly through my bonds and gasped, "Take my scarf and climb onto my shoulders. There's an open-ended pipe coming out of that ceiling thing. Block it up, for God's sake, or we're done for."

Watson was swaying like a drunkard, but after two attempts I did manage to block up the pipe and came down from his shoulders just before he sank to his knees. "But how do we get out?" I wailed. There were no windows.

"Try the door," groaned my husband weakly.

To our utter amazement it wasn't locked. I paused to turn off the tap. If the gas went through the open door of the strong-room into the rest of the house the smell would alert Angelo and we'd be well and truly in the soup again before we could escape. "With any luck though, the pair would be poisoned in their beds," John said bitterly. "Now come along before that misbegotten misanthrope of a manservant comes down here to check the results of his handiwork."

"There are still hot coals in the range," I muttered, as we sped through the kitchen.

"Of course there are. He uses it as a furnace. Now, you gather up your skirts and climb through this window. I'm going to get the monkeys, and mind you are standing outside here when I get back."

Watson handed me out one of the ornaments and then flung his leg over the sill. We had lost the bull's-eye lantern, but the streaks of an early dawn were already lighting the sky and we could see clearly which way to run. Although the load was halved between us, our progress with the gold gewgaws was very slow. I decided that, in spite of their age, Angelo and Ellen must be made of iron and have the strength of ten. John was all for taking a rest on a handy tombstone as we ran round the church and through the cemetery. But I quickly vetoed this. Not

127

only was it too reminiscent of what had so nearly happened to us, but we would be the subject of an unwelcome curiosity from any early risers walking along the High Street. Some of the shops were already opening and I could see the butcher busy getting out his wares to display in his window. In a fever of anxiety lest Angelo should raise the alarm and accuse us of burglary, we made our way to the inn, packed our bags, paid our bill and fled back to London by the first train. "We can have breakfast in the dining-car," said Watson, who had fully recovered his appetite as soon as the effects of the gas had worn off.

The next day he took the gold ornaments to Scotland Yard in a cab and explained everything to Lestrade. He, of course, pretended to know all about the theft of the sovereigns and eyed the large, heavy monkeys with distaste. Puffing out his chest, he said the Irish police had already been in touch and he had no doubt that in a day or two he would have solved the case, apprehended the culprits and returned all the money to the Curragh.

"Well, you'll have to melt the monkeys down first if you insist on the sovereigns," said John sarcastically. "Here's the address of the thieves. But I advise you when you go in with a warrant don't let yourself be inveigled into the cellar. Keep clear of the strong-room."

"What will Lestrade find when he takes his men down to that house?" I asked after Watson returned from the Yard and I'd put the tea-things on the table. "Angelo will have got rid of his gear and dismantled his murderous contraption. They'll deny everything. The place will look the picture of probity."

"I've a shrewd suspicion the police will find certain things which have been missing for years and that Angelo will have overlooked; and don't forget what you saw in the hotel in Dundalk."

"It will be her word against mine," I said, meaning Ellen.

"They'll break her down," said John complacently as he reached for the jam.

But he was wrong. When Lestrade reached the house he found Mrs. Marple had cancelled the milk, stopped the bread and told the butcher not to call. Being without Jane she said had made her feel low. She and her faithful retainer were off on a long holiday. Unfortunately she didn't say where to, or give any indication of when she would be back. But a month later I heard that her property was being offered for sale. Although in spite of all their efforts neither Lestrade, Gregson, nor even Athelney Jones could ever apprehend her agent. Inspector Mackinnon said, when he heard about the attempt to gas us, that it reminded him of a similar case he'd shared with Holmes —and how humiliated he'd been to hear from Sherlock that, if he hoped to get results, it would only be by putting himself in the other fellow's place.

"The retired colourman," groaned John. "Who'd have thought that by telling readers about that I nearly signed my own death-warrant?"

"You think Ellen and her Angelo got the idea from that?"

"Of course. At least, I'm sure Angelo did."

But the Irish Bank, having got back its money even if in such an unconventional form, intimated that it didn't want to prosecute. So, to Lestrade's chagrin, the case was closed. I guessed he had been looking forward to personally scouring the Continent looking for the villains, even though John said sourly they were probably "holed up in Margate." I was annoyed too, but extremely gratified by the size of the reward. If no effort were made to find Mrs. Marple and Angelo –especially Angelo –and bring them to justice they could be plotting all kinds of dastardly deeds. After the agony Watson and I went through, I felt they deserved the rope.

After we had been at home for some time, and fully recovered from our terrible ordeal, John came in one morning to say he'd met Neville St. Clair, he of the twisted lip, in the street and been invited to go on a fishing trip. The young doctor who rented one of our rooms had found himself a practice in Paddington so I said I'd take the opportunity to renovate it while Watson was away. The following morning, just as I was putting on my apron prior to getting to work, there was a ring at the door bell. I threw the overall onto the kitchen table, ran into the hall, flung open the front door and told the young man standing on the doorstep that I didn't want to buy anything and would he please move along.

"And I have nothing to sell," replied a well-remembered voice. It was Mrs. St. Clair –Emily Fanshaw –in a bowler hat and a grey ulster. Of course I let her into the house and we sat at the kitchen table over a companionable pot of tea and a plate of hot buttered toast. She'd come round to ask what I thought of the idea of opening an agency together.

"What sort of agency?" I asked suspiciously. With her it could be anything, and the more dubious the better.

"Why, a Detective Agency for solving crime. You seem to be quite good at it."

"And what about Watson, is he to be included?"

"He can be off visiting one of his relations if ever we're called upon to travel."

"Can't you read? He said when he first met Holmes that he had neither kith nor kin."

"In *England,* and you said, or your husband said, in the adventure you had with the Sholto brothers that all your relatives were dead. But the readers were still told you were

131

away seeing either your mother or your aunt! But I'm not going to suggest *we* publicise our activities in the same way."

Activities. Although she had been anxious to bring Leather Apron to justice her behaviour over the Duchess of Loamshire's diamonds was somewhat suspicious. How was I to know she'd always be on the side of law and order? Any more than I was when I helped John Clay.

"From what I saw and heard your own behaviour could be called into question at times," she said tartly when I raised this point. "I was more than annoyed when I found you'd given my address to A. J. Raffles."

I thought it best to let this pass and asked where would we operate from, and what about her straight-laced husband?

"You've just told me you were about to clean out a spare room. All we'd need then would be a couple of chairs, an imposing desk and one of those new-fangled things called typewriters. As for my husband, he'll be quite happy to see me doing something legit; and the lucre would make up for what we lost when…"

I asked her hastily if she'd like more tea. Obviously Holmes' embargo on her better half's begging still rankled, since she never missed a chance to mention it. But she'd forgotten, or didn't even know, that Sherlock was at the bottom of the Reichenbach Falls so it wouldn't matter now what Neville St.

Clair, a.k.a. Hugh Boone, did.

"And Watson needn't go traipsing all over the country on pretend visits?" I asked.

"Only if he's helping with our enquiries, and then we hope there won't be any pretence, unless he has to adopt a disguise for detecting purposes. Otherwise he can sit comfortably in his study reading *The Strand Magazine*. But for heaven's sake keep him well away from pens and pencils; and hide the manuscript paper."

"What about your two children while we're on a case?"

"They have an extremely caring and competent live-in governess, and can always stay with their grandparents now that my father has retired and sold the brewery."

I'd heard the expression 'looking at you sideways'. This is what I did now to Emily. Mr. St. Clair was a full blooded man still under forty. Straight-laced or not, what if he fell a prey to temptation? There'd be no live-in governess in my establishment under any circumstances, not even if she was as grey as a badger and addicted to aniseed balls. But Emily sat serenely drinking tea as if she hadn't a care in the world.

"Have you any idea when we can start?" I asked.

"Anytime you like. I've put advertisements in all the papers to say we're available."

"Giving this address, no doubt?" And without saying a word

to me first. Really, this woman was very high-handed. She couldn't know by instinct that I'd fall in with any of her schemes. But, "Not at all. I've given a box number," said Emily smugly.

"Replies to be called for at the Wigmore Street Post Office?"

An empty cup clattered onto her saucer. "How did you know that?"

"It's what always happens. Written in the stars, I shouldn't wonder."

Mrs. St. Clair got to her feet, grabbed her bowler, adjusted the ulster so that it covered her shirt and trousers and made for the front door. "You carry on getting the room ready. I'll see to the desk and typewriter. Oh, and we'll need some kind of filing system as well as a few pens and such. Leave it to me."

"Don't forget writing-paper, notebooks –and the business cards," I added sarcastically. Already reduced to the dogsbody, I wondered how long I could stand Emily's officious ways. Then I reflected that it was my house and that I'd also have Watson to back me up. It might not be so bad after all.

An hour later a furniture van arrived with a magnificent desk, upright cushioned chairs and a typewriter. Soon after that Emily Fanshaw herself came in looking radiant. "Our first investigation," she said, flourishing a large envelope. She looked so excited I half expected to see a crest on it. It turned out she had called in at the Post Office immediately after ordering the furniture and found a letter waiting. I rushed into John's study to fetch a letter opener and sat waiting breathlessly for what our client had to say.

"A lost dog," spat Emily in disgust, after reading the request twice.

"It won't hurt to start small," I said, taking pity on her disappointed face.

"Not that small." She flung letter and envelope into the kitchen stove and sulked for the rest of the afternoon.

It was some days before I saw her again, and the new office felt very lonely without Emily or John. But when she eventually reappeared, dressed as usual in her male attire, I saw she was carrying a suitcase and brandishing a piece of paper. It looked like another letter. Placing herself on the nearest chair and grinning broadly, she showed me the envelope. It was addressed in a foreign hand, and from where I stood the stamp seemed to be a green one. With a picture of a woman on it who was certainly not the Queen. "It's from France," crowed Emily, giving a second wave of the paper, "where there has been some wholesale poisoning of chocolates, and fruit, just for the fun of it."

"They won't want us, though. They've got too many cops of their own."

"That's just where you're wrong. Not about the number of *gendarmes* maybe, but this is a request from a private citizen."

"How does he know about us then, unless you've been putting advertisements in the French papers?"

"He's a wine exporter and saw our advertisements when he came to London on business."

"But he didn't come directly to us as soon as he'd finished business? Things were beginning to sound more and more peculiar.

"He'd read about our Agency in *The Times,* but before he could do anything here a wire came begging him to return home at once. Fortunately he remembered our box number."

"Emily," I said sternly, "you aren't making the slightest sense. A Frenchman wouldn't need to read about us or be interested in our box number. Neither would he need to do anything in our line "here" as you put it. Not unless he already knew of some particular crime which concerned him personally. In that case, wine or no wine, he wouldn't have left France."

Emily looked rather blank for a moment. "I grant you it's a bit of a puzzle," she said. "But the point is, someone's written to us to go over there as fast as we can and says money's no object. So pack a case and we might be in time to catch the nine-fifty boat train if you get a move on."

Well I did get a move on and, leaving a note for Watson to

pay some outstanding household bills as soon as he got back from his fishing spree with her husband, followed Emily out of the house into the pale morning sunshine. Putting two fingers between her teeth, she whistled shrilly for a four wheeler and helped the cabby haul our luggage on top. She then clambered in beside me and watched with a sadistic interest as he whipped up his horses and got us to Victoria Station only seven minutes before the train was ready to depart. Cursing softly, Emily rushed to buy two first-class tickets and I ran across the concourse to secure two seats in an empty carriage.

"The London, Chatham and Dover Line," she said breathlessly as soon as she was settled comfortably opposite me in a seat by the window and a porter had put our cases up on the rack. "That means a stop at Canterbury."

Why she should be interested in that I had no idea. I was completely winded by the rush and only too glad to know that, because Dover hadn't been tide dependent for over thirty years, we wouldn't have to hang around waiting for our ship to sail but could start from the Port almost immediately. Emily, however, sat looking out of the window with a smug smile on her face – while I tried to imagine myself opposite a real young man and not just one dressed for the part.

"A passenger ship, the *Seaforth*, went down some time ago," she said suddenly. "It was rammed by the *Lyon* in thick fog and sank within twenty minutes. And a cargo vessel coming from Newhaven foundered towards midnight during a violent gale and was smashed against the western jetty at Dieppe."

"Are you telling me all this to show off or because you're nervous?" I said crossly. "Or are you planning something else rather than going to Paris? You seemed mighty interested in the stop at Canterbury." Where a change at Canterbury West, and some even more complicated shenanigans, would get us to Newhaven in time for a crossing to Dieppe.

"Thought there might be time to visit the Cathedral," said Emily airily. "And I want to buy a carpet bag."

"Not a chance," I said. "It will probably be the shortest possible stop to take on water, and maybe mail and a few passengers."

The journey to Calais passed without further comment, although we had an hour's wait there for the train to the Gare du Nord. That station when we arrived was vast, cold and full of people in an atmosphere of smoke and perspiration. They moved restlessly between the booking office and the boards announcing arrivals and departures and looked as if worry about catching a train had deprived them of sleep. Eating, drinking, surrounded by fretful children, they sat on their luggage or on seats too crowded to be comfortable. I expected to go straight into the City and be ready to start our investigation the next day.

138

But "No," said Emily. "Surely I showed you the postmark? The letter was from Nantes."

"We'll still have to find a night's lodging at this hour." After my experience with her in Whitechapel I was determined it wouldn't be in a region like La Villette, Menilmontant or the Porte d'Italie, where even the policemen were afraid to go. Neither would I allow her to spend time watching the prostitutes working their pitches on the Boulevard de Clichy. At my insistence, we took a room in a small hotel on the Left Bank and next morning left from the Gare St. Lazare for Nantes, by way of Le Mans. I also insisted that Emily change her clothes for more feminine attire. It was all very well travelling across the Channel in trousers, but if we were to be in a hotel in a French town for any length of time I was determined it would be in the guise of two respectable young matrons.

When we arrived at our final destination, I was irresistibly reminded of Manchester —even though the sights and smells of the place were rather different. But I discovered Nantes was a seaport some thirty five miles inland on the river Loire, and that it took some time to get there. "If we had gone to Dieppe," said Emily nastily, "the train would have taken us straight to St. Lazare without all that waiting about in Calais, and it would have been cheaper."

I took no notice, busy looking for someone able to give us the name of a suitable place to stay, and reflecting that it was she who had taken charge of the travel arrangements. As we left the station encumbered by luggage, and with Emily lamenting the absence of a new carpet bag, she accosted a tall, raw-boned youth with knobbly wrists sticking out of the sleeves of his jacket and asked him for the name the town's best hotel. What with her French and his English it took a long time, and a lot of gesticulating, before the information was in our possession and I felt free to think about a cup of coffee –or even a tisane. But finally she bowed, he bowed and I thought we'd be off at last. However just as the young man turned away, after picking up a large wooden tray bearing a solitary loaf and hoisting it back on his head, she called out in a loud and very English voice, "By the way, what do they call you?"

"Maigret," said the boy, and went with a loping gait in the direction of a large bakery.

The hotel seemed opulent for the provinces, the food tasted good, and the beds were comfortable. Just before falling asleep I asked Emily if it was true her correspondent had said money was no object. With no clients up to now, our so-called Agency wouldn't stand the cost of this trip –and neither would Watson's bank balance. Her husband might have to don the red wig and make-up again and be the man with the twisted lip begging in the streets of London. But Emily said she trusted the Frenchman completely, and had already sent round a note to say we'd call on him the following morning at eleven.

"Do you have a really decent dress in that luggage of yours?" I asked, snuggling down under the bedclothes and afraid she might still go striding into a French drawing-room in her high boots and outlandish trousers after all I had said to her in Paris. All I got for my pains was a slight snore from the bed next to mine so I had to resign myself to hoping for the best. At least she wouldn't wake me up (as I knew Holmes did Watson once) to ask if I'd be afraid to sleep in the same room as a lunatic.

When we arrived at the house in the Avenue des Huguenots I saw at once that, grand as it was, it had seen better days. Two large stone pillars supported an iron gate with a faded coat of arms above it, but the overall impression was one of tarnished paint and broken tiles. Plaster flaked off from what had once been a fine façade, and everything had the appearance of neglect. Emily, no doubt thinking of her own immaculately kept house, made a face as she tugged at the bell-pull and signalled to me to keep my eyes open and my ears cocked for anything which might help us.

After a while a dour manservant eventually let us in and we found the house in chaos. The first thing I noticed in the main salon was a woman sitting in an armchair with her apron over her head. She was rocking to and fro, while muffled sounds of sobbing could be heard coming from under the cloth. Her husband, or a man I took to be her husband, stood by looking completely helpless. "She has been like this ever since our young daughter disappeared," he said wearily.

"You've been to the police?" Emily bristled importantly.

He was a tall man carrying a fair amount of flesh but nevertheless, in spite of his age, having a good and imposing carriage. Now he drew himself up and, looking down at her majestically, said in a refined voice, "Such unfortunate circumstances are best discussed privately within the family and with private individuals."

"Fiddlesticks," said Emily Fanshaw energetically. "We'll need all the assistance we can get." She signalled to me (Emily was becoming very good at signalling to yours truly to do something) and I went over to the woman in the chair, idly glancing out of the window at the unkempt garden as I did so. At first she resisted all my efforts to get her to reveal herself. But at last, by dint of soft words and stressing that the only way to help her daughter was to tell us exactly what had happened, I prevailed upon her to uncover her face. I saw at once that she was quite pretty and years younger than her husband. "That's right, my girl," said Emily with gusto. "You can trust us to find the child, but we must have something to go on."

The distressed mother began by telling us what we already

knew. That her husband had been away on business in London and she had had to send for him. Then she went on to say that the child was last seen playing alone in the garden. But when the time came for her to come in for luncheon she was nowhere to be found. In answer to Emily's question the woman said yes, the iron gate to the house was seen to be open, which was unusual, but there was no sign of any force having been used to open it. "An inside job?" muttered Emily to me under her breath. Aloud she said, "Tell us, Madame, what did you do next?"

"We, that is the servants and I, searched all through the garden and the house. Gustave, that's our manservant, went into the Avenue outside the gate and walked a considerable distance in both directions, but he saw nothing."

"No carriage and no sound of a carriage?" I asked.

She shook her head. "And no-one could tell exactly when Lucille left the garden. I was upstairs counting the linen, the servants were either in the kitchen or getting the table ready for dinner –and we now have only one, live-out, gardener who had already left for home."

"Forgetting to shut the gate after him," said Emily triumphantly.

"Certainly not," interposed a deep voice. "Laurens would use a small side gate always, and that was found shut as usual."

"No doubt out of sight of the main house," sneered Emily,

referring to both the gate and the gardener. "What makes you so sure he didn't take the child with him?"

"I have had his house thoroughly searched, and he was in the habit of going to a tavern immediately after his day's work. Hardly the place for an e*nfante* brought up as our daughter has been."

"Or indeed any young child," said Emily severely. "Well, with or without your kind permission we are going to the police. If they allow us to work alone we will do so. Otherwise..." With a small bow to Madame and a haughty look at Monsieur she swept out of the room, leaving me to follow as best I could and feeling as usual like some kind of poorly paid servant.

The police station when we reached it proved to be a large building in the centre of town. Emily asked me to give my name to the uniformed *flic* at the desk and we were asked to wait for a few minutes. We could see the young man walking towards a door marked *Commissaire*, but were unprepared for a burst of quickly suppressed laughter from a group of coppers busy filing evidence obtained from the French criminologist Bertillon's new finger-print system, or shuffling photographs of the "usual subjects". One old man, who looked ready for retirement but hadn't risen above the rank of sergeant, was struggling into his overcoat ready, as he told us, to walk the streets searching for the shop which had sold an ordinary kitchen knife to a young thug who was suspected of murdering somebody with it. "I've been at it for three months and will never give up. All these youngsters think about are their wages and how to keep warm."

"But why had they all laughed?" asked Emily, afraid it was because of her English accent.

"Because he said you wanted to see *le homard.* Sometimes the cheeky beggars call the boss *la pince.*" The old man swept out into the street grumbling, and Emily raised her eyebrows –at the same time fingering the elegant French parasol she'd bought in Paris.

"The lobster," I said, in answer to the eyebrows. "Or the claw."

"I really envy you the grasp of the language," she said kindly, watching as the first policeman we'd spoken to came out of the *Commissaire's* office and threaded his way towards us.

"It's the first thing, French, that governesses have to learn," I said, "if they're to get anywhere." I remembered that Mrs. Forrester's little girl had been quick to pick up the language. But her brother had had a bit of a struggle. Unfortunately this caused some friction in the household since the boy was very obviously my employer's favourite.

"The *Commissaire* will see you at once," said a silky voice. As soon as we entered the office I realised how the poor chap had acquired his nicknames, but Emily was busy looking at the pictures which adorned the walls. Each framed photograph had the name and number of the subject underneath. This was no rogue's gallery, however. Each man had died in the execution of his duty. Shot, knifed, pushed under a *fiacre*. If that was what happened in Nantes, it must be much worse in Paris.

The *Commissaire* came forward and greeted us warmly. It was such an honour he said for him to receive the wife of the celebrated Doctor Watson. If something in his voice told me he would have preferred John or, better still, Sherlock Holmes himself, he was nevertheless prepared to put up with me and indicated very politely that he was entirely at our, or rather my, service. "One in the eye for Emily Fanshaw" I thought, and proceeded to outline what we had been told at the wine-merchant's house.

"This is more than strange," said the *Commissaire*, tapping on the desk with his good hand, "since you say M. Clément has told you he doesn't want to involve the police in what looks like a kidnapping. He was in here very recently complaining that someone had tried to poison his wife."

Emily brought out the letter which had reached us by way of the Wigmore Street Post office. "M. Clément had been in London and seen the advertisement for our very successful Detective Agency," she said, stressing the words 'very successful' extremely mendaciously. "But before he could make an appointment to visit us he received a telegram calling him home. I assume it was because his daughter had been kidnapped, although he mentions in this letter that you have had a lot of trouble with what sounds like wholesale poisoning."

The *Commissaire* groaned heavily. "You think he wanted you two ladies to investigate the chocolate episode rather than let us do so?" A hard-done-by expression settled on the policeman's face and he sighed heavily. "I had promised him every assistance."

"That's as maybe," retorted Emily. "But I can tell you to us that at the moment it's as clear as mud." Translate that, said her expression as she glared at me over the top of her parasol.

"Tell us about the chocolate," I said hastily.

"It seems shortly before M. Clément left for London his wife received a box of chocolates," said the *Commissaire* moving slightly in an effort to make himself more comfortable in his big leather chair.

"How 'received'?" Emily interrupted sharply.

"They came with a note from her best friend. But as soon as Madame Clément sampled one she spat it out saying the taste was too bitter. Shortly after that she became ill."

"And the chocolates went for analysis?"

The *Commissaire* looked embarrassed. "Well, no. They had already been got rid of."

147

Emily groaned loudly and I looked hard at the man, who was twirling a gold coin between the thumb and little finger of his left hand. It was all he could do. There was a nasty gap where his other fingers should have been. Well, as I said earlier, that explained the nicknames. He was absentmindedly revolving the coin, which was catching the light as it moved, and I wondered if this was a ploy to mesmerise a criminal into making a confession.

"You want to know how I got this," said the policeman, suddenly thrusting his maimed hand at me so that I received quite a shock. It was more a statement than a question. "I was a young raw recruit at my first execution. When they brought the man out into the yard to spit in the basket he broke free and began running up the walls, with his hands still tied behind his back. I tell you it would have looked funny if it hadn't been so horrible. We were on him like tigers, of course. From the time the condemned man is strapped to the bascule and his head is off is normally thirty seconds. We must have done it in half that time."

Cracher dans le panier. Literally, "To spit into the basket." I moved uneasily in my chair, and dared not look at Emily. But I did wonder vaguely why we were suddenly being told this tale. It bore no relation to the investigation in hand. Perhaps the man felt obliged to mention it every time he met someone new, it

148

bothered him so much.

"I have heard," continued the *Commissaire* expansively, "that in some of our colonies where there are often whole groups to be executed at once the least guilty goes first." He spat contemptuously and said, "As if it's possible to apportion blame in that way. But here in Nantes we do things differently. We execute criminals separately and," here he paused delicately, "clean and hone the –er –apparatus between each –hum –event. We are not so uncivilised as to let one man welter in the blood of another."

Amused no end by this purple way of expressing himself, I reflected that if the cretin who was about to be guillotined hadn't already weltered in somebody else's blood he wouldn't be in that situation in the first place. Out of the corner of my eye I could see Emily stuffing a handkerchief into her mouth in a vain attempt to stop laughing. The tears ran down her cheeks, and her normally pale face reddened so much I feared she would have a fit. No doubt he thought she was weeping in sympathy with the man on the shelf. At least I hoped that was so.

"And what happened next, Monsieur?" I asked politely, partly to draw his attention away from my silly friend who was still fighting to control herself and partly because I was really interested.

He looked at me queerly. "I was young, inexperienced and

149

anxious to please my superiors. One should know better than to go too near the knife. By the time the dust settled as you English are fond of saying I saw that, along with his head, my three fingers were also in the basket."

"Action and reaction," said Emily unexpectedly. She looked as though she was trying to work out if, after they were cut off by the force of the blade hurtling downwards through the air, fingers sprang up as high as heads before toppling into baskets.

"How did you feel?" I asked, even more desperate to divert the *Commissaire's* attention away from her.

He looked at me for a few moments before replying and then said, "Why, grateful that unlike the prisoner *I* still had my head!"

Chapter Seven

Somehow or other we managed to get out of the Police Station and went down the main boulevard towards an avenue which housed most of the emporiums selling chocolates. Emily was shaking with laughter and looking in all the shop windows to hide her face from passersby. "The Avenue of Saint Anthony, now The Avenue of Henri 1V," I said, in an effort to help her recover her poise. "The Edict of Nantes, you know: freedom for Protestants in the practice of their religion." I was breathlessly trying to keep up with her lengthening stride and kept tripping over myself. "Did you know that Peter Abelard was born here?"

"That's the trouble with you governesses," she gulped, her face still red from the effort of not laughing like a hyena. "You always want to tell people things. Unimportant things," she added nastily. "I believe Holmes said a few words on the subject to that precious husband of yours. Something about not letting one's 'little attic of a brain' become overloaded with information which isn't relevant to an investigation!" Suddenly becoming serious, and glaring at me almost as fiercely as when we were in the *Commissaire's* Office, she snapped, "Freedom fiddlesticks! I do wish you would keep your mind on the job."

She had stopped walking so suddenly I almost cannoned into her. "I'm sure this is the place," she hissed, pointing to a most impressive building which quite outshone all the others.

I followed her meekly into the shop, wondering if this was how poor old Watson felt when Sherlock was giving him one of his put downs. The interior was at first very gloomy, but deliciously cool. After a while I could distinguish rows of chocolate boxes ranged on shelves round the walls and tied with the most complicated bows. Other boxes sat on pedestals, and one particularly luscious-looking one had a small lamp trained on it. Behind the counter and staring at us with anything but a benign look stood a very thin man –with the most ferocious squint I ever saw in my life. He was so willowy his spine seemed hardly capable of supporting him, and he bent over sideways like a straw in the wind. When he spoke, however, his beautiful voice made me forget all his other drawbacks. I smiled at him as if he had been the most handsome man in the world and I the most willing woman in the world to make his acquaintance. Emily, however, was busy inspecting the chocolate boxes. Without warning, she suddenly grabbed the one with the light shining on it and put it on the counter with a bang. "Did you sell another of these within the last few weeks?" Her voice had a real snarl in it, like an angry she-bear.

"Why, yes, Madame," said the sinuous shopkeeper. He looked taken aback at the ferocity of her tone. "To a little girl who wanted it as a present for Madame Clément."

"Little girl?" Emily obviously didn't believe him. "You're

sure of that?"

The man's face paled. He began to stutter, and small beads of sweat ran down his narrow forehead. "Well, no. Now I recall. It was a young *lady* who first came in to choose the chocolates and asked for a box of them to be sent to her friend. But later M.Clément himself came in with the same box, saying there was something wrong with the contents."

There wasn't a little girl then? *Au contraire*, but there was, insisted the willowy young man. She had come in with the young lady and seemed very pleased and excited about buying such a very expensive sample of what he had in the shop.

"And was there?" asked Emily. "Anything wrong with that particular box, I mean?" The glare she gave him would have frightened a much less nervous creature than he was. It even made me blink a bit.

"I did not think so. After tasting one of the chocolates I received back from M. Clément, and finding it as usual delicious, I made the rest of them up into little packets and sold them as 'tasters'. Because it was impossible, you understand, to rescue the box once it had been opened. And the ribbon could never have been re-tied in the same way. But it was a dreadful waste of such expensive merchandise. Although I hoped that, by disposing of it in that way, it would be good for business."

"Why not inform the manufacturers?"

153

"We stock very little of that particular brand. I thought it was hardly worth it."

"I can believe that," said Emily to me as we sat later at a little table on the Avenue Henri IV genteelly drinking coffee and enjoying the open air. She added rather cryptically, "The makers of the stuff would soon cook his goose. By the way, do you realise how easy it is to poison such confectionery? First a syringe with a very fine needle to put in the arsenic, or whatever it is. Then heat the needle in a candle-flame, until it's hot enough to melt a little of the chocolate, which is then smoothed over the place where you've made the jab. It usually works like a dream." She sounded as if she'd been poisoning chocolates all her life –and enjoyed doing it.

"I can understand Madame Clément not being poisoned if she spat out a chocolate quickly enough. But how come he, the shopkeeper, didn't get sick? He said he tried one. And what happened when those tasters were let loose on the unfortunate people of the town?" My coffee was already cooling and I took a sip or two of it while she collected her thoughts.

"I should imagine that not all the chocolates were poisoned," Emily said finally, through a mouthful of choux pastry. "Maybe it was only the top layer. As for the townsfolk, I imagine some of them did get sick but put it down to eating too many of them."

"That still doesn't explain all the poisoned fruit we were told about. Has anyone become ill because of that?"

"Who can tell?" said Emily carelessly, picking up her parasol prior to taking a stroll down the Avenue. "What do you say to our visiting a Music Hall this evening?"

"We can't," I said, somewhat fazed by the abrupt change of direction. "Not alone, that is."

"Whatever are you talking about? I'll be your escort."

I remembered the trousers, and a man's jacket which now hung in the hotel wardrobe. It meant we'd have to smuggle ourselves out of the hotel –and probably back in again at the end of the evening. I only hoped she wouldn't invite another couple to sit with us and afterwards be inveigled into taking a drink in an all-night *bistro*: where she'd sit in her men's clothes smoking cheroots and swopping risqué stories with a French lout while I tried to make polite conversation (if polite is the right word in such a place) with his French tart.

Well, thankfully, what I feared didn't happen. We enjoyed the show, joined in all the songs, applauded the acrobat on the uni-cycle and laughed at the dancing dogs. It was all very raucous and great fun. But when we got back to the hotel I was so tired I fell asleep almost at once and only woke up when Emily shook me by the shoulder. "What's the French word for clink?" she asked.

"*La Prison*," I said sleepily. "Why do you want to know?"

"Because he's in it."

I sat up in bed. "Who's in it?"

"Our *Chocolatier,* that's all. While you were snoring I was busy down in the hotel lobby listening to all the gossip. I was correct about the chocolates. Not many contained arsenic. But some of them did, and several people *have* been taken ill. One or two of them quite badly," she added with relish, moving over to the dressing-table and taking the pins out of her hair prior to brushing it.

I swung my legs over the side of the bed and began to dress. "Do you remember what we were told before we left London?"

Turning away from the mirror Emily said, "When you thought it was strange that M. Clément knew something was going on at home even before he got the wire?"

Carefully pulling up my stocking and fastening it with one of the embroidered garters I'd bought in Paris while she was choosing between this and that parasol, I decided it was time for a recap. "M. Clément wanted to consult a private detective while he was in London, and read about us in *The Times* newspaper. But before he could make an appointment he received a cable to return home..."

Emily laid down her hairbrush. "Yes. I still have the letter he sent us. So it seems there were two mysteries. I think now that he didn't trust the Nantes police to find out who was trying to poison his wife, or the reason why. When this more serious business of the child came up, he distrusted them even more. All that talk of the family honour was just eyewash. But why should he go to the police simply because his wife was sick? Nobody would know about arsenic until this latest outbreak. You said yourself, if he had suspected poison he would never have left home."

"I think he did suspect something more serious than a bad chocolate, although not necessarily strong poison. But as his wife recovered pretty quickly, and his business in Britain was very important, he decided to leave France after all. But before doing so he took the precaution of carrying the chocolates back to the shop. Just in case Madame Clément was tempted to try another one, in spite of the fright she must have had."

Emily finished putting up her hair and, surveying herself in the glass with some satisfaction said, "Muriel, my dear, don't you think it's about time somebody interviewed the 'best friend', the one who sent the box of chocolates to Madame Clément? I assumed it was a woman but..."

"Either way, Longshanks must be got out of jug. It's unlikely he poisoned the chocolates. Not unless he has an insane hatred for the family and wanted to finish all of them off. Madame Clément would hardly avoid sharing such a treat with her husband –and the child."

"Talking of that, who was the child who accompanied the 'young lady' when she ordered the chocolates?" Emily stood up, tidied the dressing-table top and, ignoring her own question and my answer said, "If that was the case, the shop assistant with the squint would be sadly frustrated when he saw that well-fleshed chocolate-loving man coming through the door with an opened box of the firm's finest merchandise in his fist. Do you think that would be enough to make him go over the edge and send sections of it out to murder the town wholesale?"

"And at once become even more of a prime suspect than he is at present? How do we know that M. Clément isn't as mad as a hatter with a grudge against *him* and poisoned the chocolates before he took them back to the shop?"

"According to Monsieur, his wife was already taken bad; and what would he poison them with?"

"Arsenic, of course. Nearly every household keeps some of it in the garden shed –to kill rats."

"Garden shed," mused Emily. "You don't think Laurens..."

"No, I don't. And as for your other idea, that Madame Clément has a lover, we both know that a young woman came in to buy the chocolates."

"And it's that young woman," growled Emily, "who we are going to find –immediately we've had breakfast."

So it was that after the *croissants,* the *comfiture* and the coffee were consumed we sallied forth once more to speak to Madame Clément or, failing her, the self-satisfied husband. When the sour-faced manservant opened the door Emily asked him if he had taken a box of chocolates into the main *Salon* on the day his mistress became ill. He said (with what I thought was some reluctance) that he had, and asked truculently what it was we wanted this time.

"The sender's name," said Emily crisply. "And his or her address."

The man said there was no need to trouble the family. Mademoiselle de Luc visited often. Sometimes, if Monsieur was away and it was late at night, he had to call a *fiacre* for her and give the driver directions. He laid undue emphasis on the 'de' to show his employer's aristocratic connections.

"All servants are snobs," Emily muttered. Aloud she said haughtily, "If you know the address, please give it to me."

"On whose authority?"

"Your master's. You must know he has engaged us to look into...certain things. All servants listen at key-holes."

I thought he would slam the door in our faces when he heard the scorn in her voice. Instead it had the opposite effect. Disappearing for a moment into a tiny alcove which led off from the passage, he came back with a grubby piece of paper and handed it to her meekly

"Thank you," said Emily in her grandest manner. "We are very much obliged to you."

As soon as he had gone back inside the house we scurried out of the big iron gate, taking care to shut it behind us, and hurried back towards the centre of the town. "A good address," gasped Emily as we ran. She looked again at the piece of paper in her hand. "But I can't quite make it out."

"To the left, just behind those trees." In spite of the 'de', the dwelling looked small and cramped. Emily was wrong. It wasn't a good address. More like a hovel. I wondered if Miss de Luc was a poor relation, rather than a friend, who Madame Clément sometimes took pity on and invited to the house so that she could enjoy the luxury of relaxing in more congenial surroundings.

"What excuse can we give for calling?"

"We're amateur mendicants," said Emily with a grin. "Who have come begging and aren't very good at it!"

I looked at her with a frown and said, "Two respectable and well-dressed English women? I'd be surprised if we were good at it!"

"No-one likes tramps calling on them. But I see your point. We had better say the woman has been recommended to us as a milliner. I'd love to go home in a hat from Paris."

"Only this isn't Paris," I said peevishly. "We've no idea whether or not she makes hats."

"Everybody in France makes hats," said Emily dismissively. "And they're very good at copying fashions in the provinces. Nobody at home will be able to tell the difference."

There she was, letting her imagination run away with her. Just because Emily meant to use millinery as an excuse for calling it didn't mean it would work; and if the woman was in the habit of sending poisoned chocolates to people I didn't want to antagonise her.

"Here, lean on me," said Emily suddenly.

"Whatever for?"

"I've changed my mind. You've had an attack of the vapours because a mad dog ran at you in the street. Only a glass of water or something stronger will cure you."

"I don't mind pretending to be faint. But you can forget about the mad dog. It's too extreme."

"Unfortunately yes," said Emily, "but more exciting than millinery. Imagine, if you caught rabies I'd have to take you home in a coffin."

"There's no need to look so pleased about it. And I don't intend to die here, of rabies or anything else. If I am to die young I'd rather do it in London."

By this time we had reached the door of the house. Emily

knocked hard and rapidly, while I tried to look like a person who had been taken ill suddenly in the street. It really was an out-of-the-way spot, with rows of tiny houses arranged round a number of small gardens so that the whole place resembled a street of beguines.

When the door finally opened, neither Emily nor I could conceal our surprise at seeing a little apple-cheeked woman in a white apron. "Mademoiselle de Luc?" we asked doubtfully. Somehow or other, after meeting Madame Clément and listening to the man who sold chocolates, we had expected a much younger and more stylish person.

"No-one of that name lives here." Was it my imagination or did the old crone looked startled, and more than a little on her guard?

"You're quite sure?" snapped Emily. She'd quite forgotten the mad dog charade, and that I was supposed to be feeling faint.

"Of course I'm sure, Madame. There is only myself here since my poor husband died."

She said this just as she applied the edge of the white apron to her eye, brushing away an imaginary tear. Emily meanwhile was craning her neck over the old woman's head to see as much as she could of the inside of the house. Finally she bowed and the widow shut the door. We withdrew with as much grace as possible and walked rapidly towards the nearest café.

When we looked inside everything seemed rather dingy. But there were a few tables outside in the sun. I was a little worried at being there at all, but Emily said every Frenchman knew how eccentric the English were. She only wanted to sit long enough to tell me what she had discovered.

"She said she lived alone" –this was the ancient dame in the little house –"so what was a child's doll doing in the passage?"

"Perhaps she's got grandchildren? The coffee was warm, and much better than I expected.

"Maybe she has, and maybe she hasn't. I also saw a couple of picture books on a hall table."

"So?"

"I shouldn't be surprised if they have disappeared by now. I don't know about you, but I wouldn't believe a word that woman said, wiping her eye with the corner of her apron. I never saw anything so theatrical in my life."

"Are we going back?"

Emily stood up. She had finished her coffee and put a couple of *sous* under the saucer in payment for it. "We're going to keep watch on the place."

There followed two of the most tedious days I have ever endured in my life, not excepting the times when Watson was away with Holmes. It was even, if you can believe me, worse than *that*. My companion in crime-solving had engaged a cab to

163

wait outside the café while we spent the time walking up and down pretending to admire a non-existent view. In an effort to make the time pass more quickly, I let her practice her French on me. By the time something did happen her fluency in the language had increased ten-fold.

Towards the end of the second day, just as the sun was about to set, a carriage stopped outside the house we had under surveillance. Telling the driver to wait, a young, slim and decidedly handsome girl got out and knocked at the door. This was opened a crack. After a moment the crack widened, and the woman went in. A short time later she appeared again. Only this time she had a child with her, so muffled up it was impossible to see her face. As we watched, the pair climbed into the carriage and the coachman prepared to drive off. Emily raced across to the cab she had retained and, after a frenzied few minutes, we were off in hot pursuit.

Ordering the driver not to let the vehicle in front know it was being followed, we traversed the streets of Nantes until we reached the outer fringes of the town. Here the houses were very grand, and the gardens enormous. Emily took note of the dwelling at which the carriage stopped, watched the woman and the child get out and then told our driver to take us to our hotel. I was never so glad to rest my feet at last in the confines of our shared bedroom. Which during the previous two days we had only used to sleep in. They positively burned from all that traipsing up and down, and I could almost have wished myself back in Mrs. Forrester's establishment. Where I'd have a comfortable chair, and my only problems would be how to keep the children in order and myself out of the way of Mr. Forrester.

"I'd put money on it that's the Clément child," said Emily, taking off her shoes and putting on a pair of blue embroidered slippers.

"What are we going to do about it?"

"I'm not sure yet. But that's a drum just asking to be broken by a bit faker."

I had to laugh. She was quite right about the house being easy to burgle, but a bit faker was underworld slang for a coiner. However, by the next morning she had decided to visit the place to make sure we were on the right track.

"Very well," I said, "if you'll just give me time to practice my fainting technique."

"No need for that. We're two very respectable English ladies who have read about the beautiful architecture of some parts of Nantes and would like to see round her particular bit of it."

"You'll be lucky if you don't get thrown out on your ear."

"What, with a letter from the Duke of Holdernesse?"

"The Duke of Holdernesse? Do you know him then?

Emily gave me a pitying look. "I know him enough to pinch

some of his ducal writing paper when Neville and I were on a sight-seeing visit to his Stately Home, along with about two hundred other people. It was on display in the library. I only needed one sheet."

This seemed to me to show remarkable foresight. How could she know when, if ever, it would come in handy? I guessed it was no use asking her how she'd managed such a sleight of hand under the eagle eye of the house-keeper, to say nothing of those other types anxious to see how the very rich lived. I'd only get a cock-and-bull story. So I sat and watched her hand glide over the paper as she wrote her spurious letter of introduction. She had a most elegant script. I couldn't help admiring it, and said so. Emily said with a gratified smile that she hoped it would do, carefully blotted the missive, put it into an envelope and addressed it to Mademoiselle de Luc at the number and street we had seen the day before. Then she bounded up from the desk and said in her loud, rather raucous, voice (the one she used outside Bayswater) "Time for action, Muriel. Stir your stumps."

The house again looked very grand, even from the outside, and we were surprised when Mademoiselle de Luc opened the door herself. She in her turn looked equally surprised when Emily Fanshaw explained our errand and gave her the letter. I couldn't help noticing the marked hesitation in her manner as she opened the door a little wider and showed us into a small sitting-room to the right of the vestibule. But after some reflection she decided to show us round, at the same time as she arranged for a little refreshment to be served later.

The inside of the building certainly exuded an atmosphere of wealth. Emily admired the drawing-rooms, I was greatly struck by the library, and Mademoiselle enthused about the garden. She didn't invite us to go upstairs or into the kitchens and Emily didn't press the point. Instead she concentrated on the beautiful architraves, the stained glass in the moulded window frames and the paintings on the walls. "Some of my family," said our hostess modestly. "And others because my grandfather was a connoisseur of fine art."

The back garden when we reached it was large and sloped away from the house. A small door next to a conservatory, and a few stone steps down, led across the capacious lawns to another door in an end wall. It was this second door which opened onto the main route into the town or, if one went far enough in the opposite direction, to the rows of mean one-storey dwellings with their tiny green squares that we had already visited. I made a note that it was this door which meant one could enter or leave the building without using the main entrance, and probably without being seen.

Suddenly a small fair-haired child burst out of a coppice and ran towards us waving a picture book. "We are having tea on the terrace in honour of my English visitors," said Mademoiselle de Luc. "They arrived very unexpectedly, bringing a letter they say is from an English Milord." She had carried the tea tray out herself and placed it on a table with her own hands. Now she lifted the child onto her knee and offered her a cake. "My niece," she said in a whisper as if she didn't want the child to hear.

"Did you ever see such brass-neck?" said Emily to me as we drove away from the house after what I at least had found a strained couple of hours. "That child is no more her niece than one of the little ragamuffins we saw playing in the Town Square."

There she went again. Where was the proof that the little girl was anything other than de Luc's niece and had been collected by her, after a short visit perhaps to an old servant? When we reached our hotel Emily said she was going out once more and might be some time. I was to stay put. Well, I sat in the lounge reading all the newspapers. Then I picked up a yellow-backed novel left behind by another English traveller and tried to interest myself in that, had a mild flirtation with the waiter at luncheon, went for a moody walk in the grounds and finally arrived back to our bedroom where I had a good sulk. It felt just like old times, before Sherlock went over the Falls and Watson was hardly ever in the house.

Emily, when she did arrive, was flushed with excitement. Not for her the inscrutable, hard-to-fathom look. "The case, you will be glad to know, is closed. I have the cheque in my pocket and we can leave for home as soon as you like."

"How is it 'closed'?" I was determined to let her see how fed-up I was.

"I've been to see *le homard* and told him to arrest Mademoiselle de Luc and release Longshanks. I then visited M. Clément at his business headquarters and told him where he would find his daughter. Result one child safely at home and one young lady in custody."

"All done on your say-so? It sounds incredible."

She nodded happily. "I had to act quickly in case de Luc got the wind up and took the child back to her apple-cheeked friend. Not that it would have made much difference. If Lucille hadn't been in one place the police would have found her in the other."

"Perhaps you'd be good enough to explain things to your addle-pated friend," I said crossly. "After all, I can hardly be said to have spent a very exciting day."

"It's good to be rested occasionally," said Emily soothingly, sitting down in the second armchair and gazing for a moment out of the window. "You recall that Madame Clément, her name's Ernestine by the way, was taken ill when some chocolates were sent in to her –and before her husband came to

169

London; and that the urgent request to return home was because his daughter had supposedly been kidnapped? Well, dear Ernestine arranged it all herself by taking her own child in a closed carriage to the house of her friend. The little girl was used to de Luc and even called her *ma tante*. But in case anyone suspected, they arranged for Lucille to stay for a while with the lachrymose widow. If all seemed to be going well she could be brought back to that grand house we visited this morning."

"What about servants?"

"Rather surprisingly, there were none. Except a morose old cook who kept herself to herself and minded her own business. Even if she did see the child about the house or was asked to provide a little more food than was customary (or even had the little girl in the kitchen with her sometimes) that wouldn't be anything new. But you must remember how surprised we were when de Luc opened the door herself."

"Not as surprised as I am to hear Ernestine arranged for her own daughter to disappear, and had a 'best friend' who was trying to poison her."

"Oh, but she wasn't. Trying to poison her, I mean. Madame Clément knew all about the chocolates and had strict instructions, if she wanted to allay suspicion by sampling some herself, only to take them from the bottom layer. But she got in a muddle. That was really why the child was sent away. In case

170

there was another, more disastrous, mistake."

"And Monsieur was recalled so that the 'experiment' could be continued?"

"That's a polite word for it. With only him and his wife in the house all the two women had to do was wait until he consumed enough confectionery for it to work."

"How 'work'?"

"Why, kill him you idiot."

"Are there no doctors in Nantes, no pathologists in Paris?" I demanded, stung.

"His wife would say he was depressed. Arsenic was kept in or near the house to be used on vermin and he took it on purpose. The friend, of course, would confirm the depression since everyone knew she was often in the house even when the husband was at home. Things began to unravel when M. Clément was so prompt in going to the police. But when he was equally quick at returning the chocolates to where they'd been bought by de Luc that was quite a good thing for our two viragos, especially when the shopkeeper began sending out those blessed tasters."

"How was it a good thing, if I may ask?"

"They only had to wait a while for someone to be taken ill, or even die, before the man would be arrested. That would divert any suspicion away from them, and all they had to think of then was something a little more fool-proof."

"While we were still at home you said fruit was being used to poison people. Was Longshanks also responsible for that outbreak?"

"Of course not," said Emily. "He wasn't responsible for anything, except selling expensive chocolates to rich customers. No, it was blind panic. With M. Clément suspicious and the police involved, de Luc realised the shopkeeper might remember her. She completely lost her head and sent anonymous baskets of fruit to perfect strangers, reasoning that even if the police caught up with her they would have trouble proving a motive."

After a restless night trying to resolve certain discrepancies in Emily's account, I got out of bed next morning ready to pack but feeling anything but chipper. She went to pay the hotel bill and order a conveyance, while I sat in the foyer by the luggage waiting impatiently for her to come back. Then "Miss Fanshaw," I said deliberately as we went down the hotel steps, "why were you so sure about the child?"

She brushed a speck of dust from her shoe with the end of her parasol. "I could see you didn't believe me when I made that remark about the ragamuffin. But the woman who went into the shop to buy the chocolates had a young child with her. Of course it might have been her niece –or it might have been Ernestine's little girl out for a walk with the friend. How else can you

172

explain the child's excitement unless she knew the gift was for her mother? It's my guess de Luc took the little thing home and left her to play while she doctored the goods before taking both child and chocolates back to Ernestine's. Later, when the child was sent to de Luc for safety if you remember, that personage was most reluctant to let us into the house, declined to show us all of it and paled visibly when the little girl suddenly appeared in the garden. She obviously wasn't expecting her, and I dare say the old crone in the kitchen received a rollicking for letting her out of her sight. If that doesn't convince you, why did the woman whisper and immediately give the child a cake if it wasn't to distract her from saying something that would blow the gaff? It was a very short time after that that we were shown out."

"But why involve the child at all? According to you, Ernestine lets her daughter go out for a walk with the friend who takes her into a shop and buys chocolates. They then go back to the friend's house where she poisons some of them, at the same time distracting the child's attention by giving her a few toys to play with. As soon as she's satisfied that the chocolates will do their work, the friend takes them and the child back to the Avenue des Huguenots. Once there she doesn't go in to the mother and hand over the child and the chocolates personally, as the servant might reasonably expect her to do since she is such a particular pal of his mistress. Instead she gives them to him, leaving Ernestine to bring Lucille back to her house at a later date. It all sounds unnecessarily complicated."

Emily looked nonplussed for a moment. Then she said, "It must have all been designed to divert suspicion from de Luc. After all, we don't really know if she waited for the manservant to open the door. She may have simply rung the bell and told the child to wait quietly with the box of chocolates until somebody came. The walk may have been arranged to get the child to trust the friend even more. The beautiful lady had bought very expensive chocolates for *Maman.* She had taken her home to a house with a lovely garden and where there was lots of lemonade and cake, as well as toys..."

"But that surly young manservant said de Luc visited the Clément house often."

"Yes, to see Ernestine. But she may not have seen much of the child."

"Lucille seemed quite comfortable with her."

"I didn't say she never saw the little girl. But obviously the chocolate episode, besides being part of a plan to poison Monsieur, was to impress her with de Luc's kindness to her mother and get her used to being alone with her."

"But," I protested hotly, "the manservant more or less said that the box of expensive chocolates he took into the drawing-

174

room was from de Luc."

Here Emily used a very coarse expression to mean the manservant wouldn't remember who had sent what. She was obviously tired of the whole episode and anxious to get home. I looked admiringly at her and said, "It was very clever of you to build up such a strong case against the pair of them on such slight evidence. Or, if not strictly evidence, at least a number of nuances."

"Large inferences," said Emily smugly, "can come from a collection of quite small facts."

She sounded so much like Sherlock Holmes I had to look twice to make sure she wasn't in disguise. According to John, Holmes had been a devil for disguises and I would never put it past him to dress up as a woman, tall as he was."Tell me," I said, "why did these two women *want* to poison M. Clément?"

"Oh," said Emily airily as she marched out of the hotel and climbed into the cab which had drawn up alongside the kerb, "Ernestine discovered she didn't like men, and de Luc has always been averse to their attentions. But the two of them could hardly hope to establish a *Salon des Femmes* with him around. *"*

"A *Salon des Femmes*? I thought that was only in Paris!"

Emily settled herself more comfortably inside the vehicle and called to the cabby to make sure the luggage was safely secured on the roof before driving us as quickly as possible to the station."That's only the most notorious one," she said in a sleepy voice. "My dear, there are branches everywhere." And before I could say another word she'd dozed off.

Later, as the train travelled noisily across country, I said, "What do you think will happen now in that household?"

"I should imagine nothing much will go on for some considerable time. I'm sure you recall Madame Clément sitting with her apron over her head and sobbing her heart out, and how you went so readily to her assistance? With acting talent like that she'll easily convince her doting husband she was completely duped."

"And de Luc?"

"Fortunately nobody has died, so we won't hear of *her* head spitting into the basket. But she'll certainly get a long stretch in a French prison, which will be a pretty grim thing in itself."

"All the same, I wouldn't be in his shoes when she comes out."

"Me neither. However, by that time his wife might have found a way all by herself of murdering her husband. But really, I can't concern myself with the problems of *die lesbierin* and run a detective agency at the same time."

"It's not illegal, lesbianism," I said. "At least, not in England since Queen Victoria said it was 'Impossible!' But there's still

176

one thing to be cleared up. Why did the Cléments' servant give us that first address?"

"Because he was a fool, and lazy with it. He'd been told – probably falsely –that after visiting Ernestine the friend often went out on charity work. She was probably up to something much more reprehensible since I can't see her as someone succouring the poor. But there were several addresses where she could be contacted if she was wanted. He simply gave us the first one that came to hand."

"So our turning up at the widow's was pure coincidence?"

"Beginner's luck," said Emily.

It was when we reached Victoria Station after the tiring journey through France that her behaviour really surprised me. Emily seemed suddenly to have acquired a new lease of life. She dashed through the concourse and out into the street, leaving me to scuttle behind her, after giving a porter hurried instructions to load our luggage into a cab and telling the driver to take it to the St. Clair's address in Bayswater. When I did finally catch up with her, I was amazed to see the inexplicable woman walking in a very sedate and genteel manner behind a large uncouth man. He seemed to be having difficulty with his crutch. It was obviously intended to help him to walk, but signally failed in this respect. He either wasn't used to it or it weighed much more than was customary. The crutch caught him off balance and swung him half-round at intervals. When this happened Emily dodged into a doorway, signalling me to do the same as soon as she realised I was following behind. This went on for several streets until she suddenly accosted a policeman and demanded he follow the man.

Of course he wanted to know why; but Emily said she didn't know. It was just a feeling she had. Flourishing her purse under his nose in the gathering gloom, she implied there would be money in it for him if he was quick enough to size up the situation, and that he might even 'earn his sergeant's stripe that night' if he followed her instructions. The policeman opened his bull's-eye lantern and let the single beam fall on the cripple's back. "He seems to be having trouble with that there crutch," he said.

"Never mind that," said my dear friend and colleague impatiently. "Just keep your eyes open and be ready to act if necessary." She could see the man was nervously fingering his police whistle and said maliciously, "You may need to call up reinforcements." But as we continued to travel through the streets with nothing at all happening, Emily began to look doubtful. That is, until our quarry suddenly took a quick turn into the doorway of a jeweller's which was just about to shut up shop. At the same time several furtive figures emerged from the shadows, the policeman blew his whistle, policemen arrived as if from nowhere, the indistinct newcomers vanished as quickly as they had come –and we rushed into the building just in time to see a gun being pointed at the proprietor's head. It was a gun with a short stubby barrel, the kind commonly known as a 'bull-dog'; and the man who held it was as upright and as steady as any other healthy person. The crutch lay on the floor and Emily ran towards it with a cry of joy.

"I thought so, my dear Muriel," she said in the best Sherlockian manner, picking the thing up and looking at me with a satisfied smile.

As for me, I didn't know what to think. The man had been disarmed and hauled away by three hefty policemen (including our acquaintance with the bull's-eye). The owner of the jeweller's shop was in the back helping himself to a glass of brandy and Emily was preparing to go back to Victoria Station. As we hurried along I asked her how she had got so suddenly onto the trail of a jewel thief.

"I didn't," she said. "That is, I didn't know exactly what was going to happen. But I saw that the crutch wasn't the usual wooden one. It was made of aluminium, and a singular affair at that. Aluminium is light but very strong. The man should have been able to manage his support well, unless there was something inside it."

"Whatever do you mean, 'something inside it'? And however

179

did you spot him?"

"To answer your second question first, he got out of a third class carriage of our train and went hobbling down the platform in a most peculiar manner, like someone who wasn't used to walking in that way. That's what drew my attention to him. Although aluminium is a light metal as I said, most things manufactured from it are hollow to make them lighter still. When I picked up the crutch I saw that the handle at the top had been unscrewed and that there was space enough inside for something, in this case a gun."

"It would have fallen to the bottom of the crutch," I said scornfully. "He couldn't have reached it."

"It *had* fallen to the bottom of the crutch, and was quite heavy for its size. That's why he kept losing his balance. But what was to stop the thief unscrewing the crutch, tipping it up, retrieving the gun, cocking it and then rushing into the shop? We three were some distance away and there was a deep recess at the entrance to the jewellers."

"And space in the hollow crutch where he could stash the loot," I said.

"Doubtful. It was much better to abandon the crutch as he did and stuff the proceeds of the robbery in his pockets. The men outside were obviously waiting for him, to divide the spoils once they had all run to safety, and were there to lend him a hand should anybody cut up rough."

"Do you think there will be a reward?"

"I jolly well hope so," said Emily. "I don't like chasing after criminals for nothing."

Chapter Eight

Watson was at the station when we arrived back from our sudden and unexpected, not to say unplanned, adventure of the aluminium crutch. He said he'd been there for hours. But he seemed very pleased to see us and I guessed he'd been lonely, just as I used to be when he went off with Holmes. Neville St. Clair was also there with the children and said he had planned a trip to Italy for himself and his family. If his wife would care to come with him to Cook's newly opened Travel Agency he would get the tickets there and then and reserve places for them all to leave in a week's time. Emily jumped at the chance. I'm sure she was thinking more of banditti than cathedrals and art galleries. Giving me M. Clément's cheque to bank, she fair raced out of the station again–with the children running behind and her husband pleading for a little more decorum.

As John and I left the station he took out his whistle from an inside pocket of his jacket to summon a hansom, and when it wheeled over from the opposite side of the road handed me in as if I had been a lady who (like the gentry) had all the time in the world. But, after I had explained about the luggage by saying it had all gone to Bayswater and we were both safely inside the vehicle, he disturbed me horribly by suddenly saying, "A telegram came for me this morning." After all the excitement in Nantes, the fatigue of the journey and the pleasure I felt in being home I could have wept. Surely he hadn't found another Holmes while I'd been away?

"No," said John as if he had read my thoughts. "We're wanted in Ballarat!"

Well, once we reached home what was left of the evening was spent talking endlessly about that telegram and getting used to the idea of such a tremendous undertaking as a trip to Australia. The next day I set about providing myself with a number of new outfits. I was already feeling that a journey to Victoria and one of the most famous gold-mining towns in the world could be quite exciting. It would, I guessed, be completely different from France. Even John seemed to relish the idea, though travelling by train from London to Liverpool and boarding the *SS Devonia* to New York was at first quite uneventful. Thanks to my portion of M. Clément's cheque, we were able to travel first class. This was such a luxury and so comfortable that I was surprised to see when I came out of our state room one morning that Watson was leaning over the side and looking a little white round the gills.

"What's the matter?" I asked cheerfully, moving nearer to him. "You're not seasick?"

For answer he drew me behind a stanchion. Just as a tall, hard-faced man passed us on his way to the back of the vessel. "That's him," he hissed. "Neil Gibson."

"Neil Gibson?"

"The Gold King, a man whose dastardly conduct drove his wife to suicide."

"Well," I said with spirit, "he's not going to do the same to your wife." It wasn't like Watson to be scared, and I was surprised to see him so rattled. Dodging round the stanchion, I ran towards the place where Gibson had disappeared and saw him leaning over the taffrail. He had his back to me and was gazing out to sea, moodily smoking a cigar.

"He offered Holmes any amount of cash to save the woman he loved from the gallows," whispered Watson just behind my left ear. "And when he saw that money failed to talk actually had the audacity to impugn my friend's reputation!"

"Good for him," I thought.

"And, when Sherlock accused him of lying about his intentions towards the girl, Gibson jumped to his feet so fiercely, and raised his great knotted fist with such a fiendish look on his face, I thought it best to spring to Holmes' defence before he got flattened."

I felt my admiration for Mr. Gibson increasing by the minute, in spite of his craggy, remorseless face and his cold grey eyes.

"Would you believe he had the temerity to say Holmes knew best how to ruin his own business, and had done himself no good that day? If I remember rightly, Gibson's exact words were 'I have broken stronger men than you.' He also said that no man ever crossed him and was the better for it. You can hardly blame me if I was a bit shaken to see him on the same ship as us."

"Let's go down to breakfast," I said soothingly. "And be sure to keep out of the fellow's way for the rest of the voyage." It might have been exciting to meet him, but it was obviously better for John's peace of mind if we didn't. The last I saw of the menacing millionaire he was being given the VIP treatment and going through Customs at once, while Watson and I waited on the Quay with the rest of the passengers for our more humble luggage to be checked.

There followed an exciting few days sampling the sights of New York before we caught the train to San Francisco. Not for us one of the locked emigrant carriages but a Pullman car as luxurious as the ship. I had a lady's maid almost to myself, and there were bathrooms for both sexes. The dining car was a dream. San Francisco, when we finally reached it, also seemed quite wonderful –with trolley cars competing with the many cabs plying their trade round the City. I could see John was enjoying it all and was almost sorry when we left port and, in a sailing vessel aided by steam, headed for Cape Town.

What can I say about that City? Busy, bustling, full of beautiful gardens, it was a paradise of pleasant activity. Soon, however, we were once again at sea on a seven thousand mile trip (Seven thousand *nautical* miles, according to Watson) to the Antipodes and making for Melbourne. "Will you want to get off the ship when it puts in at Pitcairn?" John asked. "It's the usual thing, and can easily be arranged if you think you can stomach a bum-boat."

So it was that our ship weighed anchor and we were rowed ashore with a number of other passengers to what seemed like an Eden of breadfruit trees, bananas and plantain. Some hard bargaining took place and, after being shown the volcano where Fletcher Christian used to sit waiting for someone to come and get him for his terrible treatment of Admiral William Bligh, I found myself going back to the ship with a bead bag and a large bunch of bananas. Watson tossed them over the side saying we had had more than enough to eat as it was, and we sailed on for some time before sighting, a week away from Sydney, the three 'King's Islands' at the northern-most tip of North Island, New Zealand. After that the ship veered west towards Melbourne and the rotting carcases of the old convict hulks in the bay.

As soon as the ship docked and all the formalities were over we made our way to a moderately priced hotel, which turned out to be not a patch on the one we would stay in later in Ballarat. It was after a dull dinner, served by a disgruntled old waiter, that John suggested we pay a visit to Queen Victoria Market. It had been opened in this very English City, named after Her Majesty's first Prime Minister, more than twenty years before.

186

"I heard she was in love with him," I said to John.

"A girlish crush," replied Watson with a grin. "She was looking for a father-figure. Albert soon came along to put paid to all that."

"Perhaps most of the love was on his side. Melbourne was certainly cut up when he left office and could no longer rely on having the Queen's ear all the time."

"She blamed him, you know, for not letting her marry Albert sooner," said my husband, careful where he was putting his feet.

The history lesson over, we strolled arm in arm along Queen's Street towards a huge building. I quickly decided that I had never before seen such a large market or such varied goods. "You can buy anything here it seems," remarked John looking round in amazement, "from second-hand clothes to a colt pistol or a tame kangaroo."

Since I had no wish to end up with another bead bag, I contented myself with simply looking at all the other shoppers scrambling for goods and asked my husband when we were going to leave for Ballarat. "As soon as you like," he said. "In fact, we can take one of these rather jolly little trolley cars to the station and look up train times now. Unless, that is, you'd prefer a cab?"

I could see he was dying to ride on a trolley so I said no to the cab and we rattled down William Street at a cracking pace, and turned right into Spencer Street. We bought our tickets for the next day at Spencer Street Station and found out that it served the rural population. In other words, the line was used by trains taking travellers out into the country. I confess that, after our long voyage by sea, I looked forward eagerly to a complete change of scene and said as much to Watson.

After a surprisingly good breakfast of bacon and eggs, coffee and (slightly burnt) toast at our hotel, we made our way back to Spencer Street, this time by cab, and were soon settled in our reserved seats and bowling along towards Ballarat. The short trip passed without incident, and also without much conversation since we were both tired. The station there, with its domed clock tower, had been opened with great ceremony two years after my marriage to John and still retained its newness. The interior seemed very elegant, and shrieked money. Over a quarter of all the gold found in Victoria had come from the reef mines of Ballarat, and the last one wouldn't be worked out until some years later although, as John told me, the only one in British hands had folded nearly forty years earlier.

We reached our destination in good time and stepped out of the Station onto Lydiard Street. John hailed a cab and told the driver to take us to the best hotel in town. This was The George, where rooms had already been booked for us. I was amazed at the evidence of tremendous wealth that I saw. Highly decorated houses, large public buildings with wonderful verandas; and The Mining Exchange which the guide told us was built the year after I first met Sherlock Holmes! "John," I said, grabbing his arm excitedly, but careful not to tell him why I was so thrilled, "There's even a theatre." How I had loved the theatre, and some of the young men who frequented it!

"The oldest in Australia," said our driver smugly.

"Not quite," muttered Watson, "Just the oldest in the Provinces."

I remembered he had been in Ballarat before, and said that all this must be very familiar to him, including the art gallery we were just passing as we drew nearer to our hotel.

"Not at all," he said. "It was all much more rural –and rough. There was a police station just here, and all these fancy buildings are simply the result of the money people made from the gold which was being dug up –and later from the tourist trade. By the time that theatre was built in 1875 we, the Sacker family, were all back in Britain. As for art galleries, well I had more than my fill of one when I worked with Sherlock on the Baskerville Case."

Shifting himself round a little in the cab so that he could watch the passers-by as well as talk, Watson went on "He had next to no knowledge of art. But when I remarked on this he denied it, and insisted on visiting a Bond Street Gallery to see a lot of rude pictures. They were by some Belgian artists of the *Avant Garde* School and really Mary my dear I wouldn't have liked you to see them. We seemed to be in there for hours, and he talked about the canvases for what seemed like hours after we left and went back to the Northumberland Hotel to await Sir Henry. As for me, I could never detach my mind in that way from any of our investigations until they were over, and sometimes not even then. I always had to go over things in order to satisfy Holmes about what or what not he wanted to put into *The Strand Magazine.* I even had to make notes for him of some other cases I never even took part in. At the time of our visit to the Bond Street Gallery we were involved with a dead body in a double coffin, I remember. Or was it a gigantic hound?"

By this time we had reached our hotel, where two flunkeys came down the steps to take our luggage and a young woman in a smart outfit welcomed us with a wide smile to Ballarat. However, the room when we reached it was not the one we expected to be in. That, we were told, would not be ready for a few days. In the meantime, the management hoped we could make do with this one? Make do? The room was the height of elegance: gold candelabra, gold fittings in the bathroom and a veranda to die for. Watson was busy inspecting a complimentary box of cigars and a bottle of Irish whiskey, while I sniffed at a gold-topped scent bottle (free to female guests) and marvelled at the thickness of the monogrammed towels placed ready for us – and at the silkiness of the monogrammed sheets on a magnificent bed. "Even the towel-rails are gold-plated," I gasped.

John said he'd go down to Reception and order dinner while I unpacked, and it was when we were sitting at a table in the Hotel's stunning dining-room that he told me why we were there. I was toying with a gold-handled fruit knife at the time and only half-listening, but something he said did at last pull me up. I caught the words "bank robbery" and instinctively felt for my purse. John grinned and said, "Relax. It was in the early eighteen fifties."

More history. I began absentmindedly peeling an apple.

"A miner named Henry Garrett stormed the bank here. He had had no luck at the diggings and his claim eventually lapsed. By all accounts he took to drink, then to the bush and finally to sticking up wagons and stealing the gold which was being taken to Melbourne."

"Alone?" I said. He must have been quite a man. It was a pity it all happened too long ago for me to have met him.

"He had a number of similar gentlemen to help him. Their biggest and most daring job was to break into the Victoria Bank here in Ballarat. Unfortunately, before the gang escaped with the gold, two cashiers were shot dead. As you can imagine, this resulted in a gigantic man-hunt. But after a great deal of hard graft by the police Henry and his five little helpers were finally caught red-handed and hanged."

I arranged the discarded apple-peel at the side of my plate, thinking what a neat red and green pattern the coils made, and cut delicately into the fruit. In such a place I was determined at all costs to behave like a lady, even though I'd heard Australian society was a lot more lax in its manners than its British counterpart, and probably even more so in this town than in Melbourne. Putting a piece of apple into my mouth and glancing round the room to see if anyone more interesting had come in, I said, "If all this happened so long ago, and Garrett and his gang are dead anyway, what has it got to do with us?"

"Someone has reason to believe a new gang want to repeat their exploits. In fact, they've already begun doing so."

It sounded like a reprise of Mrs. Marple and her Angelo. Only this time men were stealing nuggets, not coins: and those two could hardly be compared with a gang of Australian roughnecks –except perhaps in the strength of their murderous intentions if the old Garrett gang was anything to go by. I never thought I'd become so sick of hearing about such a desirable metal as gold. But I stopped gazing round the room and said in a peevish voice, "But why *me and you*? Why call us over from the other side of the world? There must be people here who can nab them?" After all, we hadn't been around in 1854. I had stopped pushing bits of peel round my plate and was now giving Watson my full attention. Surely it was his connection with Sherlock all over again which had brought us to Australia?

"Yes," he said. "Holmes did have a similar case involving mining and mobsters. As a matter of fact, he had two, one in Australia and the other in America."

"I wasn't aware that he was ever on either of those places," I said coldly. "It was you who were supposed to have done the travelling, *and* have all that experience with women."

"Of many nations and over three continents," chortled John. "Holmes allowing readers to know that certainly boosted my ego. Although I happily shared lodgings with him for some years we were very different men you know. Holmes had a lukewarm attitude towards women, although he could put them at their ease when he liked."

I had to give him that, and recalled that Sherlock had been unusually sympathetic towards Maud Bellamy when her fiancé was killed in an investigation he called 'The Lion's Mane'. I was just about to put another question to John when a waiter appeared at my elbow asking if we wanted coffee. I watched the man bring a tray across the room from the kitchens and place it expertly on our table. Everything, including the tray, was solid silver, except the cups. These carried the hotel's newly designed monogram on the outside and a small hand-painted picture of Australia's national emblem, an acacia tree with bright yellow flowers (echoing the more solid gold already in the room) on the inside just below the rim. Milk from a silver jug and sugar from a silver bowl were added to strong black coffee, before the steaming cups were handed to us with some ceremony, and the silver sugar tongs carefully returned to their accustomed place on top of the sugar lumps still in the bowl. Leaving the tray and its contents in position in case we wanted more coffee the waiter unobtrusively removed my plate with its apple core and peel before walking quietly to the next table, where a stout man and his faded wife were busy arguing over whether to have coffee at their table or a whisky-and-soda in the bar.

"Did you notice anything about that chap who served us?" I asked John.

"Only that he seemed good at his job. No clatter. No chat. He hadn't forgotten anything, and gave us the right number of spoons. He wasn't trying to get fresh with you was he?"

"Certainly not," I said, pretending to be annoyed. "It was his hands."

"Well, I can't say I noticed them. I was too busy thinking about this job."

"They weren't a waiter's hands, delicate and soft..."

"He wasn't either. Delicate and soft, I mean. More like a

heavy-weight boxer, now I come to think of it. But, after all, this is Ballarat. You can't expect the kind of servant you get in the London Clubs."

"No," I said to myself, stuck-up and as old as the hills. Terrified and ready to pounce if a woman showed any signs of coming a step further than the foyer.

John put down his coffee cup and said, "I presume you noticed something more to the point than his athletic build?"

"Yes, although that might also be important. But it was his hands as I said. I had plenty of time to observe them while he was messing about with the coffee and they were not only large but callused. More like a miner's than a waiter's."

"By Jove, you don't mean...?"

"I don't know what I mean. But he needs watching."

After breakfast the next morning, at which 'our' waiter was nowhere to be seen, John sat on the veranda outside the bedroom window studying a large map which he'd obtained free from Reception and talking most annoyingly in a non-stop detecting-type of tone. "This is where new gold deposits have recently been discovered," he said, pointing to a remote spot which must have been all of forty miles from Ballarat. "And this is the marked trail along which the wagons travel. It's an old trail, from where prospectors thought there must be gold many years ago and missed it. But now someone has found that there is gold there after all and put up the money to dig it out. Trouble is, a gang is holding up the wagons and pinching some of it."

"What about the police? What are they doing?"

John folded up the map, took a look at the crowd crawling like ants below him and came back into the bedroom. "I was told in London that this is a very secret operation, to be kept from the authorities. That's why we must be circumspect. The owner of the whole outfit wants to keep everything under his hat. He says he is unable to proceed openly against the robbers and needs our help."

I sat down heavily in the nearest armchair. Surely this didn't mean that whoever it was expected us to confront and capture a lawless bunch of bush rangers single-handed?

"The best thing we can do," said Watson seeing my stricken face, "is to take a ride out there. Pretend we're tourists. There's quite an industry taking such people to abandoned workings. They like it."

"According to you, it's not an abandoned mine. It's up and running on the quiet."

"True. But I still think we should go out there. Perhaps we could pretend we were looking for somewhere else and got lost."

Another minute of this nonsense and the room would ring with the sound of a woman having violent hysterics. Really, I was beginning to feel almost sorry for Sherlock. "Sit here," I said getting out of my chair, "and collect your thoughts. While you're doing that I'll ring for a strong drink. We both need it."

"A bit early in the day, don't you think?"

I pulled the gold-threaded bell-rope so hard I almost broke it. "This is Australia," I said, and tugging at the bell-rope again waited impatiently for a discreet knock. When the knock came, or rather, a little while before it came, a small sound made me spring to the door. I flung it open with s flourish; and was surprised to see our waiter of the night before sprawled on the mat. With a muttered curse, he got to his feet. "Listening at keyholes," I said. "A fine thing for what's supposed to be one of Ballarat's best hotels."

"Not at all, madam," he said suavely. "You rang. I came to see what was wanted."

He was bending down brushing the knees of his trousers and, young as he was, I could see clearly the beginnings of a bald patch on the top of his head. "If not listening, then looking. Probably both," I added scornfully. "By the amount of dust you're removing from your nether garment I judge you've been at it quite a time."

"Did madam ring for fun?" I realised he was really pushing it, well aware I could report him for rudeness and possibly get him the sack.

"No, for a gin and tonic. Two, to be precise."

He sauntered down the corridor, whistling softly. "Believe me, Watson," I said, "that bloke's no waiter. He lets his guard down when the boss isn't around and doesn't seem particularly worried about getting the elbow. Which must mean waiting isn't his only job."

"Maybe you're right." John got out of his chair and went to stand by the window. "Do you really think he was listening at the door, Mary? It would mean he heard our plans for visiting the hidden gold mine."

Just as I opened my mouth to answer, there was another even more discreet knock at the door. This time John opened it and a small slavey, looking frightened to death, came in carrying a tray and two drinks. I looked with amusement at the little lace doilies and the assortment of nuts in a tiny gold cup without handles; and at the two sweets side by side on a half-serviette. Gracious living in the Antipodes. Not quite right, but a good try. John patted the girl on the shoulder in a decidedly avuncular manner and slipped a few small coins into her apron pocket. "Looks as if she needs 'em," he said with an embarrassed laugh. "Little maid of all work. Who would have expected it?"

I too was puzzled. Such girls didn't usually make it to the bedrooms of hotel guests but were kept out of sight in the kitchens, doing the rough work. I wondered vaguely what had happened to the waiter. Taking my first sip of gin and tonic and at the same time handing John his glass I said, "It might be a good idea after all to find this mine as soon as possible. But we won't go as tourists or," giving him a withering look, "pretend we're lost. It would be best to come clean. Say why we're in Australia."

So sometime that afternoon we found ourselves going in a pony and trap towards the newly discovered source of fresh gold. I could see John was enjoying himself as he plied the whip but forty miles over rough terrain, with nothing but dingoes to look at, was more than a little tedious. To my surprise, however, the mine when we reached it consisted of a huge hole open to the sky. It was a stunning sight, and quite unlike my idea of what a mine should be. But, said John, open cast was cheaper than sinking a shaft.

Tiers of rock-hard sand at different intervals made ledges for a variety of wagons to stand on and to travel down laboriously in a zigzag movement whenever they were called for. And, as far as I could see, these rough wooden carriers descended to a remarkable depth. They performed a balancing act of quite terrifying proportions, sometimes with their left or right side wheels suspended in space and only righting themselves at the last minute when I felt certain they would go spiralling down into the earth and certain destruction. Their heavy loads on the way back up provided more stability, but the noise of men either screaming warnings or furiously digging sounded deafening. It was worse when great cheers added to the row as each load reached the top of the mine. They were immediately taken to huge vats, which Watson called flotation tanks, where the ore was washed away and the precious gold sank to the bottom. Men in broad hats ran about shouting, checking each new load as it arrived and seeing that it got safely into the vats before sending the empty carts back rapidly for more.

I saw that rusted implements were lying some distance from the edge of the mine, looking like huge metal saucers. Shallow pans whose sides sloped inwards so that when water was added to the ore, and the whole thing shaken, the much heavier gold gravitated to the centre. Broken 'cradles' used to speed up this process lay hidden in the tough grass, abandoned relics from a much earlier time when men thought there might be gold but hadn't been able to find it. Screwing up my eyes, I saw in the distance huge flumes of water under enormous pressure being used to wash away the side of a hill to release the gold there as easily and as thoroughly as possible.

"There's a 'long tom' by all that's wonderful," said Watson, pointing towards a wooden platform which sloped away from the mine over some tall trees and shook like something with the ague. "That's an American idea, to divert river water onto a platform and use it to wash the ore. All that riddling soon gets rid of the rubbish; and I'm blessed if I can't hear blasting in the distance. They must be dynamiting the hill to get the gold out as fast as they can."

"Considering this is supposed to be being done on the quiet it all sounds like a rather big operation." I meant the words literally. The noise was deafening. It felt as if it could be heard in Melbourne. A number of armed guards with their backs to us were standing sentinel. But they seemed more intent on keeping the miners in than any snoopers out, and it was some time before we could attract the attention of someone willing to help us.

A grizzled old miner did, however, finally spot us and showed us the way to a ramshackle office. As we went in, Watson gave such a start I thought he'd seen a ghost. I turned quickly towards a man standing behind a rickety desk which, like the rest of the place, looked as if it was on its last legs and nearly fell over myself. There, in all the malevolence of his millions, stood the Gold King.

"I know you," he said, glaring at John. "Threatened to knock me down once."

"But," stammered Watson, pulling something out of his pocket, "This letter..."

"Signed by my agent who I left in England to engage the best man he could, since I didn't want my rivals to know I was

201

leaving New York for Ballarat and had anything to do with the possibility of gold being found in this mine. As it is, I am more than reluctant to have anything to do with you either. But the situation has become so desperate since I last heard from him I'm willing to gamble on your having learned something from that devil Holmes. Although now I've seen you again..."

"Mr. Gibson," I said, stepping forward and interrupting the great man without ceremony, "you can rest assured that Watson, *with my help,* will be quite capable of dealing with any problems you may have regarding this mine."

"I can quite believe it," he said, glaring down at me with a wolfish grin on his unprepossessing face. "So all you'll need now are the details."

"Just a moment before we get to them," I said haughtily. "We would very much like to know why you've seen fit to put a waiter on our tail."

He looked nonplussed for a moment or two and then said, "You've already spotted that? It's as well to know what the enemy's up to."

"If you think we're enemies, why send for us in the first place?"

I was gratified to see that he reddened slightly under his tan. "I've already told you I didn't send for anyone in particular. Now I have to make sure you haven't been infected by that blasted detective with his high and mighty ideas of what's moral and what isn't."

"I know all about that," interrupted John gruffly, "although Holmes ventured the opinion that you might get together in holy matrimony eventually. As for me..."

"Never mind raking up old times," I said impatiently. I'd no wish to listen to something I hadn't been concerned in, and only just stopped myself from adding "It's all water under the bridge." This, of course, would have been an extremely tactless remark considering his wife had killed herself near one, and in a rather fiendish way which almost baffled Sherlock. The notoriously touchy Gold King might decide to dispense with our services there and then, leaving us to pay our own passage home.

John appeared to sense what had nearly happened and said hastily, "What is it you want us to do exactly?"

Neil Gibson sat down heavily. "Find the thieves. Stop them stealing my gold."

"A tall order," remarked Watson, mopping his brow as we climbed back into our pony and trap. Nervously jerking the reins, he drove in the direction of some stunted trees and then stopped. Under cover of blowing his nose, he stared at me helplessly over his handkerchief.

"Where and when does the gold disappear?" I asked. "Does it

happen every day?"

John scratched his head and said slowly, "It would be impossible to produce enough gold from this particular site for that to happen, even though the mine is deep and Gibson is going all out to milk it as much as he can with all that blasting and those high speed water cannons. As far as I can make out, one of the loaded wagons is being waylaid roughly every week about three miles from Melbourne, and after the others have gone ahead. The driver is tied up, while the rest of the gang grapple with the armed guards before knocking them out, grabbing the gold and making off. It's only a matter of time before someone gets killed."

"One thing's for certain," I said. The men can't escape into the bush so near a city. They must hole up in Melbourne itself."

I could see John's brain was working overtime. "Not necessarily. The simplest thing would be to slip back to Ballarat. Come to think of it, it would be thoroughly stupid if the stolen wagon load went anywhere near Melbourne. There would be no chance at all then of keeping Gibson's operation quiet."

"But what about the wagons which do get there? The same must apply to them."

"I have no idea," said Watson. "But Gibson being who he is, I've no doubt he has some scheme for hiding what he's doing."

"Then it's Ballarat for us," I said. "Let's go back there as fast as we can. The sooner we finish this job the better. It gives me the creeps."

"Then you'll never make a proper detective. As Sherlock used to say, 'Surely no man would take up my profession if it were not that danger attracts him'. Holmes and I were mixed up with Andaman Islanders as you very well know, as well as murderous union men and others who thought nothing of taking pot shots at us with the most artfully constructed air guns."

I said nothing to this. Instead I contented myself with taking over the reins and driving us back to our hotel. How we found out that the robbers weren't in Ballarat but in a Chinese settlement about fifty miles away called Ararat is a story all on its own.

Chapter Nine

As soon as we returned to Ballarat John began to make discreet enquiries about any funny business which might be going on in the area. He had the advantage over me in this because he could move freely through the many pubs and bars in the town, drinking with the men and swapping yarns about the old days. I suggested he flash his money about a bit. But not too much in case he was mugged one night on his way back to the hotel. I knew from experience that greasing people's palms often did the trick. Even so, he never told me exactly how he discovered Gibson's gold wasn't where we thought it was but about fifty miles away, in a similarly named place famous for its mountain scenery. A few days later I packed a change of clothes, Watson arranged with the manager of The George to keep our room open and we hired a conveyance which would get us comfortably to Ararat.

The first thing I noticed when we arrived was the way the architecture of the town complemented the surrounding scenery. The main street especially was set out to show visitors Mount Ararat to the best advantage; and the Pyrenean Range, together with Mount Cole, were not far behind. Watson, however, felt a little liverish. He said all those hills reminded him of his terrible time in the Lofoten Islands, Halstad to be precise, and he hoped I would not expect him to go skiing. Instead he suggested we visit a place called Stawell for a day's racing. It was the home of the Stawell Gift, a sprint which took place once a year and he would like to have a bet on it. "In my bachelor days I used to lose half what little money I had on horse racing, and once had to ask Holmes to lock up my cheque book. Maybe this time I'll be lucky."

"That's what all gamblers say."

Nevertheless, he did win something, and we returned to Ararat quite happy and ready for any amount of investigation. Chinese nationals, who had walked across Australia in the eighteen-fifties after a hazardous voyage from a southern province of their home country, had settled in Ararat. Where they managed, when all others had failed, to find very rich deposits of alluvial gold in the nearby rivers. This made the 'celestials', as they were called, thoroughly disliked. But it also made them fabulously rich. Their part of the town developed over the years into one as elegant and as gold conscious in its way as any Victorian suburb built by Europeans who had arrived more recently than the Chinese and began sinking mine shafts to get the gold out of the ground. Like Ballarat, Ararat's nineteenth century architecture was bang up-to-date and had its full share of magnificent verandas.

That evening we decided to take a walk through the town towards the north end and sample what were to us very unfamiliar sights, including a building in Girldlestone Street on the other side of the railway tracks. This place, John said, was built as a prison in 1859 but was now being used to house criminally insane men in the most appalling conditions. Well, bad as I may be, I'm no Emily Fanshaw. The thought of the comfortless life these poor devils must be leading filled me with horror. I begged to be taken back to Main Street and a more populous part of Ararat. It was while I was looking at some beautiful gold fans in the window of one of the town's biggest emporiums (just as I had stared into the window of a shop in The Haymarket to avoid Professor Moriarty) that I heard Watson gasp and felt his elbow tighten on my arm. "The air-gun man!" he gasped. "Colonel Sebastian Moran."

"The bloke you said was in Afghanistan with you?"

"I said no such thing. He was in Kabul with Major-General Sir Frederick Roberts. Readers were told I was in Kandahar, only then it was spelt slightly differently."

"It was all made such a muddle that no-one could tell where you were."

"Wasn't that the point?" said John smugly. "Moran was Moriarty's right hand man and the Professor paid him more than the Prime Minister gets."

"Have you any idea why he's here in Ararat?"

"No. But he's bound to be up to no good, and so we're

certainly going to follow him."

It was difficult to keep pace with the Colonel among the ins and outs of the narrow streets of the Chinese Quarter, or to disguise that an outwardly unconcerned and respectable looking couple were shadowing a suspect. It was also hard to make sure our quarry didn't notice anything. But after a great deal of dodging in and out of shadowy doorways every time he seemed about to turn round, we finally saw Moran enter a low-storey house very near a small temple.

There was a light burning in an upstairs window and John suggested I climb onto his shoulders and take a peek inside the room. I jumped down after a minute or two, silently signalling him to move away and follow me as I ran up a side street. When I judged we were at a safe distance from the temple I said, "Moran is sitting at a deal table with a piece of paper in his hand, giving instructions to a bunch of ruffians. I also noticed there were several sacks stacked against the wall."

"Did you hear anything?"

"Only a confused murmur –and a couple of raised voices. I couldn't distinguish the words. What about you?"

"Well while keeping you steady I had my nose pressed as closely as I could to the lower window, trying to take in as much of the room as possible. A Chinaman was sitting in an armchair, burning pastilles in a little metal pan and smoking some kind of hookah."

"Then he won't bother us for a while," I said. "Two things I will tell you. Although the light wasn't particularly bright in the room, there was something very peculiar about those sacks. They gleamed in places. And I could swear that one of the men round the table was that old miner who showed us into Gibson's office."

Watson whistled. "An inside job, by Jove. As for those sacks, what you saw were sprinklings of 'pay dirt', or in other words, gold dust. They're probably stuffed with it."

"You called the Colonel the air-gun man. Why was that?"

"You obviously never read *The Strand*. Acting on Moriarty's orders and using a gun specially engineered by the blind German instrument-maker Herder, Moran hired a room in Baker Street opposite number 221B, knelt down at an open window, poked out the air rifle and blew Holmes' head off. Fortunately he only destroyed a wax model. In reality we were right behind him with some police officers and he was arrested by Lestrade. Sherlock said he was surprised an old *shikari* could be caught by such a simple trick. The empty house was a trap and the Colonel was his tiger."

How like Holmes. The man couldn't resist embroidering everything. Aloud I said, "Interesting as all this is, it won't get us very far. We'd better go back to the mine as soon as we can

210

and warn Gibson his own men are in a plot to rob him."

Easier said than done. It was already late. The only thing we could accomplish that evening was go back to the hotel and, after breakfast the next day, travel as fast as possible to his workings. But, although the mine had been going full-tilt during our first visit, now it was as silent as the grave and the Gold King nowhere to be found.

"Well, that's it," said Watson ruefully. "No money. We can't go to the police. I'll bet my last penny Moran will already have moved on anyway. It was never part of Moriarty's plans to let any of his henchmen operate for long in the same place. Quite likely the meeting we saw was to pay the men off and make arrangements to transport the gold from the nearest port back to England. It's a sure thing Moran's papers will all be in order, even if they are forged, and he'll make a very credible picture of a prosperous merchant seeing his goods on board what appears to be a *bona fide* ship bound for goodness knows where." John's normally placid face twisted into the nearest thing I have ever seen to a snarl since I've known him. "With all the gold put into hundreds of little bags to disguise the weight," he growled. "And the wooden crates labelled 'Donations from the Generous and Caring People of Australia for the Poor of the World' I shouldn't wonder."

Back at the George Hotel in Ballarat and trying to eat a

joyless dinner, I noticed that we had a new waiter. Small, eager and with a round, cherubic face like an angel in a renaissance painting, he hurried to and fro doing his best to serve us and obviously disturbed by our lack of appetite. After asking several times if the food was to our liking he took to gazing solemnly at our untouched plates as if he hoped to improve matters just by looking at them. Although Watson had confided to me that he once told Holmes he 'kept a bull-pup', that is he had a short temper, John is the most easy-going of men. But now he asked for the food to be taken away. He felt quite unequal to eating anything he said, at the thought of having to go home broke.

That evening, while I was creaming my face prior to getting ready for bed, John asked me if I could hear a noise, "Very faint, like a mouse scratching." I turned away from the mirror and listened. Not a sound. But Watson wasn't satisfied. Signing to me to be absolutely quiet, he crept round the room in his socks, opening the closets one by one, looking out of the window, putting his ear to the wall and finally asking if I knew who occupied the two rooms on either side of ours.

"The couple we saw in the dining-room on our first evening moved into their room on one side of us, at the same time as we moved into this one. But I noticed they were still in the bar as we came upstairs. There aren't any bedrooms at this end of the corridor after this one."

Watson, looking very sceptical, went out onto the veranda. When he came back he said that, in his opinion, there was a door somewhere done up to look like an entrance to a broom cupboard – or something of that ilk. I said yes, I had spotted it but had no reason to suppose it led into anything but what it was. Even in a posh hotel like this one the cleaners had to keep their brushes and brooms somewhere.

"You remember when we first arrived they said our room wasn't ready? I think you'll find a partition made of something light, like lath and plaster, runs across this corridor making it appear a considerable number of feet shorter than it is; and that anyone with a key can open the so-called broom cupboard and go in. Wipe the cream off your face and put your shoes back on. I want you to slip along the corridor on the other side of the stairs which corresponds to this one. Then run back and tell me if you think it looks longer."

In less than a minute I was in the place he mentioned and, tingling with excitement, attempting to judge its length. It certainly seemed longer. But there might be an innocent reason for that, and I couldn't stay walking up and down to check at that time of night for fear someone might come out of one of the bedrooms and wonder what on earth I was up to. With my heart in my mouth, I flew down the stairs and up another flight to our corridor. Yes, I gasped as soon as I saw Watson, I was sure the other one was considerably longer.

Without a word, he crept out of the room and put his ear to what he had said must be a partition. Then, glancing over his shoulder, he gestured to me to join him and we both stood listening intently. "There it is again, he muttered. "Like an animal caught in a trap."

"What do you suggest we do?" This time I had heard the sound for myself.

"Nothing, until we're sure everyone is asleep."

When the maid came to turn down the quilt I was to seem as if I was going to bed while John would be sitting out on the veranda pretending to have a last pipe of his favourite tobacco, 'Arcadia Mixture'. As soon as the coast was clear we would try to open the door of the broom cupboard with what Watson described as 'a first-class set of burgling tools' which he said Holmes used when he went after the blackmailer Milverton and which Mycroft Holmes had given to him after Sherlock went missing.

It seemed like an age before we felt it was safe to venture out of the bedroom. My limbs were stiff with tension, and I badly needed a drink. Perhaps Watson was right when he said I wouldn't make a good detective, although I felt I was keeping my end up so far. As for him, all he said was that it reminded him of an intolerably long night in a house in Stoke Moran, where he and Holmes sat fully clothed listening to the distant howls of a baboon and waiting nervously for a particularly poisonous snake (which he called a swamp adder) to put in an appearance.

But as soon as he thought the coast was clear he signalled to me to creep out with him into the truncated corridor and, after going through his set of instruments twice, found what he was sure would work. In two minutes we were on the other side of the false wall and I saw that he had been right. The space behind it was at least the size of a small room, and there in the middle of it was the Gold King. He lay on his stomach with his haggard face turned towards us and a stout gag filling his mouth. A number of knotted ropes were wound round his huge body, making it almost impossible for him to move. However, as soon as he saw Watson a profound look of relief came into his eyes and he stopped trying to scratch the floor with the toe of his left shoe. Bound tightly as he was, this seemed the only movement he was capable of; and the sound was the one we had heard when we thought there was a mouse loose in our room.

John had sprung across the intervening space like a young gazelle, levered the gag roughly out of Gibson's mouth, worked at his bonds with the penknife he'd used to open the window at Mrs. Marple's house after pulling it hastily out of his trouser pocket, and now tugged at the ropes like one possessed. Even so, it took some time to cut Gibson free, and all the while Watson was making such an effort he remained completely silent. As soon as the last piece of rope fell to the ground, however, the Gold King burst into a stream of language which wouldn't have disgraced the fish market in Billingsgate, or even the environs of Whitechapel.

"Come along to our room," I said quickly, afraid someone might hear such terrible imprecations. He had been tied up, said the millionaire once we had settled him into a comfortable armchair, since soon after we left the mine. The men he'd hired had turned on him, knocked him out, brought him bound hand and foot to Ballarat –he presumed in one of his own wagons and covered by a blanket –and then left him to starve in that horribly cramped space. Where his cries couldn't be heard because of the gag, and he couldn't move because he was as good as paralysed by his ropes. Taking pity on him, I rummaged around in my handbag and found some chocolate while John rang for a stiff drink, taking care to be outside the room in his pyjamas and dressing-gown when a member of the night staff brought it, snatching the tray away and slamming the door before the man could make any attempt to get in or see that there was now a third person in the room.

"Are they all in it do you think?" asked Gibson, meaning the hotel staff.

John considered this for a few minutes and then said, "No. But I shouldn't be surprised if the waiter you sent to spy on us is. And he probably has an accomplice, somebody on the front desk who sent us to another room while they both worked on somewhere to conceal you. Also, it must be perfectly obvious that not all your men at the mine were out to rob you. Otherwise any gold you had managed to get out of it would have vanished into thin air like the rest."

"But you say the mine is no longer being worked?"

"No. So the overseer must be in on the robberies. He's pensioned the honest men off." Watson walked about the room for a minute or two to stretch his legs and then continued, "Whatever one says about The Napoleon of Crime, as Holmes used to call him, he was always careful not to be too greedy. And I dare say his Chief Lieutenant feels the same."

"The Napoleon of Crime? I think I've heard that name somewhere. Surely you don't mean...?"

"Naturally I do. Professor James Moriarty, and his Second-in-Command Colonel Sebastian Moran."

Gibson's face turned white as a sheet. Even though he was now free, and sometimes behaved very ruthlessly himself, he couldn't repress a shudder. Rising unsteadily to his feet he said hoarsely, "Call me a cab. If Moriarty's involved in all this then the gold I've lost can go to hell. I need to get back to my yacht at once. The gold I *have* got is stashed away in the hold. I'll cut my losses and head for home. I don't want anyone to change his mind and come after it before I've had time to get away, and especially anyone connected with that arch-fiend. As it is, I've managed to allay suspicion about what I've been up to by greasing the palm of some high-up in the Ministry of the Interior –who got me an export licence because he thinks I'm opening up the market for Aboriginal art."

"Is that how you've labelled your wooden crates?" I asked, with a sideways glance at John. "As Aboriginal artefacts?" Obviously it wasn't only Moran who was pulling the wool over the eyes of customs officials. And I couldn't help remembering what I'd advised John to do in Ballarat when it came to gathering information: imply that there was money to be had, but not in such a way that anyone would take the chance of cutting his throat for it.

Instead of answering, Gibson went to the door, opened it, looked carefully up and down the corridor and, in one fluid movement belied by his heavy frame and recent discomfort, slid snake-like down the stairs. After saying that he always had to call cabs for Sherlock and his clients, as well as accompany some of the latter to the ranks, John followed him without another word, and this time I really went to bed.

The next morning we both ate a very hearty breakfast. In

response to saving his life Neil Gibson had said that as soon as he got back to New York he would send Watson a banker's draft for a quite astonishing sum of money. "If he ever does get back," I said through a mouthful of eggs and bacon. "I wouldn't like to travel seven thousand miles by yacht in a rough sea, or even if the sea was as calm as a mill-pond."

"There are yachts and yachts," said John signalling for more bacon. "He'll get back home all right."

And so did we, only to find that the house had been burgled. Fortunately all John's, and Sherlock's, papers were safe. He had sent them to Cox's Bank in the Charing Cross Road before leaving for Liverpool. But the room which Emily and I set up as a detective agency had been ransacked. The filing cabinets and the typewriter were gone. Upstairs, every closet had been opened and their contents rifled. The ivory-backed hair brushes I had given Watson for a wedding present, and which he said were too precious to risk taking to the other side of the world, were missing. The cut-glass silver-topped scent bottles he had given me were nowhere to be seen, and even the aspidistra no longer sat on the hall table. In fact, there was no hall table. If it hadn't been for the promise of Gibson's draft which would easily cover our losses I would have sat on the stairs and cried like a baby.

John, of course, was all for calling the police and finding out who had done it. He wandered round the house muttering names which were completely incomprehensible to me: Steve Dixie, Barney Stockdale, The Spencer John Gang, the Duchess...

The Duchess? Surely the Loamshires weren't mixed up in the burglary of what was, after all, a modest suburban house?

"Isadora Klein, who married the young Duke of Lomond. She once sent Barney's mob to rob a house in Harrow. Holmes had told the householder, a pleasant old lady whose name I think was Mrs. Maberley, that there was something in the house she didn't know she had, and probably wouldn't have parted with if she did know. But dear Isadora knew she had it, *and* what it was. Sherlock then asked me if I read the situation in the same way. I said that I did. Much to my surprise, Holmes then said, 'Doctor Watson agrees, so that settles it'. Rather sarcastic I thought, especially as I made a bloomer almost immediately afterwards."

"Is this a revenge burglary then?" I asked. "Because of your association with that man, who I refuse to name but who is rapidly becoming the bane of my life?"

John made some clucking noises which he meant to sound conciliatory. "I doubt it. It may not even be them. But the gang's very active in that line, and nearly always broke."

"Always ready to rob, you mean?"

"I should say so."

"Do you happen to know if the Neville St. Clairs are still in Italy?" Emily might be a great help in all this.

"Yes, they are and sent us a post-card while we were away." John stooped and picked it up from where there had once been a mat. "They're staying in the country for another month so that they can see the sights of Florence and take a trip to Naples, among other things."

I took off my bonnet and flung it across the room.

"That's no good," protested Watson. "Why don't you run round to the butcher for a couple of pork chops? That is, if we still have something to cook them on."

"Or something to cook them *in*," I said fiercely, retrieving my bonnet and ramming it on my head.

It was while I was on my way back from the butcher that I realised a young man was following me and didn't seem to care whether I was aware of it or not. Affecting an indifference I certainly didn't feel I marched on, fully intending to clock him one with my market basket if he came any closer. But he was suddenly capering in front of me, his hand in the act of pulling off a shapeless hat and with a sheepish smile on his long face. I saw that he was no more than nineteen or twenty years old at the most and trying to slick down his unruly hair to make himself seem more presentable. "You're Missis Watson, ain't you?" he said.

"Maybe I am and maybe I'm not," I said. "The question is who might you be?"

He looked surprised. "Why Wiggins, o' course. I used to be one of what Mr. 'Olmes called his Baker Street Irregulars." Pulling himself up to his full height and looking ridiculously self-important the boy continued, "In fact, I was their leader. That is," he went on disconsolately, "before I 'eared 'e'd disappeared. Used to give us each a shilling 'e did to hunt, and a whole guinea to the boy who actually found whatever Mr. 'Olmes was after."

I looked appraisingly at Wiggins and said, "I think you'd better come home with me and meet –er – Doctor Watson."

"'E was a nice ol' boy," said Wiggins, falling into step beside me and offering me his arm like any gentleman.

"Well I never!" said Watson as soon as he saw him. "You've certainly grown Wiggins, although you always were taller than the other boys. I expect you still remember that steam launch the *Aurora.*"

"Black, with two red stripes," said Wiggins promptly. "And it 'ad a black funnel with a white stripe."

"So it did. I remember the advertisement Mr. Holmes put in the newspapers and which I made a note of. Well, you and the other boys were certainly instrumental in helping us trace the Agra treasure."

"I 'eard it ended up in the river," remarked Wiggins reflectively.

"Never mind that now," I said hurriedly. "Doctor Watson and I were about to eat. There's not much in the house apart from what you see in this basket, but you're welcome to share some chops. And if there's any of the jam I put up before we left England still in the cupboard here's a fresh loaf to put it on."

"A right feast, if you arst me," said the boy enthusiastically. "Give me a minute and I'll go round the corner for some reeb."

"Beer would do nicely," I said kindly, unwilling to spoil things by demanding anything better. Something I knew he couldn't afford, and not wishing to offend him by insisting on paying for something more palatable myself.

I left John explaining to Wiggins that we had just returned from Australia, only to find at the end of a long and tiring voyage that we'd been burgled and would have to eat in the kitchen as that seemed the only place where anything had been left for us to sit on. But Wiggins said a kitchen table and chairs were quite a luxury for him, and he "only 'oped he could 'elp to catch the blokes wot cracked the drum."

An exhausting week later, during which we managed to replace most of the furniture by promising to pay as soon as Gibson's draft arrived, there was a whistle outside the front door. When Watson went to investigate he found Wiggins on the doorstep brandishing a smart new cane. His linen looked a good deal cleaner, and the jacket and trousers he had on only a little worn. "I've found 'em," he said, as soon as his foot passed the threshold. "Them wot done the job."

"In Whitechapel?" asked Watson.

If anything, the boy's slouch became even more superior and the look on his face even more knowing. "Naw. Where would anybody be able to hide all that was took from 'ere in Whitechapel? After going all over London I spotted a young cove I'd seen earlier acting right silly and almost dropping somethin', while an older man stood nearby laughing his head off. Toffs they were, for all that I saw them going into a low pawnshop. As soon as they came out I went in, just in time to see the ol' nuncle putting a ticket on two very 'andsome cut-glass silver-topped scent bottles before setting them down on a convenient shelf at the back of 'is shop. Where, I might add, there was already an equally 'andsome pair of ivory-backed hair brushes." Wiggins turned suddenly to Watson and said, "Wot's your full initials, gov'nor?"

John looked startled. "J.W." he said, after some hesitation and a furtive glance at me, "J.H.W."

"The very same," crowed Wiggins. "Then I respec'fully advise you to take a cab to a well-known fencer's crib in Shoreditch. But not by 'anging on to the back of one like I did.

224

Far too much for a man of yore age and stamp."

"But where did you first see the two men?" I asked. "Before they took a cab?"

Wiggins stared hard at me, a puzzled expression on his young face. "Why, missus, the H'albany, o'course."

"The Albany? What were you doing in The Albany?"

Wiggins gave me an offended look and shifted his feet a little. "I was jes' takin' a stroll like," he said defensively. "Wiv me best duds on. Cut quite a dash, I did, wiv this 'ere new cane."

"What did the two men look like?" cut in John quietly.

"Very good-looking, one of them was. Tall and dark, wiv piercin' blue eyes. I don't think I'd like to get on the wrong side of 'im, that's for sure. But the uver one was slighter –and younger." Wiggins suddenly burst out laughing. "An' he 'ad ears like a rabbit."

"Not quite," smiled Watson. "But they certainly stick out more than somewhat."

"D'yer know 'im, then?"

"Yes," John replied grimly. "Him *and* his friend's address. I'm much obliged to you Wiggins. Mr. Holmes often gave you a guinea. But that was quite a long time ago and the cost of living has gone up considerably since then. So I'm going to give you two. You can spend the money on a smart new cravat to go with that swagger stick of yours." To which Wiggins replied delightedly that he knew where he could get a whole new suit and a posh pair of boots for as much as that.

Patting the boy kindly on the shoulder, Watson went with him to the front door and, while Wiggins went strolling down the road like a man of means without a care in the world, John and I stood on the step looking at each other in amazement.

"Raffles," he said. "Who would have believed it?"

The man we had first seen at the Duchess of Loamshire's dinner party and who I was sure had taken a pot-shot at Emily from outside the Hammer and Pincers. "He's certainly come down in the world if he's reduced to robbing people like us," I said bitterly.

"Well, there's only one thing for it," said Watson grimly. Grabbing his jacket and signalling to me to put on my bonnet again he went outside and whistled for a hansom. "The Albany," he said tersely. "Get there in five minutes and I'll double the fare."

At first I thought he meant to confront Raffles and demand restitution. But no. Leaving me to act as a lookout he went round the back of the building and, using a jemmy, prised open a window. "Watch out for the porter," I called anxiously. If I hadn't known John so well I would have said his reply was distinctly vulgar, and certainly not fit for a lady. I was left cooling my heels on the pavement for quite some time. But at last Watson appeared hot and flurried and with a large bruise on his left cheek. "Nothing to worry about," he said hastily. "I fell over using the stairs. Hadn't time for the service lift. Besides, I didn't want the Johnny in his little cubby hole to see me and insist on operating it."

"Did you accomplish anything?" I said, trying hard not to put any emphasis on the last word.

"Raffles was nowhere to be seen, and our furniture isn't in the flat."

I never expected it to be, Raffles looked so elegant and so well-heeled. His own furniture was probably *le dernier cri* and, commodious as the Albany apartment must be, there wouldn't be room in it for ours as well. "There's only one thing for it," said John just as he had outside our front door. "The pawnshop in Shoreditch." This time he whistled for a growler and didn't offer double the fare for a quick trip. "I need time to think," was all he said when we had settled ourselves inside and he'd rapped on the roof.

"What about?"

"Whether or not we can get our things back for nothing and charge it to Raffles. He'll have the tickets to collect them."

"If he ever does."

"Why shouldn't he?"

"It might all be part of an elaborate joke. Or it might be part

227

of some piece of crookery, a way of ingratiating himself with a fence before persuading him to get rid of far more valuable stuff."

You can imagine our surprise when, on arriving at the shop in Shoreditch, we saw Raffles and Bunny coming out of it. They stared at us for a moment and Raffles said to me, "Didn't I see you at the Loamshires? Somewhere in the garden I think?"

I bowed coldly. If he was going to pretend he had never come to our house when Watson was under the weather to demand the Duchess's diamonds then I wasn't going to remind him. John, on the other hand, looked as if he would have liked to grab either of the men by the throat. Raffles, however, suddenly became very haughty and said he objected to being glared at as if he were a double-dyed villain and what was the meaning of it, if he may ask?

"Why you utter cad," said Watson. "Burgling a gentleman's house, a gentleman you have dined with I might add, and stealing his wife's wedding presents. I've half a mind to knock you down."

"Street and number *if* you please," said Raffles, sounding for all the world like a London bobby.

Seeing the nasty glint in his eye, I told him hastily where we lived and had the satisfaction of seeing him blush. "Wrong street, wrong number, wrong house," he groaned ruefully. "I'm afraid, Bunny, that Bert Stevens and his gang are no longer in my employ. Perhaps you'd be good enough to go round in the morning and tell him so."

Bunny, looking as if that was the last thing he wanted to do, nevertheless mumbled his assent and Raffles said to Watson in a puzzled tone, "What wedding presents?"

"Ivory-backed hair brushes and silver-topped scent bottles, as you very well know."

"How could I be aware such trumpery things were wedding presents?" Raffles fished in the watch pocket of his cutaway coat and pulled out two pledges. "Here you are," he said, "with my compliments. In the name of Doctor Theobald, which is quite fortuitous seeing as how you're a medical man."

Having scrutinised the two crumpled pieces of paper and satisfied himself that they were genuine John stalked into the pawnbroker's, while Raffles and Bunny set off down the sordid street trying hard not to show how ruffled they were. As for us, we took the two parcels (which had been hastily wrapped in dirty sheets of newspaper) home as quickly as possible. On the way Watson kept muttering angrily that it "was a bit much" to have to pay to get back his own property after it had been stolen by someone else. He 'd been so discomposed he'd neglected to demand that Raffles go back into the pawnshop and redeem the pledges himself.

But that was nothing to what awaited us when we reached the house and saw a Black Maria outside the door and Inspector Lestrade standing on the doorstep.

Chapter Ten

Nearly everything that reminded John of Sherlock Holmes restored his good humour and as soon as he saw Lestrade he said, "Come in old chap. It's a long time since we saw you last, the Duchess of Loamshire's place wasn't it?"

I, however, was alarmed by something in the policeman's manner. This was increased when, once inside the hall, he produced an official-looking piece of paper and said pompously, "I have a warrant here for your arrest and must warn you...."

Watson, his eyes nearly popping out of his head said, "Come, come my dear fellow, on what grounds?"

Lestrade laboriously consulted his note-book. "Imitating a medical man," he said. "Setting up surgeries and treating patients although unqualified to do so."

My feelings when I saw John carried away in that black van were indescribable, although as a favour to me Lestrade dispensed with the handcuffs. Watson went docilely enough. He looked bemused, as if he had been unexpectedly hit on the back of the head by a brick. I dashed round to Emily Fanshaw's, as I nearly always regard her, but before I could open my mouth she started telling me about the family's wonderful holiday in Italy. After visiting Florence and Naples they had finally got to Rome and she was sitting with her husband and children on the *Corso,* sipping coffee and sampling antipasta one lunch time, when they made the acquaintance of a cardinal.

"Tosca, his name was. He seemed to my detective eye to be in deep trouble. Don't you think it would be fun if we could persuade the Vatican to pay for an investigation to get him out of it?"

But how could we know for certain that a cardinal was in deep trouble and needed to be got out of it? Trying to persuade the Vatican to finance something which may not need paying for seemed far too premature. I said hysterically that I had no interest in compromised clergy for the time being. At that very moment my husband was on his way to prison and I had come to ask her what were we going to do about it?

"Oh good," she said. "Now we'll both be free to..."

"No we won't," I screamed. "I've come here to ask you to help me get him out."

"We'll spring him," said Emily. "Is it Newgate or Cold-Harbour? There are some nasty things going on there," she added appreciatively, "what with the cockchafer and the crank and all."

"He hasn't been accused of murder –yet," I said crossly. "And Newgate's closed. As for The Fields you're a bit out of date, and anyway the less said about that dreadful place the better." Even if I managed to get John out of prison before his trial we'd be fugitives for the rest of our lives. "Perhaps you could just come to court with me," I ended weakly.

Some weeks later, while John was still remanded in custody, I wired the Gold King for money to pay for his defence. I must say that the draft came quickly. Neil Gibson's gratitude for being rescued from a lingering death in Australia hadn't dried up, even though he was busy again making rings round his business rivals in New York. He sent a sizable amount of cash, and I engaged Sir Edward Carson to act for John. Of course there was a tremendous amount of publicity. As the time for the trial approached this reached such a pitch that I began to worry whether Watson would get a fair hearing. The former friend and helper of the most famous detective in the world was being accused of fraud. And Sherlock Holmes (the archetypal investigator whose integrity was now said to have been without parallel) was in danger of having his credentials called into question because of the old saying 'Birds of a feather flock together'.

Letters for and against Watson were being published daily in *The Times* and in the provincial papers. Crusty old gentlemen in all the London Clubs from White's to the Garrick, and others which hadn't yet attained that stature and degree of respectability normally given to them simply on the grounds of antiquity, bemoaned the present atmosphere of decadence. They did this even while they made appointments with their mistresses, or secret arrangements to attend illegal ratting contests. The wags down in Whitechapel went about saying how it proved you could never tell with a toff and handing out scurrilous ballad sheets to anyone who had a ha'penny to buy one with.

When the day of the trial arrived after weeks of worry and I went into the court-room with Emily, I was ready to faint. Although I knew she would despise such weakness, and I was none too pleased about it myself, I kept a small bottle of smelling salts handy. Just in case I should suddenly keel over and distract everybody from the important job of getting Watson off. Meanwhile Emily gazed round the room with undisguised interest. Pointing to a large wooden structure in front of us she said under her breath, "It's like being in church."

"Except that that's the witness box and not a pulpit," I hissed, worried about just how many of the mean-spirited crew would be called to testify against poor John. Just below the desks for the lawyers there was a low seat. It was placed there for the convenience of court officials, who could whisper information into the ear of the leading counsel in the case. Anyone occupying it would have his back to us and be facing the judge. But in any event he would be invisible to spectators because our seats were so much higher. How many damaging facts about Watson would this horrible man cause indirectly to be conveyed to the Bench? I felt hurriedly for the smelling salts, and looking up saw with horror that the gallery was as full of people as there were downstairs. Emily and I, heavily veiled, had managed to get a seat in the well of the court, while all around us those who had been able to get tickets laughed and joked as if they were at a peep-show. Called to order by an usher and told to stand as the judge took his seat on the Bench, they afterwards settled down to enjoy the proceedings. Some of the crowd, like the official court reporter who sat in a box level with the judge and would record everything, even took out pieces of paper ready to scribble down the more scandalous revelations which they hoped would come out. It would never do if they were unable to describe in detail what was going on to those friends who hadn't managed to get tickets, although I noticed the scribblers were trying carefully to keep what they were doing out of sight of anyone but themselves.

Outside the court an immense crowd was milling around, with some people still wearing their black arm-bands in mourning for Sherlock Holmes and blocking every avenue leading to the court-house. There was such a clamour it was a wonder anything could be heard inside. I caught sight of one enterprising youth who had climbed onto a window sill and was leering through the glass at us. Until a constable pulled him down and no doubt sent him about his business with a flea in his ear. I learned later that

Sir Edward Carson himself had the greatest difficulty getting into court. He had had to use his fists and elbows (as well as those of his clerk) to get through the almost hysterical throng. He arrived dishevelled, hot, and angry –which wasn't a good sign for Watson, even though I'd secured such a hefty sum of money to pay the man to defend him.

A long, slow period then began as the jurors filed into their box, gave their names and were solemnly sworn in. There were no dissenting voices. Nobody wanted to be excused. As soon as all that was thankfully over, Emily drew my attention to the dock –digging her elbow painfully in my ribs after several ushers had shouted for silence. A door had slowly opened. I held my breath and saw Watson appear, walking shakily up some steps.

I watched the top of his head move slowly into view and hastily crossed my fingers. When he had negotiated the last step and arrived in full view of the court he stood with his hands resting lightly on the brass rail. There was no smile on his face, no genial twinkle in his eye. He looked deadly serious and there was a worried line between his brows. But I suddenly felt a lump in my throat and realised I was rather proud of him. His soldierly bearing, back straight as a ram-rod, and calm demeanour must impress the jury –and the judge.

After Watson had confirmed his name and address, the

Prosecuting Counsel rose slowly to his feet. "John Watson?" he said sarcastically. "Surely you mean Ormond Sacker?" There was such a sensation in court that the judge, banging his gavel angrily for silence, threatened to clear us all out if we didn't keep quiet. He then glared malevolently at the dock. Looking back at him in return, John said calmly, "My father changed the family's surname quite legally, and I prefer to be called John rather than Ormond."

"I should think you would mate," said a cockney voice at the back of the court. Its owner was immediately jumped on and ejected by an usher, who had the greatest difficulty in stopping a replacement lurking in the corridor from getting in. "And you practised for many years as a doctor?" went on the Prosecutor as soon as the hubbub had died down, "even though you were not qualified?"

"I felt that I was qualified for the little doctoring I did," said Watson. "After all, I worked at Netley for a number of years."

"Ah yes, Netley. We are coming to that. I have here Exhibit One. Perhaps you would be good enough to glance at it for a moment?"

I saw a photograph being passed to Watson across the rail. He looked at it briefly with a puzzled frown and then politely passed it back The Prosecutor ruffled his papers. "You see nothing of interest?"

"Only a group of wounded soldiers being wheeled out from the Chapel towards Southampton Water for some fresh air."

"Officers and other ranks are in the chairs. You can tell by their uniforms. But do you know who is doing the wheeling?"

"Any ancillary staff that could be got. The faces are very small and indistinct."

"Perhaps this would help?"

The Prosecuting Counsel passed the photograph to John again. Only this time he also sent over a large magnifying glass. I was irresistibly reminded of Sherlock Holmes crawling about the ground on his stomach looking for clues, and waited anxiously while Watson peered through the lens and then at his tormenter. Who said suavely, "Second from the left, right at the back."

John's shoulders sagged. He suddenly looked old and tired.

"It is you, isn't it? In your ward orderly's white jacket." Try as he might, the Prosecuting Counsel couldn't keep the triumph out of his voice, while I was left wondering how he had known of the existence of such a damming piece of evidence.

Watson nodded dumbly. But I sat there willing him to return to being upright and confident before everything tumbled about his ears. However his ordeal wasn't finished yet.

"You treated a number of railway guards while in your so-called practice near Paddington Station," went on the inexorable voice. "On one occasion you also ministered to an engineer who had lost his thumb. I think you'll find that The General Railway Workers Union will be uncomfortably interested in the first, and as for the other..."

"The young man with the severed thumb was hysterical," said John suddenly pulling himself together. "All I did was give him some brandy and water. Then I cleaned and sponged the wound, put a dressing and some wadding on it, and covered the whole with bandages soaked in a weak solution of carbolic acid. Any competent first-aider could, and would, have done the same."

"Indeed, but not one posing as a doctor. And, to make matters worse, putting the letters M.D. after his name instead of the more commonly used M.B. When, as everybody knows, the title of 'doctor' is then only a courtesy one. What would have happened if your 'patient's' wound had suppurated? He might have lost his whole hand, or even his arm."

"About the M.B. and the M.D. business, I felt that if I was going to do anything at all I might as well go the whole hog. As for Mr. Hatherley's wound, well it didn't suppurate. Which I see as a point in my favour. Of course, he has had to go through life minus one digit, but I believe he now has a very successful Practice."

This was a mistake. "A Practice," said the Prosecuting Counsel, "which he is *well qualified* to fill. I believe Mr.

239

Sherlock Holmes, the unfortunately late Mr. Sherlock Holmes himself, told you to your face that you weren't entitled to the appellation M.D. But, in spite of having no qualifications at all, did you not also treat Baron Gruner when a certain woman of the streets threw vitriol at him?"

"After bathing his face in oil," said John, "and, as with Vincent Hatherley, covering his wounds with cotton wadding, I gave the Baron a shot of morphia..."

"Which it is illegal for a layman to use. The Baron is here and wishes most earnestly to testify against you. He feels that, treated by an expert who was really a medical man, he could have recovered from his injuries, if not completely at least better than he has done."

There was a gasp of horror as the Baron was helped into the witness box by his personal attendant and everyone could see his glazed fish-like eye and ravished face. Even his neck, and part of his right hand, showed signs of having been burnt. It was obvious that only his clothes had prevented even further injuries. Although the acid had been aimed deliberately at his face with such devastating effect, much of it had also disfigured him in other parts of his body. It was said that he was never normally seen in public without hat and gloves, as well as high boots and a mask. Now his head, hands and face were bare and it was obvious he wanted to incriminate Watson as much as possible.

His hair, still thick and black in spite of his age, his figure (although not much above middle height) graceful and well-knit, the way he carried himself in spite of his injuries–all proclaimed that he had once been something of an Adonis; and when he spoke his voice, though thickly accented, was low and musical. I could feel Emily stirring beside me at the seductive tone and, much against my will, I too felt the effect of the Baron's allure. But that face...

Without a trace of embarrassment, he explained what had happened to him and why. But now he could no longer attract women with, or even without, money. His livelihood was gone, and all because of that Jackal in the dock. At this point the Baron's voice rose to a scream, definitely marring the initial effect of his beautiful way of speaking. Sir Edward Carson rose to his feet and after a glance at John said in a grave voice, "My dear sir, immediately succeeding the –hem –accident didn't you cling to my client as if you felt he was your saviour?"

"I was in agony," said Baron Gruner. "Blind in one eye, with a red mist before the other which didn't clear for many weeks. I instinctively clutched at anything –and anyone –that could help me. In addition to his other impostures the villain had gained access to my house by pretending to be an expert in Chinese curios. He tried to sell me a saucer belonging to the Ming Dynasty. I am glad to say he utterly failed to do so."

"Was it genuine?" asked the judge with some interest.

"Certainly, my Lord. Only it wasn't his to sell. The whole plot was a ruse by that interfering swine Holmes to steal some of my property."

There was another interruption from the Bench. "Vitriol is a dreadful thing, as we can see from your injuries. But it seems to me that this man Sacker, Watson or whatever he calls himself did his best for you in the circumstances. Although," and here His Lordship glared at John, "it beats me if he was on a visit to discuss saucers why he should have oil and morphia, to say nothing of hypodermic syringes, about him. Unless you're a drug addict," he added sternly and addressing Watson directly.

"By no means. It's Sherlock who was the..." John coughed suddenly into his handkerchief and went extremely red in the face. I heard Emily chuckle and trod viciously on her foot. She retaliated by giving me another prod with her elbow, and for a few moments we both lost the thread of the argument. Until finally we contented ourselves by giving each other a ferocious glare.

Although the trial continued for some time, with Sir Edward Carson doing his best by making several points about courage, ingenuity, British enterprise and the dreadful strain of having to live a lie, the judge's intervention was what finally told in John's favour. There was a general feeling that it was impossible to look like him and be a drug addict. After what seemed several hours, but which was in reality only one, the jury brought in a verdict of guilty but with extenuating circumstances. They recommended a heavy fine rather than a prison sentence, and said that in addition Watson must sign an undertaking never again to practise as a doctor. Well, that would be easy to do. My relieved husband was carried from the court shoulder-high, while I was left wondering how everything could have come out. Although John had spilled the beans to me I had, for obvious reasons, never mentioned a word to a living soul of what he had said.

The next day I received an urgent telephone call from Emily. Her husband was out, pursuing his legitimate business, the children were at school and she needed my advice as soon as possible. Leaving a very relaxed John to read the papers, I rushed off to find out what this hurried summons was all about. When I peeped into her drawing-room from the hall while taking off my cloak I was amazed to see a Roman Catholic priest sitting there. At least, I took him for a priest. But not one of the Anglican Persuasion.

"Wants to know if I have ever met Cardinal Tosca," she whispered as she took my cloak and hung it up on the hall stand. "I told him what I told you just before we went to court at the beginning of Doctor Watson's trial. That I had seen His

Eminence only once when, suspecting we were English, he had politely greeted us on the *Corso* in our own language, at the same time telling us who he was."

"That sounds a lot more than a simple 'good day'. I wonder if he had a reason for attracting your attention so particularly."

"I haven't the faintest idea, but apparently the worry of the Cardinal's sudden disappearance has done for the Pope. He had asked the British Embassy in Rome if Holmes could look into the matter, but as we know..."

"That gentleman has fallen into the Reichenbach Falls. It's possible the Vatican is aware we're colleagues and thinks Watson or, failing him, his wife is the next best thing. That's maybe why this man has called on you. Although, if he had come to us, he could have spoken to John quite easily."

"Maybe all that publicity at the trial put him off. Anyway, somehow or other the clerical gentleman sitting in my drawing-room is aware that I run a detective agency and is almost on his ecclesiastical knees begging me to help him. For all he knows, Cardinal Tosca may be as dead as the Pope, who was at least ninety by all accounts. The missing man can't be far behind. It doesn't take much to kill off such very old persons."

"Does the bloke in there think that Tosca's dead?"

"I'm sure he suspects it."

I passed into the room and took a good look at the visitor,

who rose to his feet at once when he saw me. The man was short, slim, swarthy, handsome –and young. His dog-collar, set into his shirt so that only a small band showed above his soutane, was whiter than white, and he wore a pair of stout black boots. A line of black self-buttons rimmed with purple cloth ran down the entire length of this cassock-like garment, and he wore a small cross on his chest. Emily introduced me as her 'business partner' and signed for us to sit down while she demurely took her place at the tea table. Tea was brought in, and ratafia biscuits. Balancing his cup on the arm of his chair, the young man said, "I expect you are wondering, *Signora* Watson, why I should come all this way to ask *Signora* Fanshaw such a simple question as did she know Cardinal Tosca? But the truth is, she and her family were the last to see him before his inexplicable vanishing act."

"How can that be?" asked Emily. "The *Corso* was crowded."

"But he actually spoke to you, and weren't you and your family sitting at a table which was next to a narrow alley? It was the Cardinal's custom to take that route off the *Corso* on his way to the *Piazza Venitzia* and the culmination of his daily walk – and we have no reason to think that he followed anything other than his normal routine on that terrible afternoon."

"Vanishing Act?" said Emily, who had been momentarily distracted by her duties as hostess. "We're discussing the *disappearance* of Cardinal Tosca?"

The priest's face lengthened so much he looked as if he was about to burst into tears "Yes, *Signora*, and on the point of taking part in the election of a new pope. It is better to think of him that way rather than dead. At least until you have managed to find out more."

"That's unfortunate for you," said Emily with relish. "Maybe, being old and confused, he's committed suicide at the thought of helping to elect a new pope."

The young man turned and looked steadily at her. "We do not think there is the slightest cause to think His Eminence would consider such a thing, and for such a cause. It would go against all his most cherished beliefs. He has helped to elect a number of men to the highest office the Church has to offer. He would, he will, be only too delighted to take part in another Conclave. Why, he could even be elected Pope himself!"

"Not if he was being blackmailed."

"There would be nothing to blackmail him about," said the cleric firmly. While I sat wondering where on earth Emily was getting her ideas from.

"Have you considered the possibility of a heart attack, or an accident of some kind?" I said, thinking she had been somewhat out of court with her suggestion of suicide, to say nothing of blackmail.

"Cardinal Tosca was in the best of health for his age. As for an accident, we have scoured all the hospitals without success, and have helpers searching all Rome in case he has been hit on the head and robbed by some heinous felon. We can't find him anywhere, dead or alive."

"He's left the country," said Emily decisively.

"What, on the very eve of the Conclave, and without his passport? It's unthinkable."

"According to you he vanished before anyone knew there would be a Conclave."

"Ours is a detective agency," I said, glancing sternly at Emily. "What do you want us to do?"

"Come to Rome," said the young man eagerly. "And with the expertise you must have acquired from your husband's association with Sherlock Holmes help us to find our dear Father-in-Christ."

"A somewhat emotional young man," muttered Emily after the priest had drained his tea-cup, finished his biscuits and taken himself off to the Italian Embassy. "What do you think of it all, *Muriel?*"

I smiled at her use of the old name. "If I were Sherlock, I'd say it was a three pipe problem. But since we're two respectable middle-class matrons perhaps I ought to call it a three cups of tea problem."

"Not on your life," growled Mrs. St. Clair. "I'll fetch some glasses and a bottle of brandy."

Brandy in the middle of the afternoon makes me feel sleepy. Nevertheless, I was beginning to get the germ of an idea. "Tell me, Emily, do you remember what the Cardinal looked like?" I caught my breath as I said this and coughed as the brandy went down the wrong way. "Did you happen to notice if he stooped, a scholar's stoop from bending too much over books or, in the Cardinal's case, probably medieval manuscripts in the Vatican Library?"

"I only saw him for a minute or two before he disappeared down that alley."

"Think, woman, think." It was my turn now to be the bully.

"Well, I'm almost sure he had a stoop, but no more than any other tall man of his age. As for the rest, he was very thin, and not particularly priest-like."

"Whatever do you mean by that?"

"He wasn't benign. Or jolly. In fact, as I told you soon after we returned from Italy, he looked rather frightened and in deep trouble. I guess his natural expression when his face was in repose would be one of melancholy."

"Not malignance?"

"No, no, certainly not that. But he did look scared."

"Perhaps he was being followed?"

"I saw nobody. But of course I did have the children to attend to."

"What about Mr. St. Clair?"

"Oh him, he had his nose in a newspaper and kept trying to tell me about Italian politics."

"If Cardinal Tosca looked frightened it may be that he had some inkling of danger, some premonition. That could be why he was so anxious to attract your notice."

"Why not say something more then, or sit down with us for a moment? In any case, I don't think he was that anxious, just wanted to make sure someone had seen him."

"Do you mean he needed an alibi?"

"Not unless he was up to no good himself. But if anyone was after him he probably had some vague idea he would be safer if that person saw him speak to us. If we heard something had happened to him we might remember and go to the police."

"Emily," I said gripping her by the elbow, "if all that you've said so far is right we have got to get to Italy as quickly as possible." I went into the hall to retrieve my cloak while she promised to meet me at Victoria Station for the train to Paris first thing in the morning. Looking her straight in the eye, I said sternly, "No men's clothes, and put a black outfit in your luggage as well as a mantilla. Remember this is Rome we're going to."

Chapter Eleven

When I reached home and told John where Emily and I were going he wanted to come too. He said Rome was a busy city. Parts of it were also rough. It wasn't the place for two unaccompanied ladies. He couldn't trust us to protect ourselves. But I said he badly needed a change of air. Why didn't he write to Colonel Hayter, an old soldier he met at Netley and one of the men he used to wheel round the grounds on warm days? It was this Hayter who had told him all about Afghanistan. The Colonel, John once told me, had taken quite a fancy to him and said they should keep in touch. Why didn't Watson invite himself down to Surrey for a while?

"That was a bright idea," said Emily as the train sped between Paris and Milan on the way to Rome. "I persuaded Neville to take the children to Bournemouth. It was difficult at first because he said he couldn't afford it, especially after Mr. Sherlock Holmes..."

Talk about raking up old sores. "I hope you did pack that mantilla," I said. And for the rest of the journey buried my nose in a Baedeker.

The first thing to do when we got to Rome was to find a modest *pensione.* It had to be modest said Emily because we hadn't been handed a blank cheque, even though she didn't expect to be in Rome for very long.

"I don't know why not," I said. "This could be a tough nut to crack."

Relying on our previous success, in spite of saying earlier that we'd had beginner's luck, she insisted the case would soon be closed. Cardinals didn't just vanish into thin air.

It seemed as if she was right. Dozens of them were in and around the *Corso,* or could be seen everywhere in Rome talking, arguing, gesticulating or quietly reading their breviaries in some secluded corner of a garden. They were all in what Watson in his role of an old soldier would have called 'mufti' or civilian dress, their cassocks subdued and their hats of an unobtrusive colour. Very old men were tottering about the city accompanied by their chaplains, and in a few instances their confessors, while younger men from all parts of the world –those in their late fifties and early sixties – strolled about discussing the latest baseball results or the fearful increase in the price of sheep.

We had the greatest job in finding any lodgings, modest or not. Not only was Rome full of clerics and its own citizens, who naturally wouldn't need them, but crowds of people besides us had descended on the City.

"Since that young man, Father Tomaso, begged us to come here to find his precious Cardinal the least he could have done was find somewhere for us to lay our heads," grumbled Emily, nearly pushing an old woman off the pavement. "Have you any idea where he is? I suppose we could try St. Peter's."

Gathering up our skirts, we ran across the *Piazza San Pietro*. It was so jam-packed with pilgrims and sight-seers we couldn't do anything: and the Swiss guards in their fancy dress and strange helmets were everywhere, keeping an eye on things.

Emily ran towards the Vatican where more Swiss were standing to attention, their faces impassive, and with their pikes upright and gleaming in the warm sun. Panting after her, I saw that she had found a small door leading into the building. Before she could approach it, two enormous halberds with their terrifying hooks gleaming clashed crosswise in front of our faces, only just missing our noses and chins. Emily sprang back as if stung and, cursing volubly, asked two guards what they thought they were up to.

"No-one enters the Vatican unless they have a pass," said one.

"Well we haven't got a pass," said Emily crossly, while I lifted my dress a little to see what the glimpse of a shapely ankle might do.

The answer was –nothing. But just as we were giving up in despair the door opened and who should come out but the very man we wanted to see. He looked at us with a puzzled frown but when Emily smiled sweetly at him he recognised her and come towards us with a broad smile on his ingenuous face.

"The Cardinal, our dear Cardinal Tosca, is found," he cried

within a few feet of us. "Found in time for the Conclave." He looked as if he would like to embrace us both, until he saw Emily glaring at him. She had changed from sweet to sour in the space of a second and said, "So we've made the journey from England for nothing?"

The priest's jaw dropped. He offered us a thousand apologies. It turned out that in all the excitement of the Cardinal's recovery, coupled with the enormous work which had to be done before a new Pope could be elected, he had completely forgotten his request for our presence in Rome. Well the Conclave explained the enormous crowds, the large number of cardinals in Rome and why we hadn't been able to find suitable lodgings.

"You must stay with my sister," said the priest eagerly. "She has a house in the *Via Labicana*. I will take you there, and tomorrow see that you have a place in St. Peter's for the opening ceremonies."

"Have you seen Cardinal Tosca since he was found?" I asked.

"No, but my American friend Father Josh Melia has seen him."

"He knows the Cardinal well?"

"I do not think that well. It is Father Josh's first visit to Rome. We met when I was studying in Johnsonville, and we keep up a great correspondence –mainly about baseball."

"There's no chance of our meeting him today?" I was curious

to see if Emily's description of the man as 'melancholy' was the right one.

"I'm afraid the Cardinal is spending the day resting in his room," replied Father Tomaso regretfully. "Although he is safe, it has been a terrible ordeal for an old man. He has given out that he will see no-one because he wants to be at his best tomorrow."

So it was a very short time then since the Cardinal had been found.

Suitably attired, we were driven to St. Peter's Basilica the next day by Father Tomaso's sister and her husband the *Cavaliere de Santo Spirito*. They had seats nearer the main altar and left us to squeeze into our places between a mayor and his wife, who came from an obscure village near Naples. Emily had been impossible all the previous evening, complaining for hours about our wasted journey –with no investigation and consequently no fee at the end of it; and she bit my head off when I said that we should treat the interlude as a little holiday. Hadn't she just come back from Italy, she said; and think of all the proper investigations we could be doing in England. I was glad when she finally climbed into bed and I could get some sleep.

Once we were safely settled in St. Peter's, I looked curiously round at all the dignitaries being shown into their seats, trying to recognise anyone (such as an ambassador or a royal representative whose picture I might have seen at some time in *The Strand Magazine*) while Emily sat yawning beside me and saying that all this pomp offended her Protestant sensibilities. "Study the architecture then," I hissed.

I was looking at Bernini's extravagant Baldachino with its magnificent canopy covering the Papal altar. Where several cardinals and archbishops were celebrating Mass. The edifice – that was the only word for it –had been commissioned by a Barberini Pope, and gold Barberini bees decorated its massive columns. The bees were part of his family's motto, in the same way as the three Golden Balls were the motto of the Medicis. The barbarism was that the stones for these columns had been taken from the Parthenon. The red robes of the cardinals flamed out from their seats as they sat in rows on each side of the nave waiting for the ceremonies to end and their imprisonment to begin.

I craned my neck to see which one might be Cardinal Tosca. Old, thin, rather sad-looking, there were several who fitted the bill. But there were others who I felt might look rather jolly in different circumstances, and some who were both short and well-covered. In any case, I was too far away to distinguish any of them clearly.

As the Mass drew to a close we all stood up and watched Their Eminences file into the Sistine Chapel where they would cast their votes. Trestle beds, on which each would sleep every night until the election of a new Pope, had already been taken into the Vatican's Audience Halls –the *sala regia* and the *sala ducale*. The Chapel windows had been boarded up and covered on the outside with canvas, and every chimney in the entire building except one had been blocked up.

Father Tomaso told us earlier that, once the cardinals were safely immured, a rather strange ceremony would take place. Or, rather, an ordinary ceremony conducted in a strange way. Once all those eligible to vote were settled, a Master of Ceremonies would write each man's name on a small slip of parchment, roll it up, stick it in a hole in a small lead ball so that only the end was showing and then drop the ball into a large bag. The bag would then be well-shaken and three balls taken out. I wondered if this young priest was pulling my leg. But he said no, such ceremonies had first been decreed by Pope Gregory X and had been in operation since 1274. The three men whose names came out of the bag would be Scrutinisers and ensure the Election for a new Sovereign Pontiff was properly conducted.

"Would they still be in with a chance?" asked Emily. "To become Pope themselves, I mean?"

"Of course," said Father Tomaso. Only a cardinal who was discovered to have voted for himself would be out of the running. There was also a special way of recording votes. Each man took a piece of blank paper from two large silver basins placed on a side altar and wrote his name at the top of it. He then folded the paper over just enough to hide the name and wrote his *motto* at the end of the sheet. This was then turned upwards from the bottom as much as it had been turned down from the top in such a way that there was a space between the two folded parts. This space was where the voter was expected to record the name of his choice. When the votes were scrutinised the cardinal's motto, along with his name, acted as a check against fraud.

Emily said she would need a diagram to explain all that, although it sounded to me rather like the parlour game we used to call 'Consequences'. And what was to prevent the two folded sections flying open and destroying the secrecy of it all?

"They have to be sealed at each end with candle wax before the chosen name is inscribed in the centre of the ballot paper," said Tomaso,

"And how long does this go on for?" Emily's questions were becoming somewhat brusque. I began to feel rather sorry for the poor priest.

"For as long as it takes to get a unanimous or at least a majority vote."

"How do you know when that happens if they are all locked up? Come to think of it, *why* are they all locked up?"

"If the vote is undecided, the discarded ballot papers are mixed with straw and set alight. Black smoke, which can be seen clearly in St. Peter's Square, comes out of the one chimney which is left unblocked. If a certain proportion of the ballot papers agree, they are burned without adding any straw to them. The smoke coming out of the chimney is therefore white, and the people will know they have a new Vicar of Christ."

Again, that explained the vast crowd in the *Piazza* even before the election began. A crowd which might have to turn up every day for a week to be the first to see the white smoke, or even longer judging by past disputed elections.

"That is how we know," said Father Tomaso, "by the white smoke. As to why the cardinals are locked up, in a perfect world that would not be necessary. But they could be unduly influenced, or even terrorised, by different factions if they were free to wonder about Rome while the period of election was in force. Pressure could be put on the voters. The election might be said to have been rigged. As it is, some countries already let it be known who they would *like* to be pope. But that's not the same as forcing the matter. Anonymity is very important. Imagine what might happen to a cardinal when he returned home if people knew he had made an unpopular choice."

Now the cardinals were quietly and calmly going into the Sistine Chapel. But at the last minute an old man, looking very frail and unwell, came into the Basilica leaning heavily on the arm of a young priest. Was this Josh Melia and the old man, whose red robes seemed to hang on him and whose head was lowered as if in pain, Cardinal Tosca? The congregation moved uneasily and a faint cheer went up. Some people were obviously in the know. At the entrance to the Chapel the old man was carefully handed over to the Master of Ceremonies, the doors were slammed shut and locked from inside and out by two officials (the *conclavisti)* in charge of two sets of keys, and the Conclave of Cardinals became sequestered from the world. They would not be seen again until they had elected a new successor to Saint Peter.

But although I had never seen Cardinal Tosca I felt vaguely uneasy. Turning to Emily, who was idly picking at her copy of the Order of Service, I said, "That *was* Cardinal Tosca wasn't it? The man you met on the *Corso.*"

"I think so," she said, giving me a bored look. "But as I keep telling everybody..."

"You didn't get a really good look at him."

"The cardinal who nearly got himself locked out of that chapel is ancient. He stoops. He is tall and thin. His face, as far as I could see his face, looked as miserable as sin –if I'm allowed to mention such a word in here. As far as I'm concerned that's the only difference between him and Tosca I can recall

259

after this length of time. My cardinal didn't look sinful, and for all I know they may all have to look miserable on these occasions. It's a serious business."

"But his neck, did you notice anything about this man's *neck?*"

"It was long and stringy, if that's what you mean."

"No. I don't mean his neck do I?" I said desperately. "It was his head, oscillating from side to side. He tried to control it but...Emily that was *not* Cardinal Tosca. It was Professor James Moriarty."

"Professor what?"

"*Moriarty,* the most dangerous man in the world. The 'Napoleon of Crime.' as Sherlock Holmes once called him, a person who would stop at nothing to gain his ends. We've got to get out of here and warn somebody."

This proved easier said than done. The Basilica was packed to the rafters, and it was obvious that we wouldn't be allowed to move until all the big-wigs had preceded us out of the Church. Unfortunately, none of them seemed in a hurry to do so. In any case, it all had to be conducted according to a very strict protocol. It might be hours before we got out, and if Moriarty was elected on the first ballot...

"Calm yourself," said Emily who, anything but calm, was using her knees, elbows and the inevitable parasol in an attempt to reach at least to the end of our row. Seeing someone she thought looked vaguely clerical she yelled, "Stop the Election!" And again, in an even louder voice, "Stop the Election." If anything was guaranteed to get us out of the place this was it. The choir boys stopped moving in all directions now that they were no longer needed, the thurifers stopped dispensing incense, the altar boys who had been playing five-stones behind a pillar ever since Mass ended came running out to see what all the excitement was about and a dozen Swiss Guards came tearing up the main aisle towards us. Emily was unceremoniously ejected from the Basilica as a Protestant trouble-maker and bundled out of the building like so much dirty washing.

Clinging desperately to her skirt, I managed to get out with her before we were both arrested by two of the Swiss Guards on duty outside. The people in the *Piazza* looked ready to lynch us as we were hurried away. But all I could say distractedly was, "Where is Father Tomaso? Take us at once to Father Tomaso."

"He's gone back to his office because he has a hell of a lot to do," growled one of the guards, "far too much to attend to the likes of you."

"He has already been in conversation with me and this lady," I said haughtily. "Ask your colleagues who were on duty yesterday and saw him with us."

"I've no doubt you accosted him in the street. The reverend

father is very compassionate. He would never give the brush off at once to a pair of lunatics."

"Now listen here," said Emily. "If we're lunatics how come we are both lodging with the *Cavaliere de Santo Spirito* and were given seats in Saint Peter's Basilica?"

The younger of the two men spoke rapidly in his own language. It sounded like the Italian equivalent of "Pull the other one, it's got bells on." But the older man suddenly looked thoughtful and said slowly, "I believe the *Cavaliere* is married to Father Tomaso's sister..."

"So what? We've no proof these women are speaking the truth."

Emily stamped her foot. "While you two boobies stand here arguing, the world is in the greatest possible danger. This lady is married to Doctor Watson and we are in Rome to investigate the disappearance of Cardinal Tosca."

"Wife to the friend of the celebrated Sherlock Holmes? But Cardinal Tosca is in the Sistine Chapel."

"Except that he isn't. Now will you take us to Father Tomaso?"

The Vatican is a large, sprawling building. We went along endless passages, while I fumed with impatience as the two Swiss Guards opened doors to rooms which proved to be empty. At last, groping our way towards the end of a particularly narrow and dark corridor with a low ceiling, we came to a small office which, when one of the guards flung open the door, proved to be that of Father Tomaso. He was sitting at a small desk littered with papers and writing so busily that it was some moments before he realised he was not alone. Filing cabinets stood all round the walls. There were more papers and some heavy ledgers on the floor; and when the priest did raise his head he looked older, and more tired, than when we had last seen him. He seemed surprised to see us, and even more so the Swiss Guards with their pikes at the ready.

"It's about Cardinal Tosca," I blurted out.

"Did Josh manage to get him as far as the Chapel?"

"Yes, if it was Cardinal Tosca. No, if it wasn't." This I knew sounded extremely muddled. Josh had managed to get somebody as far as the Sistine Chapel. Somebody who might have been Cardinal Tosca, or who might not.

The young priest was holding his pen in the air at the kind of angle that meant he had no time to spare in idle chat and needed to get back to work with no loss, not even a second, of time. "I don't quite understand you, *Signora* Watson."

I could see the Swiss Guards relax as Father Tomaso confirmed by his address that my name really was Watson. They no longer stood to attention with their weapons at the ready but leaned against the office wall in off-hand attitudes, while Emily and I tried to explain things. I said we had reason to believe that the world's wickedest man had wangled his way into the Conclave by imitating Cardinal Tosca and might at any moment be elected Pope.

"The cardinals have their favourites, and as I told you the rulers of certain countries have expressed an interest in a number of men they would like to see elected as the Head of the Church. All except Britain, who has said she wouldn't dream of interfering in something which was of so little concern to her. But in the long run the electors are guided by God. The Holy Spirit won't allow such a thing as a false election to happen," said Tomaso all in one breath.

"God helps those who help themselves," said Emily tartly. "I won't go so far as to say this Professor I've only just heard of will make rings round such an August Personage as the Holy Ghost, but it's your duty as a priest to do something at once to prevent the remotest possibility of such a thing happening. Or even the idea of it."

"Moriarty will mesmerise those poor old men into electing him," I said desperately.

"Is that who he is, the murderer of Sherlock Holmes? A man who is supposed to have gone over the Reichenbach Falls with him? But all the cardinals are locked in the Sistine Chapel until the end of the Conclave. It's forbidden for any of us to invade the building."

"It's that, or world domination by the Devil. Or rather the Devil in the shape of an ex-lecturer in mathematics."

The upshot of it all was that centuries of tradition were swept aside. The Sistine Chapel was hurriedly unlocked. And the people of Rome were treated to the unedifying spectacle of an old but suddenly agile man, with his red robes tucked up to reveal grey stove-pipe trousers, tripping over the leads and dodging between the statues on the roof of St. Peter's Basilica while being hotly pursued by Swiss Guards and some of the younger American priests.

These latter, however, were unable to keep up in spite of being star members of the Vatican's newly formed baseball team. With a loud cry, Moriarty suddenly disappeared over the edge of the roof on the side away from the Square. A deathly hush descended on the *Piazza*. It was broken only by the sound of horse's hooves and iron carriage wheels fading rapidly into the distance.

"That was the hell of an adventure," said Emily, relaxing in the comfort of the whole of a first class carriage on a train back to London. She looked smug and self-satisfied. As well she might. There was a very large cheque in her bag which she would share with me. After all, we had saved the world. "A shame we won't get to meet the new Pope," she said with a grin.

265

"I rather fancy myself in a black mantilla and dress, kissing a Pontiff's ring."

"A bit of a difference to your usual outdoor garb," I said, "and what's happened to your Protestant principles all of a sudden?"

"My dear Muriel, just because you haven't got the legs for trousers..."

The Conclave had reassembled after even more stringent checks than usual. Enough food for a siege had been brought in, along with a myriad of cooks, clerks and confessors, before the doors of the Sistine Chapel were locked on each side once again and all Rome waited breathlessly for the election of their Father on earth. This time hopefully without a hitch, although everybody admitted that the chase over the leads had been most exciting. Many of the on-lookers were still miffed at not being able to join in. But how were the authorities to know they weren't some of Moriarty's henchmen in disguise, intent on impeding his capture rather than in handing him over?

"A pity about poor old Cardinal Tosca though," I said. He had been found battered to death in a really dreadful den in the vilest quarter of Rome. Stripped to his shirt, trussed up and jammed into a cupboard, his clothes and pectoral cross, along with his biretta, were nowhere to be found. But the small amount of cash which he carried in a belt round his waist was still there, proving that he had been murdered for something more than money, and on the orders of someone who had no respect for his age or his office.

"Did you know," I said, desperate to shake the image of a distressed old man out my head, "that when a pope dies someone taps him on the forehead three times with a little hammer and calls his name? If he doesn't answer he's officially dead."

"Cardinal Tosca was tapped with more than a little hammer," said Emily callously, even though at first she'd been quite affected at such a ghastly death of someone she'd met even if only briefly. "But the things you know!"

"You think I should keep only useful data in my 'little attic of a brain' don't you, as you told me my not so favourite somebody once said?"

"No, no. It is all most interesting," said Mrs. St. Clair, and immediately fell asleep.

Chapter Twelve

For at least a month after we got back from Italy I saw neither sight nor sound of Emily Fanshaw so was surprised to find her one afternoon on my doorstep. I thought at first she had come to sort out whether or not there were other investigations for us to undertake and was amazed at such a burst of energy. She had certainly looked, in the train from Rome, as if she needed a good rest. I knew I could do with one before embarking on the next case. But no, as soon as we were settled in the drawing-room she announced that she had solved a mystery all by herself. She would play fair, however. I'd have half the fee. Our partnership wasn't to be jeopardised just because she'd had a bit of luck.

Coming back from a visit to the shops one morning, walking with her usual swift stride and keeping her eyes open for any signs of what she termed an 'adventure', Mrs. St. Clair had been suddenly accosted by a street musician busy plying his trade in the Bayswater Road. At first she thought he wanted her to give a coin to the monkey perched cap in hand on top of a barrel organ, and was in two minds whether to oblige him or tell both of them to clear off and make their dreadful noise somewhere else. But it turned out to be quite a different matter.

"He said that, if I didn't do something about it, his wife was going to kill him."

"Why you," I said, pouring her out another cup of the best

Pekoe.

"Who knows why any madman acts as he does," she said, taking an uncharacteristically genteel sip of her tea. "I told him to leave his monkey chained to the barrel organ and took him into the garden. I could see as we walked that he had a club foot..."

"The same as Lord Byron..."

Emily cut me short. She was obviously in no mood to listen to anything I might know or not know about such an uninteresting person as Lord Byron when she had something so much more exciting to tell me. "I tried not to make it obvious that I'd noticed it, but I couldn't help myself. He saw me looking and when we sat down in a pair of out-door chairs the gardener had left in the summer house he specially drew my attention to his deformity. Said he wasn't much of a man with such a foot and that his wife often passed remarks about it. Well, he was sick of such remarks, had lost no time in making his feelings felt and was sure she would certainly murder him if something wasn't done soon."

"Difficult to see how you could solve a crime *before* it was committed."

"The whole idea seemed crazy to me, and I was certainly glad we were out of doors. If he'd tried any tricks I felt I'd be able to yell loudly enough to attract a passerby, in spite of our high hedge. I did, however, say with perfect sincerity that I thought his reason for thinking his wife was about to kill him seemed somewhat inadequate. Why didn't he just clear out? He asked me where to, since he'd spent all the money he had coming to England from Palermo. I was very much struck with the coincidence of being involved with another Italian after all that business with Cardinal Tosca and asked him his name."

"Nectarino Ambrosio Ricoletti, and my wife. She is *abbominabile*!"

"I nearly fell out of my chair. Did those incredible names mean his mother thought she was feeding her newly born infant the food of the gods? I all but choked trying not to laugh."

I remembered Emily coming out of the police station at Nantes after our interview with *le homard* and could quite believe it. "Did he say in what way his wife was 'abominable'?"

"By making fun of his foot I suppose."

"Then why did he marry her? Come to that, why did she marry him?"

"It seems that after the unification of Italy most of the Italian refugees went home. Instead of London being full of them, as Ricoletti expected, there were very few left. He was lonely and thought he was in luck when he found an Italian landlady, one who could cook spaghetti in the Italian way."

"Are you trying to tell me he married a woman on the

strength of her expertise with pasta?"

"No. Ricoletti spun the family quite a yarn. They thought he would have money, cash coming from Italy as soon as he was settled. It was the daughter of the house who married him. But then, of course, they found he had even less lucre than they did."

I passed over her use of underworld slang and said, "She could take the foot with the money but not without it."

"That's the impression I got. Perhaps the monkey and the barrel organ were the last straw. Actually, apart from his deformity which does seem to worry him rather a lot, Ricoletti is a handsome man. Big, with black curly hair and very dark eyes. He'd be quite a catch for anyone if he wasn't so poor. He says that's partly why he didn't clear off as soon as he suspected his wife was out to murder him. He genuinely had no money to pay for anywhere else. He couldn't even get back to Palermo. A few pennies and half-pennies after a whole day working the streets was all he could raise. Considering how much we are plagued with the things there can't be much in organ grinding. Too much competition."

I reflected that Emily's husband Mr. St. Clair had managed to amass quite a lot of cash by posing as a beggar without the help of a monkey and a barrel organ. But then, he had done himself up in quite an arresting way, with a red wig and a pitifully fake scar across his face. I thought, not for the first time, that it was a

271

strange world we lived in where the real thing could attract little remuneration and a false deformity a great deal. I asked Emily how she had tackled the problem of the potential killer, since I judged that the case had already come to a successful conclusion.

"I said I would like to come to the landlady's establishment and meet Ricoletti's wife. He was very reluctant for me to be seen in the house. But at last we agreed that we would all three meet in Hyde Park. I walked across and found the couple sitting by the fountain. Well, I did get a shock. They were both obviously dressed in their best, even if their gloves were darned and their boots mended more than once. But whereas he looked big and almost prosperous she looked so scared and insignificant I couldn't imagine her murdering a mouse, let alone a man."

"Appearances are deceptive sometimes. She needn't take a hammer to him. Not with all the poisons there are about."

"If you'd seen her you would know the very idea would frighten her to death before she had time to do anything."

"So you thought his story was so much eye-wash?"

"I didn't know what to think. There might be something in it. After all, it takes courage for a man like that to accost a well-dressed woman in the street. People of that kind are a forelock-touching lot. They contrive to look grateful *and* humble for any notice one takes of them. The monkey pockets the money while the man carries on turning a handle to produce what he tries to persuade us is music. I might have called the police."

"But instead you invited him into the garden. Are you sure it wasn't his big black eyes you were interested in?"

Emily put down her cup so hard she almost cracked the saucer. "You ought to know, Muriel, that where our Detective Agency is concerned I am completely single-minded."

So she hadn't been making eyes at all the Swiss Guards then? I picked up the tea things, carried them into the kitchen and kept my thoughts to myself. When I came back she was standing by the empty grate ready to go on with her story.

"In spite of the man's being so against it, I insisted that I couldn't help him unless I saw where he lived and had the opportunity to speak to each member of the household alone."

"But what was the wife doing all this time?"I said in amazement.

"Pleating her skirt, as far as I could see. Her husband had told me that our meeting in the Park had to be 'accidental'. I was one of the fine ladies who helped to administer a charity, and had first met him when he came to ask for help."

"And had given him sixpence no doubt," I said sarcastically. I was well aware of all the old biddies who sit on committees and who get a kick out of preaching to the poor before, if they're lucky, passing over a pittance. Getting blood out of a stone wasn't in it. These well-to-do ladies with time on their hands made the whole process so painful (parting with the money that is, not the preaching) a person could be forgiven for thinking it came out of their own pockets.

"No particular amount was mentioned," said Emily repressively. "In any case, the wife looked so cowed I was sure he could have told her anything. I even doubted at the time if she was listening to the conversation. Whenever I glanced at her she was looking at the hungry sparrows almost under our feet as if she had some fellow-feeling for them and would like a few of their crumbs."

"That's hardly anyone's idea of a woman who wants to murder her husband, and it's beyond belief that she knew the purpose of the meeting in Hyde Park."

"Of course she didn't. Not the true reason, that is. It was a way of seeing her for myself and summing her up."

"And did you?"

"Did I what?"

"Sum her up."

Emily stamped her foot impatiently. "Of course I did. Haven't I just finished telling you she's such a milksop that I thought her husband must be out of his mind to imagine she'd be able to murder him?"

"Yes, because she's incapable of harming a fly, and I said in that case Ricoletti's story is a load of rubbish."

"Which was why I wished to see and speak to everyone in that family." Emily seated herself on the sofa, searched in the pocket of her dress for a small notebook and went on, "First of all, I had to find out where they all lived. Ricoletti mentioned a place somewhere in Shoreditch and, brushing aside all his objections, I arranged to be there at two o'clock in the afternoon of the following day. That way I could be sure they'd had their crust before I arrived, and could be gone again before they felt obliged to ask me to tea. They both looked so down and out I didn't want either of them, or any of the rest of the family, to be put to even the smallest expense on my account. In spite of the spaghetti, I was sure money was tight not only for the organ grinder and his wife but for the in-laws as well."

"What were they like, the in-laws?"

"Well, I started off on the wrong foot by calling the mother *Signora*. A voice from the back kitchen bellowed that she was no such thing, and a large ugly brute came into the room. He had obviously just been delivering eel skins to somewhere unspeakable because the smell of them on his duds would have knocked over a horse.

'She's plain Missus,' he roared, 'married to a plain Mister. So no more of the *Signora* if you please.' "

"Emily," I said hysterically, "however did you get yourself

275

into such strange company? The brute marries an Italian, he allows his daughter to marry an Italian. And then takes umbrage when you call his wife by her Italian title..."

"Calm down, Muriel. I assume that the brute's daughter is a *Signora,* or would be if ever she went back with her husband to Italy. But of course I was completely wrong to call her mother by that name. I suppose, after what the organ grinder told me about the Italian landlady and the spaghetti, that I assumed the whole family were of that ilk. However, once everything quietened down, I was able to get a good look at them all and came away quite satisfied."

"Yes," I said, "but did anything happen?"

"If you mean was anyone murdered, then I'm afraid the answer is yes."

"Ricoletti, his wife or his in-laws?"

"Take your pick."

"You can't mean they were all..."

"Why not?"

"Because I can tell by the look in your eye that you're pulling my leg."

"A most un-ladylike expression," said Emily with a grin. "Actually it was wholesale blood-letting, with only one survivor."

"Ricoletti!"

"Try again."

"The brute."

"It must have taken some doing," said Emily reflectively. "But..."

"The Italian landlady who cooked such good spaghetti." Then, as Emily still sat there looking smug, "You can't mean...?"

"The abominable wife. She was found unconscious and all of a heap behind the kitchen door. But her injuries were only superficial. She soon came round and responded to treatment."

"Who found them?"

"Why I did, of course."

"I don't see that there's any 'of course' about it. It's not an area you would be often seen in."

"Since my organ-grinder friend swore he was in danger from his wife in spite of appearances to the contrary, I arranged for him to show me a sign every day to prove he was all right. This could easily be done by leaving a scrap of paper in our hedge as he plied his trade. Well, one day there was no scrap of paper. At first I thought he'd been chased away before he could do anything by neighbours fed-up with the noise. But when another day went by without any indication that he'd been near the house I hurried round to his address and made my way in by the front door. To my surprise it was not only unlocked but half open. You can imagine my shock when I found the place in a shambles. There was blood everywhere. Naturally I called the police. But not before I'd had a good look round for possible clues. When the police did arrive and pushed me out I was surrounded by a lot of ghouls trying to get a glimpse of what was going on. I managed to wangle my way back in by saying I ran a Detective Agency, and had been retained by Ricoletti because he thought his life was being threatened."

"More than threatened, as it turned out," I said drily. "But it doesn't prove it was the wife who did it."

"She had been seen in a gin shop on more than one occasion while her husband was out trying to earn money with the help of his monkey. Just as importantly, she was with a man who others said was a stranger to those parts."

"It's the quiet butter-wouldn't-melt-in-their-mouth ones who are the worst," I said. "But don't forget she was also attacked. You say her injuries were superficial. Maybe the murderer (or murderers) was disturbed before he could finish her off."

"Perhaps," rejoined Emily sceptically. "The person she was seen with was big, black-bearded and burly –quite up to killing anyone if only strength were needed. The shop boy told me he spoke with an American accent and said he came from the coal fields."

I had risen and was pacing about the room. Now I sat down

with a thump. "Emily Fanshaw you, a lady, never went alone into a gin shop?" Places which as like as not were cheek by jowl with opium dens such as the one in Upper Swandam Lane. I remembered how much at home she had seemed in Whitechapel when we were searching for Leather Apron, and how she often went about in men's clothes.

"You can't be a good detective unless you are prepared for anything," she said. "As it was, it gave me a lead over everyone else. When I asked if the man had any other distinguishing features besides the beard (which he could easily shave off) I was told he was wearing a medallion round his neck. Quite a small one but my informant was sure it was solid gold, and certainly not something to be shown openly in those parts. That's why he remembered it so clearly. Thought it was a good thing the man was huge enough to take care of himself, otherwise he'd soon be relieved of his jewel. And as like as not of his life as well. As it was..."

"Being hefty, bearded and American is not proof that the man committed such a terrible crime as the one you discovered in the Ricoletti house."

"Ah, but before the police arrived I had made a thorough study of the place including the kitchen. After the bodies had been removed to the mortuary and Mrs. Ricoletti taken to the Infirmary I retrieved the medallion. I had taken it from where it was lying on the floor under her petticoat and secreted it in the dresser.

"Then it must be as I said. The murderer was disturbed and either didn't realise the medallion had been pulled off in the struggle or had to flee before *he* could retrieve it instead of you. The mystery is what was he doing there in the first place? He might know there was nothing worth stealing, unless Mrs. Ricoletti had spun him a yarn to make herself seem more important."

"I have great respect for your opinion Muriel," said Emily unconvincingly. "But it is a mistake to theorise without sufficient data."

Shades of Sherlock Holmes! Did she know more then?

"Yes," said Emily. "While the men were downstairs busy with the bodies and a woman was ministering to Mrs. R. before the ambulance arrived, I crept upstairs into the Ricoletti's bedroom and found something in an old desk. I had to break the desk open but it wasn't difficult."

"Come on then, spill the beans," I almost said. But I remembered Neville St. Clair's wife was a somewhat complex character. She had a thorough knowledge of the seamier side of life, but assumed a mantle of the strictest propriety when it suited her. "I mean," I said hastily, "tell me what else you know."

For answer she pulled a piece of paper out of her pocket. "Following an idea, after I found this I went down to the Steamship Company. It's a receipt for two tickets for the *Caronia* which sails regularly from Liverpool to New York. The tickets are in the name of Mr. & Mrs. Douglas, and the Company confirmed the sale. It's my belief the abominable wife planned to recover from her 'injuries' very quickly and then to go to the United States on a false passport with her paramour."

I have already mentioned Sherlock Holmes. Now I was suddenly reminded of Mrs. Marple since she was the last person on whose lips I had heard that word. Looking Emily straight in the eye I said, "Why did she have to arrange for everyone to be killed before she went off, and why was Ricoletti so sure he would be the only one in the house to be murdered?

"He doesn't seem to have been a very sensitive man, but he somehow knew he was in some kind of trouble and that the trouble would come from his mouse of a wife. Perhaps he had treated her badly and feared she would retaliate, on the principle that every worm turns eventually. Of course, he never suspected she had someone big and burly enough to do the job for her. Nectarino Ambrosio was on the alert for poison in his food or drink, not for a bludgeon."

"But why kill her parents?" I said in a horrified voice.

"Wanted to make a thorough job of it I suppose," said Emily

281

in an off-hand voice. "After I finished in the gin shop I went into an adjacent 'Uncle's' and discovered that a 'Mrs. Douglas' had pawned a useful set of eel skinning tools the day before the murders. That would be enough to get tickets for her and her lover to Liverpool."

"And if they pawned the medallion that would have paid for their tickets to New York and set them up for life in the Italian Quarter."

"You are becoming a little muddled, my dear. Black beard was no Italian, and the woman had only one Italian parent. Besides, who in that part of London could pay them anything like what the medallion was worth?"

"If she had learned as much from her mother about cooking spaghetti the Italian Quarter might still have suited them. They wouldn't need to sell the medallion to make a living, and perhaps they had already pawned something else to pay for the tickets for their transatlantic crossing. I honestly don't understand why the woman didn't just leave."

"Maybe she thought Ricoletti would come after her."

"Why should she, and what with? According to you he thought she was out to murder him, a very good reason for being glad to see the back of her; and he had no money for foreign travel."

"Perhaps black beard enjoyed killing. After all, he is a

Scowrer. And who's to know she didn't enjoy it too, by proxy that is. I have an idea that the medallion meant more to the man than any amount of money," Emily continued musingly, "and rather than stay in New York he'd go straight to the Valley.

"What did you call him just now?"

"Who?"

"Black beard."

"A Scowrer. That is, a member of a terrible gang which has operated a protection racket in a place called Vermissa Valley since before 1875. They would think nothing of boiling their own grandmothers for breakfast. Would you like me to read a description of the place, with its many coal and iron-working areas?"

I nodded dumbly and Emily glanced at her note-book. "According to my information 'Vermisssa Valley is a gloomy land of black crag, scarcely penetrable woods, and high mountains all white snow and jagged rock. These mountains tower on either side of a long, winding, tortuous valley'. And now listen to this description of the settlement itself: 'In winter it is desolate enough. From the top of it one has a view not only of the whole grimy, straggling town but the scattered mines and factories blackening the snow.' It would serve Ricoletti's abominable wife right if she had managed to get there."

"It sounds no worse, minus the forests and the mountains,

than certain parts of London," I said. "But they would never have got away with it. Not with the police on the job. And you," I added politely.

"They thought they would," said Emily calmly. "Perhaps black beard did. The ship sailed last week, and there's a man answering to his description on it. But one of Pinkerton's men will be there to meet him on the Quay in New York and he'll be sent straight back under guard."

"Pinkerton?"

"The Director of an American Detective Agency as famous as ours is going to be," said Emily complacently. "They have had men working in the Valley for a very long time, in the hope of pinning something on the criminals. But the townsfolk are too terrified to testify, and of course the gang members cover for each other when it comes to saying where perpetrators of a particular outrage were at any one time. It's usually 'in McGinty's bar with us' or else in the home of another member of the Lodge who, if he doesn't swear his soul away, is in for some pretty rough treatment."

Not being particularly enamoured of the glint in her eye, I hastily changed the subject. "Where's the money coming from for all this work you've done, the money you said you would share with me?"

"The Federal Government. McGinty (that's his real name)

isn't just a Scowrer. He's *the* Scowrer, and wanted for many murders committed by himself and members of his gang."

"What was he doing in one of the seediest parts of London?"

"Looking for new recruits, I shouldn't wonder, but didn't bargain on falling so heavily for Little Miss Mouse."

"What puzzles me, Emily, is how you know about the Scowrers."

"There was an illustrated article about them in *The Strand Magazine* some time ago. No photographs of the members but pictures of their regalia, including one of the thing McGinty left behind when he tapped his lady-love on the head just enough to stun but not to kill her. I must say, I almost admire him for such precision. It may be he was concentrating so hard on not doing her any permanent damage that he didn't realise he'd dropped his precious badge. Their Lodge, as they call it, poses as the ultimate in philanthropy when, unknown to the Editor of *The Strand*, it is just the opposite. And they have all kinds of esoteric rites, just like the Masons. One of these rites consists of wearing a gold ornament round the neck at their meetings, or some kind of jewelled emblem pinned on their jackets. Some of them wear bright coloured sashes. If one of those is discovered in Mr. McGinty's luggage, as I suspect it will be, that will certainly clinch things. By the way, would you like to hear something of their initiation ceremonies?"

"No I would not," I said hastily. "And I don't wish to hear any more about how you know about them either. I'll lay money it wasn't all from *The Strand Magazine*."

"I'd love to visit America," said Emily wistfully. "I've heard Long Island is really interesting. We could investigate the Cave Mystery there. I understand it's mentioned briefly in an adventure story in *The Strand* called 'The Red Circle'."

Chapter Thirteen

Sometime after Emily left for home after telling me the tale of Mr. McGinty and the abominable wife of the murdered Nectarino Ambrosio Ricoletti, a note arrived for John while I was studying *The Times*. Tucked away in an obscure corner of the newspaper was the announcement that a particularly saintly man had been elected Pope at the first ballot. The world would have nothing to fear from him. It was a relief said Father Tomaso, the Vatican's Press Secretary, to know the Holy Spirit was still hard at work in the service of the Church. Just as I finished reading this I heard a groan and looked up to see Watson waving a telegram about and gazing at me in a most miserable fashion.

"Not another investigation," he said wearily. The adventure in Ballarat and that terrible trial had tired him. And the burglary had left him apprehensive, even though he knew Raffles was behind it and it had been a mistake. He looked worn and old. Glancing over his shoulder, I read: 'Come at once to Upper Swandam Lane.' There it was yet again. Upper Swandam Lane. Like a bad penny, or a horrible omen. I saw that the note was signed 'Emily'. She must have written it as soon as she reached 'The Laurels', the somewhat unimaginative name Neville St. Clair had given to their house. It always reminded me of Mr. Pooter and Auguste Poirot.

"Now what could she want?" groaned Watson. "It's barely a fortnight since I gave her some quite good advice about the Loamshire diamonds."

"Put on a warm coat and a stout pair of boots," I said, "while I call a cab." It was best to get the whole thing, whatever it was, over and done with as quickly as possible. A few miles and there we were, back in a district I have already said was sordid. It was also an unfriendly and abnormally quiet neighbourhood for the time of day. Run-down, and decidedly sinister. 'The Bar of Gold', perhaps so called to give the impression to passersby that it sold booze and had nothing to do with drugs, lay between a gin-shop and one selling old clothes. Something I forgot to mention in all the excitement of my first commission from Moriarty was that Upper Swandam Lane itself was a vile alley behind some wharves to the east of London Bridge and had a steep set of steps leading down to its entrance.

"It seems incredible, but she must mean to meet us *inside* the opium den," whispered Watson in a horrified voice since Emily was nowhere to be seen. We had both been there before, and I was on tenterhooks lest the lascar should recognise me. We walked together down the crumbling steps, worn smooth in places by countless feet, and knocked at the rough door with its heavy iron lock. It was opened at once, and we were suddenly confronted by the Danish thug Watson whispered was an assistant there. His hair was a bedraggled yellow, and the look on his face was one I hope never to see again on any human countenance.

He ordered John and me inside with a most uncouth gesture and led us past the kitchen where the opium pipes were busily being prepared (whatever went on in other parts of the City it was always night in this place) and down a very narrow corridor. Which looked as if it had been added to the house as a secret hiding place for protesting workmen fleeing from the law at the time of the Chartist riots in 1848.

"Quite like the defiles in Afghanistan," remarked John gazing at the damp, hard as a rock and mildewed walls which were busy sprouting a kind of creeping fungus.

"How do you know," I hissed nastily, "since you've never been there?"

"I can read though," said Watson huffily, his boots sounding loudly, too loudly, on the flag-stoned floor. Was it hollow? There was no time to pursue that uncomfortable thought because I suddenly felt something cold and hard pressing into the small of my back.

"Don't you dare try anything," grated a familiar voice. "With my gun in your ribs you'd be dead as a herring in a moment."

A chilling laugh, quiet but penetrating, accompanied this pleasantry. Moriarty! What fools we'd been. Hadn't he told John just before he made that trip to Norway to find Sigerson that he'd get even? By this time we'd reached a trap-door let into the flags. The huge Dane stood on the further side of it, still clutching the wicked knife with which he'd been threatening my husband, prodding him viciously to make him move. Bending down, but still keeping his eye on Watson, he prised up a stone slab and gazed gleefully at Moriarty in the half-light of a guttering candle. The upended flag stood like an old monument in a ruinous cemetery, only kept in position by its own weight. From where I stood I could see green, evil-smelling, stagnant water. Water which I guessed was very deep.

"I ought to have remembered this," whispered Watson ruefully. "After all, I had been warned by Holmes. In fact, I can give you his exact words. 'There is a trap-door at the back of that building, near the corner of Paul's wharf, which could tell some strange tales of what has passed through it upon the moonless night.' I asked him if he meant *bodies*. 'Aye, bodies, Watson. We should be rich men if we had a thousand pounds for every poor devil who has been done to death in that den. It is the vilest murder-trap on the whole river-side.' I tell you, my blood ran cold."

"Shut up," said Moriarty, pushing his gun further into the small of my back, "and let's get on with it." He sounded quite demented.

"I haven't got it," said John in a last desperate attempt to placate our enemy. "Mary told you a few weeks ago we haven't got it."

"Diamond necklaces," yelped the Professor. "Who needs diamond necklaces when revenge is so much sweeter?" He danced about in an agony of anticipation, the gun pressing into me at intervals something cruel. "Didn't your wife and her fiendish friend rob me of far more than paltry diamonds? I could have been master of the world, with more power than any number of diamonds could give me. Eventually all the churches of every denomination would have come under my sway, and then..."

I felt there was an element of wishful thinking in this, even if Moriarty had managed to become pope. But "This is it," I thought despairingly as I was pushed nearer and nearer to that gaping hole and almost overcome by the dank smell wafting up from the water. Then, just as I had given up all hope, there came a terrible smell of chloroform, followed by the thud of a falling body and the sound of a gun hitting a stone floor.

At the same time the Dane received a blow from behind from a heavy cosh. To my intense relief our old acquaintance A. J. Raffles stepped out of the shadows and, signalling to us to stand aside, rolled the two recumbent bodies into the Thames. He closed the trap-door with a crash, leaving only a slightly wider gap between it and the next flag to show where it was, sprang over it and ran with us out of that cursed house with Bunny, busy stuffing a stinking handkerchief into his overcoat pocket, bringing up the rear. Galloping like crazy, we didn't stop until we'd left Upper Swandam Lane behind us and turned into Fresno Street. Where John, the oldest and heaviest of us all, had to stop to catch his breath.

"Raffles, old man," he said at last. "*You* can have the Duchess of Loamshire's necklace. You deserve it."

Raffles tried as hard as he could to look modest. "It was the only thing to do in the circumstances, especially after sending that pack of fools to the wrong house and letting them steal all your stuff."

"But it's a sure fact," said Watson, "that Emily Fanshaw (as she sometimes calls herself) doesn't want it. That husband of hers has become so sanctimonious since he stopped posing as a beggar that he'd only ask awkward questions if he found out about her goings on in the Hammer and Pincers, as well as all the other places she's been in and all the other things she's been up to. I told the woman only recently to deposit the necklace in my bank vault at Cox and Co. I want you to go there right now and take it out."

"What, become a bank robber?" asked Raffles with a grin, as if the thought of being such a thing had never once entered his head.

"No, no." Watson took a scrap of paper out of his pocket and wrote rapidly on it with a pen he borrowed from Bunny. "This is my authority for you to collect a certain box. Not an *old tin box,*" he continued nostalgically, "just the ordinary cardboard kind." He hesitated. "Of course, I expect you will have to sign for it."

"Then I shall be Inspector MacKenzie," said Raffles gaily.

"Too dangerous," muttered Bunny, "with Scotland Yard already after you."

"Then how about Glasspool?"

"You used that name when you stole the Velasquez."

"So I did," said Raffles, looking hard at Bunny. "I seem to remember you caused no end of trouble on that occasion with your damned interference. But I shall have to use some name other than mine own." And he and Bunny went off arm-in-arm in the direction of Charing Cross Road humming a little tune between them, while Watson and I went home in a hansom cab.

During the drive I asked my husband why he hadn't passed on the necklace to the new Duke of Loamshire's trustees. After all, it formed part of the estate and we were compounding a felony.

"Rats," said John, with uncharacteristic warmth. "The damn thing has caused enough trouble as it is, and may cause more.

293

As A. J. Raffles will find out. We're through with it, and as far as I'm concerned that's all that matters."

The next day, while Watson was at the races, I received an unexpected visit from his literary agent. "If it's about the skis you lent John to take to Norway," I said, showing him into the drawing-room, "or if you're hoping for any more work from my husband he's still away searching for Sigerson." I didn't mention all the other episodes we'd been involved in since. Or that he was betting heavily somewhere.

Arthur gave a start which shook his whole massive frame. "But Sigerson is Holmes," he said, "lying low and in great danger from Sebastian Moran now that the Colonel has served his jail sentence."

"Don't tell me that beggar didn't go over the Falls either," I said bitterly, meaning Holmes. As soon as he thought the danger was past he'd be harrying my husband with more investigations. Yours truly would be pushed in the background, and what a background, again. "After what Moriarty told me…" I stopped suddenly. I didn't want *him* to know the Professor and I were acquainted. But it was too late.

"If you believed him, you'd believe anything," said Arthur.

"That's no longer relevant," I replied haughtily, "now that he's been drowned in the Thames." I didn't say who'd drowned him.

"And I'll believe that," said Arthur, "when I hear his body's been washed up in Gravesend. By the way, are there any of Watson's unpublished manuscripts lying around? I had in mind something about a Ritual, the Musgrave Ritual I think it is, one of Holmes' earliest investigations before he met your husband."

"I have no idea," I said. "Sometimes he says his stuff is in Cox's Bank, and sometimes it's on a shelf in his study." Afraid Arthur would ask me to make a search, and knowing that all John's manuscripts had gone to the bank before we left for Australia, I rose hurriedly with an excuse that I needed to visit the butcher, the same one who'd alerted me to the Irish bank robbery. "If you want to place anything more you'll have to write it yourself."

We bowed each other out. I made a pretence of going round the corner to the High Street, and he hurried off in search of a two-horse bus to take him to London Bridge Station and home. But not before he had said rather cryptically that he would like to bring 'a friend' to see me.

When I mentioned this to John he said, referring to our narrow escape in Upper Swandam Lane, "After that little episode I feel we both need a holiday. But I suppose it would be best to see this 'friend' first." He had taken off his boots and put them on the fender as usual, and I was busy brewing tea with a dash of rum in it. Placing the teapot squarely in the centre of the tray and bringing out the chocolate biscuits, biscuits I thought I'd never taste again, I handed him a steaming cup of the best tea money could buy and said, "I couldn't agree more." But at the same time I was as intrigued as he was to discover who this mystery person might be that Arthur was bringing to see us.

Well, he came to the house. Arthur came with him. And we were confronted with the most decrepit-looking old man I have ever seen in my life. Even worse than Professor Moriarty, though considerably shorter in height and looking rather less malevolent, with a curved back and white side-whiskers.

"I know *that* disguise, said John, springing out of his chair. But before he could come any nearer the old man had whipped off his whiskers, straightened his back and legs and revealed himself as –Sherlock Holmes!

The first thing he said to me was, "I hear you have been taking my advice, Mrs. Watson, and indulging in some detective work."

"And I heard," I retorted boldly, "that you'd gone to your death over some Falls."

"If I may suggest that you take the trouble to read my account of what happened there you will see, not that I escaped from the Reichenbach Falls, but that I was never in 'em."

"Your account?" I was busy remembering how, when John made his confession to me, he said he would be 'as fulsome a usual' when he wrote about his friend's death for *The Strand*; and there was no doubt he had given me more than a slight impression he wrote up Holmes' investigations.

"Of course they were my accounts," said Sherlock, carefully lighting his first pipe. "Who else do you think wrote all that stuff? Not Watson, whatever he says. I saw through him from the start, as soon as I realised he had bribed young Stamford to pass himself off as his dresser. How could this stranger be at Saint Bartholomew's Hospital at the same time I was there studying chemistry, and in the same labs he would use as a trainee doctor, and yet we never ever met? However, I admit it took me a while to solve the puzzle. He looked like an old soldier, and had obviously hurt his shoulder in some way. But both those things could be explained if he had trained, as he said he did, in Netley Hospital. Perhaps as an orderly, or something similar. As for the tan, he could have got that wheeling wounded officers round the gardens in sight of the sea and Southampton Water. A fact I believe was brought out at his trial. I decided to make a deliberate mistake by telling him he had been in the tropics and, considering what was in all the newspapers at the time, quite possibly in Afghanistan. When he made no attempt to correct me by saying that Afghanistan isn't in the tropics I knew I had my man, *and* something to hold over him if I needed it."

This all sounded rather clever. But it was also mean and I looked a poor old John's face as he sat there, taking it on the chin without a word of complaint. "Why did you ask him to say he wrote everything then?" I said angrily.

"I didn't want my own name to appear. So it was the only way we could get paid."

"What rot. Your name was in all the accounts more, much more, than once."

"No it wasn't," said Sherlock calmly.

"I know from all the times you tried to make Watson look small, and all the times you tried to show how much cleverer you were, that you're a particularly nasty piece of work. But I never realised until now that you are completely cuckoo." I felt like throwing a cushion at him.

"I assure you I am no such thing," said the infuriating man haughtily. "When I say my name is not Sherlock Holmes then that is exactly what I mean." He took a small piece of paper from his waistcoat pocket, scribbled on it and tossed it over to me. Well, the initials were the same at any rate.

"We formed a kind of triumvirate," went on Sherlock grandly. "Like the ancient Roman Republic. I made up the stories, Watson signed them and Arthur acted as his agent in order to get them into *The Strand Magazine*."

"His agent," I said impatiently. I had no desire to listen to anything about Roman history.

"Why yes," said Sherlock. "Arthur has written some well-received historical novels, about the Monmouth Rebellion and suchlike, so a lot of Editors know him and trust his judgement. As to why I made up the investigations, have you any idea how wearing it can be to get up in the morning and immediately have someone knocking at the door asking you to find a lost fiancé or a set of trumpery jewels? Someone who prevents you from enjoying concerts, visits to the art galleries, quiet little dinners in exclusive restaurants or leisurely walks in the park? A man or a woman with a footling problem like a riddle or a poisonous snake (to say nothing of being in the clutches of a blackmailer) which will delay that interesting trip to Persia or Tibet or the work I wanted to pursue in Montpelier? All of which had nothing to do with sleuthing. It was only by pretending I already had so much work of that kind and telling the public all about it that I was able to have any life of my own at all. Watson will tell you he felt the same. On cold and frosty winter nights when we'd just managed to get the fire going really well and were sitting discussing the latest racing results over a large glass of whisky and soda the door would burst open, bringing in horrible flurries of wind and water and somebody wanting to root us out immediately from our comfortable arm chairs and go with them into exterior darkness. In other words, hell."

"I remember one evening particularly well," said John, speaking for the first time. "There was a raging storm, with the wind sobbing like a child in the chimney. That was a nice touch of yours, Holmes, 'sobbing like a child.' It was when you came to describe what might have happened if we'd bothered to answer the door bell or if Mrs. Hudson had been at home to do so. I was thankful to sit by the fire reading one of that American author's stories. Clark Russell I think his name is, with you sitting so companionably on the other side of the hearth reorganising your index system..."

"Yes," said Sherlock smugly. "It was a 'nice touch' as you so rightly observe, my dear fellow. But as a matter of fact I got it from the author you admire so much. Clark Russell actually wrote that the tempest 'shrieked like tortured children at the hall door and the window casements, and roared like the discharge of heavy ordinance in the chimneys.' I flatter myself my style is a tad less over-blown."

"Organising his index system fiddlesticks," I thought to myself. He was more likely making notes for his imaginary tales, and in addition scattering titles around wholesale to make it seem he was even busier than everybody thought he was. That was how it must have been. I recalled John's weak attempt to write 'The Riddle of the Rotterdam Packet', with its borrowed sentences and broken-off ending. I should have realised then that he didn't write anything for Sherlock. No red-blooded man, however bored or short of money, would voluntarily record the rebukes Holmes flung at him all the time or, worse still, the sarcasms he heaped continually on his head. Although John might be happy to put his name to something which brought in enough cash to keep both of them in cigars, whisky, newspapers, concert tickets, Turkish baths and the rest, as well as paying the rent and putting money on the nags.

"I suppose you'll want him to start all over again," I said wearily to Sherlock Holmes. "Visiting Baker Street so that you'll always have someone there you can try out your ideas on." I remembered a passage in *The Hound of the Baskervilles* addressed to John. 'It may be that you are not yourself luminous but you are a conductor of light'. It seemed incredible that after we were married Watson often just sat in one house while I nearly died of boredom in another. What about Mr. Forrester? What about the Agra treasure? Had I imagined all that?

"No, no," said Sherlock soothingly. "You know that was real because, after all, you were involved in the investigation yourself. So was the work I did for your employer Mrs. Forrester. Watson and I investigated several little matters together. A red-headed pawnbroker, the twisted lip affair, somebody who had lost a thumb, the Tor Bridge business, something concerning Edward VII's natural daughter ("The

Gruner case," interpolated John) and one or two others, including all that nonsense which ended at the Reichenbach Falls. ("I was absolutely certain you'd gone over," said John). But the whole thing was becoming so exhausting, I feared very much for my health. It was much better to use my imagination. Which you must admit is considerable."

Oh, I admitted that all right. I also remembered John Clay, the two pairs of boots behind the curtain in that blackmailer's house and Upper Swandam Lane. But I didn't want to lose John for long periods all over again.

"Nor will you," said Holmes. "I'm retiring." He turned to Watson with a smile. "You remember that little cottage I told you about on the Downs..."

"I certainly do, by Jove," said Watson heartily. "It will do you good, and I've heard it's a wonderful place for bees."

"Bees?" said Sherlock reflectively. "Now there's an idea."

This was how John and I ended up in East Yorkshire spending a week in a place called Beverley while Sherlock went off, hopefully for good and all, to Sussex. I had already given my dear husband a rollicking for not being entirely frank with me about who wrote what on that terrible evening when he revealed his name wasn't Watson and that he hadn't ever been an assistant-surgeon in Afghanistan but a ward orderly at a Military Hospital near Southampton. As it was, he said he would much rather go to Scarborough than Beverley. In fact, he seemed strangely reluctant to visit the East Riding. But I wanted to see The Minster and so carried the day. After settling in our lodgings and making sure the bed was well-aired, we spent the evening reading the papers. Something John said he was well used to in his days with Holmes. "Only he was always asking me to read them aloud."

"Well, I won't do that," I said, busy looking at the latest fashions, surprised the see copies of *The Ladies Home Journal* so far North. The next day, refreshed and invigorated after a good night's sleep and a hearty breakfast, we walked towards the Minster, with John still exhibiting a strong desire to be elsewhere. Once inside, I stood gazing at the beautiful windows, the chancel with its high roof beams and the many monuments. One in particular, in the South Aisle of the nave, intrigued me, although Watson held back and pretended not to see it.

'Sacred to the memory of the men of the fifteenth regiment of foot who lost their lives in Afghanistan in 1880', I read. As my eye swept down the list of names I saw that the last but one was *John Watson*. White with fury, I turned on my cringing husband. "So you, or your father, stole a dead man's name," I said.

"There are lots of Watsons everywhere."

"Yes," I said, "but the date, and the place. The fact that this man was a soldier, and serving in Afghanistan. Was this Arthur's idea?"

"Of course not. I met Arthur after I'd changed my name and before he consented to become our go-between with *The Strand*. But he agreed that Watson was better than Sacker, especially for literary purposes."

"What about the 'H'? At the moment I can think of all kinds of unpleasant names that could stand for. Names it would be the greatest pleasure to me to call you."

"It doesn't stand for anything," said John trying to assert himself. Even though he knew he was completely wrong-footed and had been callously opportunist. "Although there have been several suggestions from *Strand* readers and others. Henry, Horace, Herbert, Hamish, Hopley…"

"You used that name in 'The Adventure of Black Peter', John Hopley Neligan," I said accusingly. "Even though it was the middle name of that unfortunate man who got struck by lightning on a railway platform in Ingleton. And you've used several other names from this monument. At least Sherlock has. But you must have told him about them, or even said something to Arthur."

"Arthur told *me* some things," corrected Watson. "For example he was married at a place near Ingleton and knew that the vicar there is called Thomas Sherlock. It was the vicar's father Ralph Hopley Sherlock who was killed in a thunderstorm. But that was ten years before Arthur could have heard the story. So many people waiting on the station witnessed the event that they must have still been talking about it."

I ignored this and said, "How could you be Henry since you let Holmes tell everybody that was your elder brother's name?"

"His first name, and my second maybe," said John weakly.

"Henry John and John Henry," I said sarcastically. Really, I was quite beside myself and wished we'd gone to Scarborough after all.

"I thought the 'H' would distance me a bit from this poor chap after I saw the inscription," said John piteously. "But I can quite see now..."

"Next thing you'll be saying is you put it in because you didn't want to pinch his whole identity." I was already marching resolutely out of the Minster. It had certainly lost its charm, for me at least. And John, I now knew to my cost, had had an excellent reason for steering clear of it. He followed at a safe distance, knowing I couldn't bring myself to speak to him, until we reached our hotel.

But, angry as I was, I realised it would be useless to continue quarrelling with Watson forever. I was also very annoyed with Arthur. If he knew about the monument I felt he ought to have persuaded the man who became my husband to change his name a second time –before the partnership between him and Holmes became so famous. John's first two reports, or rather Sherlock's, were published in quite ordinary journals. One of them was relatively obscure and the other an American periodical.

When the silly pair became involved with that Adler woman, if they really did and she wasn't a figure of the imagination, and Sherlock hit his stride as a writer he could have persuaded Watson to call himself anything. Or even resurrected his given name of Ormond Sacker in spite of what Arthur had said about such an outlandish label. Surely no-one else in the whole wide world would have been called that. It wouldn't have mattered what name Watson, both as the supposed writer and the receiver of cheques, used to sign his stories so long as the Editor of *The Strand Magazine* knew it was the same as the one on his bank account. A thought suddenly struck me that Sherlock hadn't only persuaded him to continue using the name he'd borrowed from the memorial but had also realised that there was a ready-made history for someone he wanted to pose as an old soldier.

Later in the week, after we had become firm friends again and done rather a lot of sight-seeing together, I whispered my news to John, just like any other coy Victorian wife. Of course he wanted to pack up and go home immediately, wouldn't let me drink any more wine, insisted I have a nap in the afternoon, and altogether made himself a thorough nuisance. Until I said I wasn't that fragile and would crown him if he didn't stop fussing.

"Well," he said expansively, thumbs in his waistcoat and boots in the fender, "At least there'll be no more sleuthing."

I wasn't so sure. What crook could suspect that a youngish matron quietly pushing a bassinet through the London Streets was on his trail? It would be a walk over.

Also from MX Publishing:

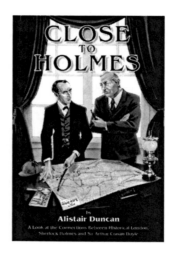

Alistair Duncan

Close To Holmes

A Look at the Connections Between Historical London, Sherlock Holmes and Sir Arthur Conan Doyle

Also from MX Publishing:

Alistair Duncan

Eliminate the Impossible

An Examination of the World of
Sherlock Holmes on Page and Screen

Also from MX Publishing:

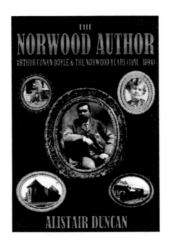

Alistair Duncan

The Norwood Author

**Arthur Conan Doyle
and the Norwood Years (1891 - 1894)**

Also from MX Publishing:

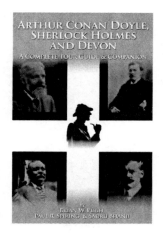

Brian W. Pugh and Paul R. Spiring

Arthur Conan Doyle, Sherlock Holmes and Devon

A Complete Tour Guide and Companion

Also from MX Publishing:

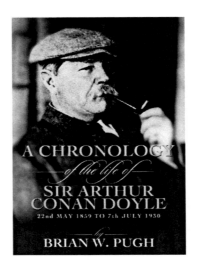

Brian W. Pugh

A Chronology of The Life Of Sir Arthur Conan Doyle

A Detailed Account Of The Life And Times Of The Creator Of Sherlock Holmes

Also from MX Publishing:

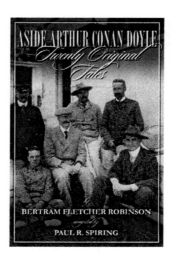

Paul R. Spiring

Aside Arthur Conan Doyle

Twenty Original Tales By Bertram Fletcher Robinson